To Dye For
A Mortician Murder

Greta Boris

Cryptik Press

Copyright © [2022] by [Greta Boris]

All rights reserved.

No portion of this book may be reproduced in any form or by any electronic or mechanical means, including information storage and retrieval systems, without written permission from the publisher or author, except for the use of brief quotations in a book review or as permitted by U.S. copyright law.

Cover by Mariah Sinclair, www.mariahsinclair.com

Edited by TwilaBeth Lambert

Ebook ISBN 978-1-958088-00-5

Print Book ISBN 978-1-958088-03-6

ASIN B09WG2SVDC

This book is a work of fiction. Names, characters, businesses, places, events, locales, and incidents are either the products of the author's imagination or used in a fictitious manner. Any resemblance to actual persons, living or dead, or actual events is purely coincidental. Brand names are the property of the respective companies; author and publisher hold no claim.

Contents

Dedication		V
1.	Harry's Hair Stop	1
2.	Greener Pastures	6
3.	The First Corpse	10
4.	Open Arms	14
5.	Harry's Request	19
6.	The Big Day	24
7.	Trudy's Last Dance	30
8.	Post Life Services	37
9.	On My Toes	42
10.	El's Bells	48
11.	Humming Along	52
12.	Pending Nuptials	59
13.	A Purloined Letter	64
14.	Problems of the Heart	71
15.	Haunted Hair	78
16.	On the Back Foot	85
17.	Nightmare on Elm St.	90
18.	Unintended Consequences	94
19.	Attack of the Killer Chorkie	99
20.	Battling Microbes	104
21.	Relative Problems	109

22.	Double Indemnity	117
23.	Bloody Heaven	123
24.	Killer Coincidences	129
25.	Welcome to the Twilight Zone	134
26.	Corpse Caffeine	140
27.	Cat Fight	144
28.	A New Customer	151
29.	Gossip Grist	155
30.	Unnatural Causes	160
31.	A Cold, Cold World	165
32.	All's Well That Ends Well	172
33.	Tribal Alliances	176
Also By Greta Boris		182

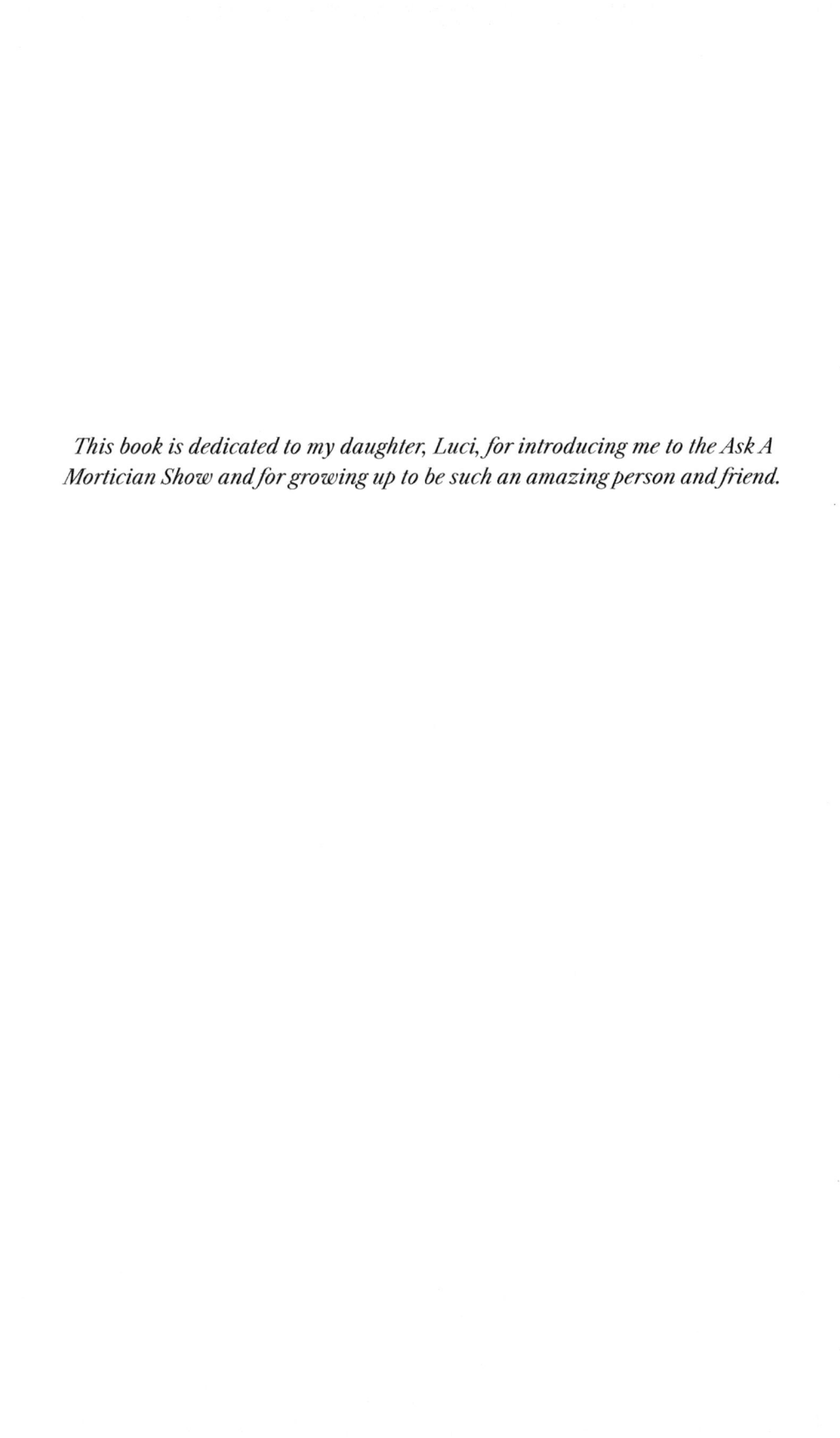

This book is dedicated to my daughter, Luci, for introducing me to the Ask A Mortician Show and for growing up to be such an amazing person and friend.

1

HARRY'S HAIR STOP

It's hard to build a business when your clients keep dying. Take this morning, for instance. Harry—he's the owner of the salon I work in—handed me a note. My 10:15 canceled. Last minute. And I couldn't even get mad at her. She was dead.

I waded to my aqua-blue, faux-leather chair through a sea of gossip, dumped my patent leather purse in the cupboard under the lighted mirror, and sat. My reflection stared back at me, wearing an annoyed expression. I adjusted it to solemn.

I felt heartless. Honestly, I liked Trudy. She was one of my favorites, but when all your clients are seventy-five and over, you can't let yourself get too attached.

Maddy glanced my way and batted her eyelashes, quite an accomplishment considering the amount of mascara she coated them with. "You heard about Trudy?"

I nodded. "Third one in seven months."

"It's going around."

"I'm starting to feel like a jinx."

"It's not just you, sweetie. We've all lost at least one."

"Imogene." Harry's smoker's voice bounced off the checkered linoleum floors and yellow walls. He only called me Imogene when he was with a client.

"Yes, Harry," I said.

"Can you take a walk-in?"

My spirits lifted. Maybe the morning wouldn't be a total loss after all. In the mirror I saw Harry, hips swishing dangerously close to Camille's shears, coming toward me. Behind him was a fragile looking, white-haired lady—guesstimate eighty-five. I sighed.

"This is Imogene," he said to her. "Don't let the tattoo fool you. She's one of our best."

The white-haired lady eyed the Rosie the Riveter tat on my right bicep. A frown formed on her face. I don't think she approved, but she hiked herself into the chair with Harry's help.

"So what can I do you for?" I immediately regretted the stupid expression. I'd picked it up from my grandmother's boyfriend, Phil. He's a walking cliché. A nice one, but still, he's contagious.

The woman patted her short curls and said, "I need a toner. My hair has gone brassy."

Ah, a blue-hair. She must have moved to Orange County from a small town where they still turned their seniors into Smurfs.

A half hour later, my new lady wore blue hair and a grimace I believed was intended to be a smile. "Very nice," she said, and handed me a tip. Five percent—which must have been the going rate in the forties. I loved my seniors, but most of them were stuck in the past when it came to tipping. I couldn't imagine how I was going to afford my own place at this rate.

I had an appointment to check out a studio after work. It was small, one room and a kitchenette. Fingers crossed, I might be able to swing the rent. I had a little nest egg put away. I hoped it would be enough for first and last and a security deposit. My monthly income at Harry's was inconsistent, what with the increased attrition and all. Consequently, I still lived with my grandmother, which was a whole other problem.

After the Smurf lady left, I walked to the front desk to check on my schedule. Harry was on the phone. "Of course, of course," he said. "She'd be honored. Harry's Hair Stop is honored."

I hoped I wasn't the *she* he was referring to. My experience with Harry had taught me if honor was being offered, payment wasn't. "Genie, darling, I have a special event for you." I was the *she*, then.

"Yes?" I said, cautiously optimistic. Special events could be lucrative.

"Gertrude Rosenblum requested you for her funeral."

I stared at Harry, who didn't look up from the papers he was shuffling. I had the impression he was avoiding my gaze.

"Trudy is dead," I said.

"If she wasn't, she wouldn't need you for her funeral, would she?"

"I'm sorry, Harry. I don't understand what you're saying. Am I supposed to style the pallbearers? Her family? Trim the priest? What?"

His eyes finally meet mine. "No. Trudy wants a wash, blow dry, and her makeup done." I'd heard about stylists taking funeral gigs, but I'd never known anyone who did it.

"You'll be overseen by one of the mortuary staff, and they'll prepare the, ah, Trudy, for you. She requested you, Genie. It's an honor."

I wished he'd stop with the honor stuff. "I don't..." I didn't know how to end the sentence. I don't feel comfortable? I don't know how to do up a corpse? I don't want to? All were true.

"Genie." Harry shook his head, disappointment etched into his features. I hated it when he called me Genie. No one but my grandmother was allowed that level of familiarity. "You wouldn't deny a woman's dying wish, would you?"

Why did he have to put it that way? He waited for a beat and, when I didn't respond, said, "Good. You need to be at Greener Pastures by five on Friday. The service is Saturday morning—open casket. I'm counting on you to make Trudy look her best. The funeral director said we could put business cards by the guest book."

I tried to swallow, but there was no moisture in my mouth. Then a vision of a mailbox with my name on it entered my mind. I managed to rasp out my one burning question. "How much?"

It was dark by the time I left Harry's. I plugged the address of the studio apartment into my phone and followed the directions onto El Toro Road. Seven minutes later, I turned onto Elm street.

Elm was in one of those early Saddleback Valley housing tracts that had just graduated from old to retro. My heart had skipped a beat when I'd read that. I mean, retro is my middle name. I love swing dancing, big band music, Betty Boop, and pretty much everything from before the year I was born.

The homes here were big, the architecture sixties stucco, and the trees large and mature. It was a nice change from Liberty Grove, where I currently lived. Don't get me wrong, Liberty Grove was a beautiful, well-manicured community. The only problem was no one under fifty-five was supposed to live there unless they married in. I was twenty-six and single. I'd sneaked in after an unfortunate stint with a roommate. Gran would never turn me away.

A man stood under a street light halfway up the block. I glanced at the number on the curb, 27651. This was the place.

"Imogene Lynch?" he said.

"Peter Daniels?" I stuck out my hand. We shook. He was pleasant looking and appeared to be in his late fifties. Young, thank goodness.

It wasn't that I was opposed to older people. On the contrary, my life was filled with them. So much so I was afraid I was becoming one of them—an old woman, trapped in a young woman's body. While Peter Daniels wasn't exactly my age, at least he was more of a father figure than a grandfather one.

"We're not quite done with the improvements, so you'll have to use your imagination." He led me to a white wooden staircase built against the outside wall of the garage.

The treads were worn. The paint thin. I thought it gave the place a beachy air. At its top was a red door. A niggle of excitement ran through me. I'd always imagined myself living in a home with a red door. All the doors in Liberty Grove were painted by the association. They were beige.

Peter unlocked the door and gave it a kick. It burst open. The smell that wafted out reminded me of summer vacations, and I smiled. I already loved the coastal vibe of this place, and I hadn't even seen it yet.

Peter felt around on the wall next to the door and flipped a switch. A dull, yellow light popped on. "I've been meaning to replace the bulbs," he said.

A small room opened before me—small, but large enough for a couch and an easy chair or two. I could have friends over. Not that I had any friends. At this point in my life, all my friends were actually Gran's. If I lived here, I could make my own.

To my right were two large windows. They were dark now, but looked like they'd let in a lot of light during the day. Between them was a perfect spot for a hanging plant. I'd always wanted my own plant.

"Here's the kitchenette." Peter waved a hand toward a small laminate counter that separated the living room from a playhouse-sized kitchen. If I was the squealing type, I would've squealed. It was adorable. There was a tiny fridge, several small cupboards, and a miniature sink. I wasn't much of a cook, but I could imagine myself there whipping up a pot of soup or a salad for the friends that came with the apartment.

"I love it," I said.

Peter beamed. "It'll be available at the end of the month."

We talked money. The security deposit was a bit more than I had, but I thought I might be able to swing it after the funeral gig. I wasn't looking forward to the mortuary but had to admit it came at an opportune time. For me, I mean. Not for Trudy.

"Can I call you in a couple of days?" I said. "I have to move some money around."

"Of course. Of course. We still have work to do, so no hurry." We shook hands again, and I headed home.

A half mile from Gran's was a supermarket shopping center. I pulled in, turned off my engine, locked the car, walked up the block and through the guarded gate into Liberty Grove. An unknown neighbor had noted my car in the lot near Gran's place at night and reported me to the LG Homeowners Association. I'd parked at the grocery store ever since.

This was another reason I had to move. Despite all appearances to the contrary—my tattoo, darkly dyed hair, and penchant for wearing black—I was a rule follower. When I was a child, I was the classic goody-two-shoes and lived in dread of displeasing adults. I had nightmares about being yelled at by anybody other than Gran. I'd never completely outgrown it.

From the street, I could see a dim light in Gran's window. Nobody home. I remembered she'd said she had book club that evening. Good, I wasn't ready to face her. I hadn't figured out how I was going to tell her I was leaving.

Harley, her bloodhound mix, met me when I entered the living room. He used to meet me at the door, but he, like everyone else around here, was slowing down. "Hey there, buddy." I patted his head. He wagged his tail and looked at me through hopeful, droopy eyes. He followed me into the kitchen and sat by the cupboard where his treats were kept. I gave him a few, then scoured the refrigerator for something for me.

Gran had left a plate covered in plastic wrap and topped with microwave instructions written on a sticky note. A pang hit me while the chicken, mashed potatoes, and Brussels sprouts heated. I would miss this, miss her, but it was time. Gran would understand.

While I ate, I mused about how I'd break the news. A dozen soliloquies pranced through my mind, but none seemed right. I continued to ponder it as I put my dishes into the dishwasher. On my way up the stairs, procrastination settled comfortably on my shoulders like a well-worn bathrobe. I would tell her after I signed the lease. No sense upsetting her if things fell through.

2

GREENER PASTURES

On Friday afternoon I pulled through the big, black gates of Greener Pastures and followed signs to the mortuary. Headstones and mausoleums dotted the verdant landscape like stone flora. Despite the warm spring weather, I shivered.

I'm not superstitious. I believe when we die; we die. That's it. Poof. We're gone. My grandmother is the one who swallows all that afterlife stuff, but I guess she has to. She was one of the original Jesus people, brought into the fold in the 1970s, which, according to her, makes her about forty-seven. I don't think that's what's meant by "born again," but who am I to argue?

When I reached the stucco building marked MORTUARY, I parked. It was 4:30. I'd been jumpy all day and figured it was a good idea to get there early. Better to relax and get used to my surroundings before wielding an eyeliner pencil. I hefted the strap of my makeup bag over my shoulder and exited my car.

I pushed open the mortuary's double doors and entered a hushed environment. Deep carpets and heavy draperies swallowed the timid light peeking through the windows. A song by some long-dead sixties band, the homogeneous rendition familiar although I couldn't place it, flowed through hidden speakers. Eau de flower-shop perfumed the air. I knew the atmosphere was intended to be soothing, but it wasn't working.

I followed brass arrows that said OFFICE to the right. I passed two chapels, The Jubilee and The Remembrance, according to the placards. Both rooms were empty. A third, The Sistine, housed a shiny, white coffin surrounded by mounds of roses and lilies. I hurried past, rounded the corner, and walked into a slim, bespectacled woman carrying a clipboard.

Her features molded themselves into professionally sympathetic lines. "May I help you?"

"I'm looking for the director, Carlton Baldowski," I said.

"Do you have an appointment?"

"I do. At five. I'm early."

"I believe he's wrapping up with a client. Follow me." We wove through a labyrinth of hallways to a waiting room with a door at its far end. "Have a seat." She gestured to a floral print chair. "Can I get you anything? Coffee? Water?"

I shook my head as I sank into the chair, and I don't mean that metaphorically. The cushions were so soft and deep, it felt like I was being eaten alive. I anchored my elbows into the arms in an attempt to prop myself up.

It was only a couple of minutes before the door at the far end of the room opened. I heard a comforting rumble of words. "It will be a lovely service. I'm sure Roy will be pleased."

A tiny, mouse-like woman scurried into the room. "I do hope so. Roy is, was, very particular. Very particular. He stuck to a rigorous schedule, coffee at six, walk the dog from six-twenty-five to seven, eggs and—"

"Rye toast, no butter at seven-oh-five," the male voice said.

"Yes, and he wanted his newspaper folded just so. I never could do that right," the woman continued without missing a beat. "Are you sure the coffin lining isn't too showy? Roy didn't like things to be showy. He liked things to be high quality, but plain, very plain."

"The sheen is subtle. I think Roy would approve."

I started when the speaker entered the room behind her. Because of the bass rumble, I'd expected a large, barrel-chested man, but he was only a few inches taller than the mouse woman.

Carlton Baldowski, for that must have been who it was, was a diminutive sphere of a man. Everything about him was round, his belly, his face, the overly large glasses balanced on his round nose. He reminded me of a fat Elton John.

"I don't know." The woman's nose twitched. "He wouldn't even wear silk ties. Don't you have any fabrics with less shine?" She turned as if to re-enter the office she'd just left, but Carlton blocked the doorway.

"I assure you, once the coffin is in use, very little of the lining fabric will be visible."

"Roy can be difficult when he doesn't like something," she said.

Carlton looked over her head at me. "Ah, Imogene Lynch, isn't it?"

I struggled out of the man-eating chair. "Yes."

He put a hand on mouse woman's arm and steered her toward the hallway.

"I'm not sure about that lining," she said.

Carlton's smile looked lacquered on.

"I'm not trying to be difficult, but Roy—"

He patted her hand and gave her a gentle shove toward the exit. "I understand completely."

"Good. Because Roy—"

"We'll see you next Wednesday, Mrs. Rolland." Carlton Baldowski raised a hand in a princess wave as she retreated from view.

After a moment, he turned to me. The smile dropped from his face with an almost audible thump. "Now, Imogene—do you mind if I call you Imogene?" He didn't wait for me to answer, but continued. "I won't be able to spend much time going over things with you. But you're a pro, right? Don't need me. Today is an exceptionally busy day. Full moon, you know."

I nodded, as if I had a clue what he was talking about. *What do full moons and mortuaries have in common?* That sounded like the beginning of a bad joke.

"Walk with me." He bustled from the lounge, and I followed. "I'll take you to the basement. To the embalming room."

I didn't like the sound of that but followed the bouncing ball. To the left, at the end of the hall, was a door marked EMERGENCY EXIT. I found this comforting. Not that I expected anything to happen, but it's always best to have your exit strategy mapped out in uncertain situations.

"I see you've brought the tools of your trade." Carlton hadn't stopped talking since I'd laid eyes on him. I wondered if he was trying to distract me from what was ahead, the way a phlebotomist does before they stick you with a needle. "We have quite a bit of makeup, but maybe you know the deceased's favorite shades? We attempt to make them as lifelike as possible, but we're at a disadvantage. One you don't have." He pushed open the heavy door.

A shaft of dying sun shined into my eyes, blinding me for a moment. I stepped through the doorway, and my vision cleared. I was in a stairwell. A yard or two in front of me was another glass door leading onto a parking lot bordering the grassy hills of the cemetery. To my right were flights of ascending and descending stairs. We descended.

The basement of the mortuary was as unlike the upper floor as the Mojave is from the mountains. Upstairs was encased in fabrics and carpets and warm colors that ate up light and sound. The cellar was stark. Fluorescent light gleamed off pale tile floors and white walls and steel-framed doors. Our footsteps echoed through the passageway.

"Our disadvantage, of course."—Carlton's voice seemed to rise several decibels—"is we rarely know the deceased before they are. Deceased, that is."

I had to jog to keep up with his short, pumping legs.

"We have photographs, even film, but there's nothing like seeing the client in the flesh." He halted before a steel door and fixed his gaze on me. "Much better than seeing them out of the flesh," he said in a fair imitation of Boris Karloff's lisp, his face is as serious as death. I took a step backward. He chuckled. "Sorry, a bit of mortician humor." He threw open the metal door.

The room was cold. Not just sterile, but actually freezing. I wished I would have worn a sweater.

The floor and halfway up the walls were covered with the same pale tile as the hallway. At the far end of the space was a stainless steel counter fitted with a sink of the same material. I blinked. At first I thought all the grout lines were making me dizzy, then I realized the floor canted toward a drain at the center of the room. Near the drain was a metal table on wheels. On the table was Trudy.

"Here she is." Carlton's cheer ricocheted off the walls. "Looks pretty good, doesn't she?"

Other than the pallor, she didn't look too bad. I mean, I could tell who she was. She wore a green dress I recognized. She'd purchased it for a New Year's Eve party and brought it to the shop the day I did her hair and makeup for the event. She was concerned about the color against her skin. "I'm afraid it makes me look ill," she'd said. Seemed ironic in retrospect, but I knew just the makeup to use today.

Her gray hair had been washed and combed, but whoever had attempted to arrange it didn't know a thing about the way she'd worn it. It was all wrong, and the magenta stripe I'd given her for the New Year's party had faded to a rusty brown.

Her skin shone in the bright lights, but had no color. Trudy would've hated that. She never went anywhere without Ravishing Red lipstick applied in thick coats to the region near her mouth.

"Her features have been set, so she's ready for your artistic touch." Carlton waved at Trudy and spun toward the door.

"You're not leaving me alone?" I blurted out the words.

Carlton's face broke into an unpleasant grin. "She won't bite."

3

THE FIRST CORPSE

The door closed behind Carlton with a metallic clank. I stared at it for a long moment. I needed to get to work, but my limbs felt like I was pushing them through water wearing those weights they use in water aerobics classes. I'd taken only one class in my life, but I'd never forgotten it.

I'd just broken up with Bad Boy Chad for the first time. He was the kind of guy girls like me have to date because we're too stubborn to learn from other people's mistakes. Anyway, I'd been moping around the house for a week. Gran doesn't do moping.

She dragged me to the YMCA to take her early morning Aqua Boot Camp class, which she swore would perk me up. "Nothing like exercise to get rid of the vapors." I believe those were her exact words.

It was a horrible experience. It didn't get rid of my vapors, but I never let Gran get a whiff of them again. I now leave the house if I want to indulge in a pity fest.

I made my way in slow motion to the gurney in the middle of the room. My first impression was Gertrude looked peaceful. Her face was serene. Her hands were clasped over her belly. Her feet were shod in her best pumps.

Her feet were a problem, though. They weren't turned out like a napping person's should be. The toes pointed directly to the ceiling.

It was a small thing, but it bothered me. A lot. It looked unnatural. Like the Wicked Witch of the East's feet after the house fell on her in *The Wizard of Oz*. I turned my back on them and tried to block the image from my mind. I studied her face instead. After all, that and her hair were the reason I was here. The feet weren't my department.

It was then that I noticed her expression wasn't as serene as I'd first thought. Her eyes bulged a tad too much under their closed lids. There was a glint of a clear substance under her lashes that looked disturbingly like dried Super Glue. Her jaw was tight. Her mouth molded into a Mona Lisa smile.

Trudy had never smiled that way. Her smile was big and white. "Gotta show off the implants," she'd always said. She'd paid a small fortune for them and wanted to be sure they were appreciated.

I swallowed the nausea rising in my throat. Could I do this? I wanted to. For one thing, I needed the money, but for another, Trudy was one of my favorite clients. I couldn't leave her so colorless and plain. She'd be mortified if she had to attend an event in her honor like this.

I walked behind the table. Trudy's hair was always one of her best features, soft and white as a cloud. It still was. I lifted a lock and gasped. Something like an electric current jolted through me. I dropped the hair. What the heck was that?

I circled the gurney looking for a cord or an outlet thinking the table might be electrified to keep the body cold. I had no idea how these things worked. There was nothing.

I reached for her head with tentative fingers. As soon as I touched her hair, pain shot through me again. This time, it was accompanied by rage. I released her hair as if I'd been burned. When I did, the feeling disappeared as quickly as it had come.

What should I do? I couldn't fix her hair if every time I touched it I got zapped. I stood for a long moment, staring at Trudy. Then I had an idea. I dumped my bag of tricks onto a nearby metal cart and opened it. I rummaged through, found a box of rubber gloves and snapped on a pair. Like a child jumping into a cold pool, I held my breath and grabbed Trudy's head. Nothing. No pain. No anger.

I exhaled with relief. Could Trudy's body contain pent up static electricity? Did that happen? I'd have to ask Carlton.

I found the magenta color I'd used last time I'd done her hair, a mixing bowl and brush, and stirred up a small amount of dye. I covered Trudy's upper body with an apron to protect her dress, and myself, just in case there were any stray currents coming off her, and felt a bit better. A minute later I'd painted the lock with a fresh coat of color, and I was in my groove.

I believe the beauty industry is a calling. I know stylists have reputations for not being the most intelligent people on the planet, the kids who couldn't hack college. The stereotype has merit. Some of the girls I went through school with were as dumb as an empty lipstick tube. But there were also the artists. I humbly included myself in that category.

I walked to the deep metal sink and turned on the tap. The excess dye bled from the bowl and circled down the drain in maroon clouds. Maybe I should have dyed her hair hot pink or navy blue. This color took my imagination places I'd rather it hadn't gone.

"Buck up," I told myself. It was time to do her face. I pulled on a clean pair of gloves, retrieved foundation and a sponge from my bag, turned, and stopped short. Trudy's head, which had been facing straight up to the ceiling just like her toes, now tilted to the left.

I stood still, hands in the hair. A shiver rippled up my spine.

Had I done this? When I do a client's hair, I often adjust their head for better accessibility. Had I done that without thinking, so wrapped up in the project I hadn't noticed? I couldn't imagine how else it could have happened.

I'd heard stories about corpses that twitched or made noises, but I believed it had to do with gases leaving the body. Surely that kind of thing had been over days ago. Trudy died on Tuesday. Today was Friday. Could gas hang around that long? Or could it be the weird electrical current I'd felt? I had a sudden vision of a body jumping under defibrillator paddles.

I set the makeup down and, with extreme caution, placed my hands one on either side of her face, grateful for the latex that separated us. I held my breath and pushed—ever so slowly—to the right. Trudy's head clicked into place.

Okay then.

I wiped my hands on my pants. I'd be more careful.

Carlton told me her skin had been moisturized earlier in the day. I hadn't asked why. I didn't want to know. But it did help the foundation go on smoothly. I dabbed color onto the apples of her cheeks, and along her hairline and chin. She began to look a little more lively. My shoulders relaxed. I hadn't realized how tense they'd become.

"You're going to be the hit of the party," I told her and was sorry I'd spoken out loud. My voice rang in the empty room. I was used to working to the music of the salon. I missed the hum and titter of voices, the oldies Harry favored floating through the speakers, the buzz of hair dryers, the spritz of hair spray cans, and the snip of shears. It was too quiet here.

If I did this again, I'd bring a speaker for my phone. *Did this again?* What was I thinking? Once was enough. "For you, Trudy. Only for you," I said.

I tossed the sponge in the trash, stowed the foundation and pulled out eyeshadow, liner, and mascara. I decided to do a smoky eye. Yes, Trudy was a bit old for glamour, but she never thought so. The first time I met her was at the Neutron Dance Hall, a studio in Irvine. I was there for a Lindy Hop lesson with Chad. He's a great dancer—only good thing about him.

And here comes this gray-haired lady who moved like a twenty-year-old. Scratch that, better than most twenty-year-olds. She sashayed into my life that night with her beautiful, bouncing white hair, and I couldn't wait to get my fingers into it.

That was the only time I ever walked up to a stranger and tried to sell them my services. I'm an introvert. But that night, I danced my way close, handed her one of my Harry's Hair Stop business cards, and told her to call me. She did, and the rest was history.

The memory made me smile, until I faced Trudy again. "Damn it." The words shot from my lips.

Her chin rested on her chest. It wasn't that way a minute ago. I'd adjusted her head. I'd pointed her nose at the ceiling. Why was this happening?

I must have knocked something loose when I was doing her hair. Now her head was flopping around like a rag doll's. Cold dread stirred in my stomach. What if it did that during the funeral?

I could just see it, her son stands up to give the eulogy, and Trudy shakes her head at him. That could scar somebody for life. Parental disappointment is demoralizing enough when the parent is alive.

I put a cautious finger under Trudy's chin and pushed her head up. I hated to do it, but I was going to have to say something to Carlton. He needed to staple her in place before she traumatized her family.

I hurried through the eye makeup, applied her favorite Ravishing Red lipstick, and stood back to admire my work. She looked great, if I did say so myself. I half expected her to jump off the table and pull me into a sugar push.

The timer on my phone split the air. I jumped. "Geez." I fumbled for the off switch. It was time to rinse the dye from her hair, blow the strand dry, and style her.

I'd noticed a large bowl on the counter earlier and decided to rinse her hair in that. I wouldn't bother with shampoo. It wasn't like this hairstyle had to last. I filled the bowl with water, turned, took three steps toward the gurney, and dropped it.

The clatter was earsplitting.

4

OPEN ARMS

Trudy's hands were no longer clasped over her navel. Her arms had fallen open. They hung off the table, palms up, in a supplicant gesture. It was as if she was beseeching heaven, or me, to—damn it—do something.

I did. I ran to the heavy door and pulled it open. I wish I could say I was calm and controlled, but I wasn't. My lizard brain had taken charge of my body, and I no longer had options. I escaped into the corridor and raced toward the stairwell.

Before I reached it, a man barged through the door. I had a fleeting impression of size. This was a man of mammoth proportions. Good. I need big and strong right now. He was also dressed in a beige uniform. Good, again. Uniforms always engender a feeling of security unless they're pulling you over on the freeway. His hand rested on the gun at his waist. Not quite as good. Guns make me nervous, and I didn't think Trudy was dangerous. His face registered alarm as his eyes fixed on mine.

"Something's wrong," I managed to say.

He raised an eyebrow.

"Something's wrong," I repeated.

"What's that?" he said.

I couldn't explain. I didn't know. I was done talking. I grabbed his hand and dragged him into the embalming room. As soon as I saw Trudy, arms dangling over the sides of the table, I shuddered yet again.

The man's eyes scanned the room. His gaze traveled everywhere but to Trudy.

"There." I pointed a shaking finger at the gurney.

He looked at the corpse for a long moment, then turned a questioning face to me.

"She's moving," I said, my voice just above a whisper.

He narrowed his eyes. "Moving?"

"Yes, moving."

"What exactly do you mean by moving?"

I lost it then. I did a frantic jig and waved my hands in his face. "Moving. Moving. What the hell do you think moving means?"

"She did that?" He backed away from me.

"No. Of course not." I closed my eyes and tried to calm myself. After a long moment, I opened them and told him everything that had happened over the past hour—the electric shocks, the twitches. I ended with the *coup de gras*. "I went to the sink, and when I got back she was like that—arms open. Like she's, like she's asking for help."

The expression on his face as I related my story was intense and intelligent. His eyebrows met in an angled arch above a furrowed forehead. His lips pursed. This gave me the courage to ask what I'd been afraid to ask. "She couldn't be alive, could she?"

He grinned. Okay, forget my earlier assessment. The man obviously didn't have two brain cells to rub together. "It's a gravity thing," he said. "Sometimes arms don't want to stay where you put them. They flop out. Amy Lee, she's our head embalmer, usually ties their thumbs together. She must have forgotten to do it with..." He waved at Trudy. "Your friend here."

I wasn't ready to give up on Trudy. I couldn't shake the impression she was calling for help in the only way she could. "How do you explain the head then?"

He shrugged his shoulders. "You probably gave it a knock when you were fixing her hair."

I took a deep, embarrassed breath and let it out slowly. "Can you check?" My voice was soft. "Just to be sure?"

"You mean if she's alive?"

"Yes." I stared at my shoes.

He softened his voice to match my tone. "She's been embalmed. If she was alive when they brought her in, she isn't anymore."

"That's not something a person can live through?"

He shook his head. "No. See that machine over there?" He pointed to a device that looked like an overgrown blender. "They fill that with a cocktail of formaldehyde, methanol, and other poisonous chemicals and pump it into her veins."

I felt a little ill and a lot foolish. "Oh. Sorry for the stupid question."

He waved away my words. "Everybody gets the jitters in the beginning. It took me a week to get up the courage to visit Death Valley."

"Death Valley?"

"That's what we call the basement." He put out his hand. "Elmore, but everybody calls me El."

"Imogene," I said and shook.

I was finally calm enough to take a good look at him. He had a nice face. Too all-American for my taste, but open and handsome in an Eagle Scout kind of way. His dark blond hair was close cropped, but several strands had fallen over his forehead in all the excitement. His eyes were blue, his nose ski-sloped, his chin dimpled.

"So are you the new embalmer's assistant?" he asked.

"Me? No. I'm a hairstylist. Trudy, ah, the deceased, was my client. She asked if I'd get her ready for the funeral. It was a dying wish kind of thing."

"Oh, that explains it. No wonder you freaked out." Freaked out wasn't the expression I would have used. Frightened. Horrified, maybe. Freaked out made me sound like a hormonal teenager. "It takes a while to get used to socializing with the dearly departed."

He walked to the gurney, picked up Trudy's left hand and laid it on her stomach, did the same with the right, then gave them an affectionate pat. "You stop scaring the help," he said to her, then turned to face me. "Are you done here?"

How I wished I was, but I wasn't. "No. I have to wash the dye out of her hair, blow it dry, and style it."

"Sounds interesting. Mind if I watch?" He walked to the back wall, grabbed a handful of paper towels and began mopping up the water I'd spilled.

I was sure he wasn't interested in styling hair. He thought I needed company, hand holding. I bristled at the thought, but realized he was right. I didn't want him to leave.

He handed me the bowl I'd dropped when I thought Trudy was coming back from the dead. I took it to the sink. "So, how long have you worked at Greener Pastures?" I asked, attempting to start a conversation.

"About three years, but this is temporary. Just until I get on the force."

I carried the bowl to Trudy and began rinsing the dye from her hair. "The force?"

"Yes. Law enforcement. That's my ultimate goal, but you gotta pay the bills meanwhile." A cop. Made sense. It fit with his whole here-I-come-to-save-the-day persona.

"How do you do that? Become a cop, I mean?" I wasn't interested in how someone became a cop any more than he was interested in styling hair, but it seemed polite to ask.

"I'm in school now. Getting my degree in criminal justice." He paused, and I could swear I saw his chest expand. "I'm also taking some online classes in police procedures. When I'm done with school, I'll take a PEP class—Pre-Employment Preparation—and then apply for the academy."

I dumped the water I'd used to rinse Trudy's hair into the sink, returned to the table, pulled the dryer out of my bag, and plugged it in. There was a break in the conversation while I blew dry Trudy's hair, and it gave me a chance to think.

I knew El had an explanation for why her body moved, but he hadn't offered any plausible reasons for the shock I'd gotten when I touched her. He'd only squinted his eyes.

She wasn't alive. I believed him there. But now, as I styled her hair, I noticed how my hands moved, how I touched her head. If anything, this was more disruptive than lifting one lock of hair and painting it with a brush. Yet her head stayed still.

What did this mean? I had no idea. A thriller movie I'd seen recently on Netflix was rolling through my mind. In it, a group of students stumbled on a drug that brought people back from the dead. Of course, they didn't come back unscathed and pandemonium ensued, but forget all that. I wondered if there was a drug that could be taken before you died that, while it wouldn't bring you back, might make you twitchy after death. You know, like corpse caffeine.

This sounded absurd, I was aware. But when I flicked off the hair dryer, I couldn't help myself. "El," I said. He looked my way and smiled. "Is it possible that Trudy's twitches could be some kind of chemical reaction to, say, the embalming fluid?"

His smile faded. "I've never heard of anything like that."

"It's just, I was really careful when I was painting on the dye." I paused. "I didn't want to touch her. You know what I mean?"

El studied the ceiling for a long moment. "I guess I could ask my Forensic Science teacher."

I brightened. It wouldn't bring Trudy back, but it would be nice to know I wasn't crazy. I finished her hair and stepped away from the gurney to take in the final product. El walked over and stood next to me. "You're good," he said, admiration in his voice. "Our clients aren't usually this lifelike, but don't tell Amy Lee I said so."

She did look good. So good, it was hard to wrap my head around the fact she was dead. I felt my first stab of grief. I'd been so focused on Trudy's grooming, I'd forgotten the woman. In life, she'd been a bundle of dancing, laughing energy. I was going to miss her.

The last time I'd done her hair, for that New Year's party, she'd told me her heart was as strong as a race horse's. Said it was all the swing dancing she did. Which proved the point, you can't predict what life—or death—will throw at you. Only four months after the party, and she dies of a heart attack. Strange world.

5
HARRY'S REQUEST

"Genie." The voice wouldn't go away. This was the third time it had called my name. I opened one eye and closed it again. Gran stood near my bed with her old flip phone in her hand. "Genie, it's Harry."

"Why is he calling you?" I mumbled the words into my pillow.

"Because your phone is turned off. Here. Talk to him. Phil just got here. I need to go downstairs."

I reached out a hand and pawed for the phone without opening my eyes. "Hello," I said when I made contact.

"Genie, get up. You've got a funeral to attend." Harry's voice was at least a half octave higher than usual.

"Why do I have to go?" I opened my eyes.

"Because the artist should attend her opening." He chortled. Until this moment, I'd only read about chortles. I seriously didn't care if I ever heard another one.

I heaved myself into a sitting position and pushed the bangs from my eyes. "What are you talking about?"

"You, darling. Carlton says your work is fabulous. He wants you there. I want you there. Gertrude was a popular lady. This could be the biggest event Liberty Grove sees this season."

"And you want me to do what?" I said, although I thought I was beginning to understand.

"Represent us, Genie. Smile, be sympathetic, flex that tattoo, and make sure everyone knows you were the one who transformed Trudy."

"Are we angling for live clients, or dead ones?" I was being sarcastic, but Harry didn't seem to notice.

"Both," he said with enthusiasm. "This could be a whole new market for us, Genie darling. *Look like a million bucks in the here and the hereafter.* I'm thinking of running an ad in The Liberty Grove Gazette." I didn't like that idea at all, but I didn't have a chance to argue. Harry was on a roll. "Make sure you stop by the salon for a stack of twenty percent-off coupons. Hand them out with the business cards. They don't say anything about our post-life services, but you could mention it."

Post-life services?

"I had no idea you had this hidden talent," he said. "You've been holding out on me, you sly thing, you."

"Harry—"

He cut me off. "No more chatting. You have a funeral to get to." He sounded like the fairy godmother in a fractured fairy tale.

"Harry—"

"Make yourself beautiful, which won't be difficult."

I was shocked into silence. Harry had never complimented me before. In fact, I'd always had the impression I would be the first to go if there were cutbacks at the salon. I pulled myself together. "Harry—"

"You do have something appropriate to wear, right? Basic black? Maybe a strand of pearls?"

"Harry." I yelled into the phone. He finally stopped talking. "How much?" I said.

By the time Harry and I were done dickering about my fee for becoming his new Diplomat of Death, I really had to hurry. I jumped from bed, and in two short strides, I was standing at my closet door.

My room was small. Gran's condo was small. I needed a place of my own, for both our sakes. This thought made me feel only slightly better about selling my soul to Harry.

I surveyed my wardrobe and shook my head. *Do I have anything black to wear?* His question only proved he never actually looked at me when I was at the salon. My closet was a sea of black interrupted only by a handful of red polka dots, pink stripes and aqua blues from my Lucille Ball inspired days.

I pulled on an A-line skirt, a scoop-neck sweater and wide leather belt. I glanced in the mirror. My hair had been recently dyed, no blond roots. I was a symphony of ebony. I put on ruby red lipstick to break up the monochrome and headed for the door. I stopped, hand on knob. Shoes. I ran to the closet and grabbed a pair of red heels. Not for the funeral. The ballet flats I wore were for that.

These were for the after party. I happened to know the staff at Neutron Dance Hall were planning a Lindy Hop in Trudy's honor. I would be there.

Gran's voice interrupted my descent to the kitchen. She sounded angry. "I don't like it, Phil."

"Now honey, an ounce of prevention..."

"Most of that stuff is poison. It'll cure your problem alright, if it doesn't kill you first."

"Dr. Foster is a good doctor." Phil's tone was reassuring, but I didn't think Gran would buy his argument. Gran had no faith in traditional medicine. When she'd turned sixty-five, her doctor told her the best thing people could do for their health as they aged was to stay away from doctors. She'd taken him seriously.

"The AMA is in the pocket of the insurance industry. Doctors are just high-paid pill pushers. If you'd cut back on the red meat and start drinking the turmeric-ginger tea I made for you, you wouldn't need that stuff."

Harley slunk past me up the stairs. He hated conflict. I was tempted to follow him, but I had a funeral to get to. I cleared my throat so Gran and Phil would know I was coming.

They sat at the dining room table, uneaten bagels in front of them. I edged past to the kitchen and the coffeepot.

"Want a bagel?" Gran said, a false note of cheer in her voice. "Phil bought them at that place you like."

"I don't have time," I said.

"There's a blueberry with your name on it," Phil said.

"Save it for me. I've got to run."

"So where are you going all gussied up?" Gran asked when I returned to the dining room.

"Looks like you're going to a funeral." Phil said that every time he saw me. He's not a fan of black. But, hey, I'm not a fan of his white loafers.

"I am."

His smile faded. "Oh. I was just joking with you. Didn't mean to—"

I waved away his words. "It's okay. It's kind of a work thing."

Gran stood, picked up their mugs, and muscled past me. "What do you mean, a work thing?" she said from the kitchen.

"One of my clients died." I raised my voice and told her the whole story, omitting the part about Trudy's extraneous activity. I didn't want to get her started. Gran, as I mentioned, believed in the afterlife and spirits and all that. I didn't. I was sure there was a scientific explanation for what I'd experienced and hoped El would find it.

She returned to the dining room with full mugs of coffee. "So Harry expects you to spend your Saturday hanging around a funeral parlor hawking Harry's Hair Stop?" She had that mama-bear edge in her voice. "I hope he's paying you."

"He is."

"But is he paying you enough?" Phil said. "Saturday is a big day at the salon, isn't it? You need to consider the cost of lost appointments against what you'll be making today. Don't be penny wise and pound foolish."

Harry's had a different schedule due to our clientele, who were all retired. Weekends at the salon were typically dead. There was a joke in there somewhere, but I was in too much of a hurry to find it. "It's not just the money," I said. "It's also about Trudy."

A strange look crossed Phil's face. "Trudy?"

"Yeah. Gertrude Rosenblum. My client."

Phil turned almost as white as Trudy had been before I did her makeup. He swallowed. "Trudy is dead?"

Guilt hit me like a sock in the gut. I hadn't realized he knew her. That was no way to hear about a friend's death.

"Trudy Rosenblum," Gran said. "Wasn't she your neighbor?"

Phil nodded, then looked at me. "What happened?"

"Heart attack," I said.

Phil and Gran locked eyes for a long moment. Tension rolled off them in waves. "I gotta go." I kissed Gran on top of her head, and she patted my hand.

"Love you, baby," she said.

"You, too," I said and escaped.

The great outdoors smelled like grass cuttings and wet dirt. Saturday was gardening day in Liberty Grove. I waved to Mr. Rogers, who was out in front of his place pruning roses. Yes, I did say Mr. Rogers. It took me a long time to call him that without giggling. He wore the same kind of sweaters as the man we all know and love, but that was where the resemblance ended.

This Mr. Rogers, Mr. Alfred Rogers, didn't want to be my neighbor. I was pretty sure he was the one who'd turned Gran into the association because I lived with her. Thanks to Mr. Won't-You-Leave-My-Neighborhood, I had to park my car outside the gates at night.

"It's a beautiful day," I said as I passed him.

He scowled at me and snipped a dead rose from a stalk. For someone who had the hots for Gran, he wasn't especially warm and friendly to her granddaughter.

"Just stopped by to see Gran. Now I'm off to work." I smiled sweetly. There were no rules about how often, or what times of day I could visit. There were also no rules about how much of my things she could store. Unless Mr. Rogers was prepared to sit up nights with a camcorder, he couldn't prove a thing. I enjoyed rubbing his bulbous red nose in it.

I continued on my five-block trek to the car, feeling better than I had all morning. So I had to spend a few hours at a funeral. How bad could it be?

6

THE BIG DAY

The winding road that led to the mortuary was lined with sedans, and the parking lot behind the building was full. I guessed Harry was right, Trudy's funeral was the biggest event of the Liberty Grove season. I drove to a lot deep inside the cemetery and hiked back.

By the time I got there, a trickle of sweat slipped down my spine, and my hair hung damp on my neck. The cool, dim interior of the mortuary was a relief. Carlton had told me last night the service would be held in the Sistine Chapel, so I headed that way. As soon as I made the right, I saw a crowd milling around a mountain of flowers in the wide hall outside its doors.

There was an easel in the center of the floral display. On it was a picture of a woman I recognized as a young Trudy. Her brown hair curled around her head in a similar style to the one she wore today. Her eyes had the same sparkle, and her smile the same impish tilt as the Trudy I'd known.

My assignment was to stand next to the guest book and assault unsuspecting mourners with Harry's Hair Stop discount cards. Before I took my post, I glanced inside the chapel. The rows were only about half filled.

I noticed Doris Miller, who sat close to the front, dabbing her eyes with a tissue. She must be devastated. She and Trudy had been inseparable, much to Trudy's consternation at times. Three rows behind her were Norman Fielding and Rita Tarkington, two other close friends. Trudy, Doris, Rita, and Norman were all Neutron Dance Hall members and often drove to classes and open dance nights together. I wondered why the three remaining members of the quartet weren't sitting together. It seemed strange, but I didn't give it a lot of thought. I was there to check on Trudy.

Her body in its green party dress was encased in a satin lined mahogany casket. She looked like an emerald in a jewel box. It was hard to see the hair and makeup from the doorway, but I could tell her head was where it should be—nose to sky. I breathed a sigh of relief.

A line of black-suited seniors milled around the large poster boards flanking the Sistine Chapel entrance. On the boards were photographs of Trudy. Trudy in a bridal gown on the arm of a handsome, dark-haired man. Trudy with a fat baby in her arms. Trudy, her husband, and two bundled up school-aged children standing by a snowman.

Some pictures reflected her life after the death of her husband. There were shots of European vacations, Christmases with grandchildren, and several of her in swing dance outfits. An unexpected lump formed in my throat. I would miss her.

I handed out ten of Harry's discount cards before a piano rendition of Amazing Grace called everybody into the chapel. I took a seat four rows from the front so I could see Trudy up close and personal.

I bent to slip my purse under the pew, and as I straightened, someone slid onto the bench next to me. I glanced over. It took a minute for me to recognize El without his uniform. He looked even larger, if that were possible. He wore a black golf shirt and dark jeans. Not entirely appropriate for a funeral, but I was transfixed. In the long-sleeved uniform, he'd looked powerful, but I couldn't tell how much of his girth was muscle. Today I could. He was cut.

The music stopped. I dragged my eyes from his arms and focused on the chaplain, who'd just stepped up to the altar. El wasn't my type, I reminded myself. I always dated smaller, leaner guys—okay, short, skinny guys. He leaned toward me and whispered, "I talked to my Forensics Science teacher this morning."

"What did he say?" I asked, but before he could answer, the chaplain began the homily. El sat back and drummed his fingers on his thigh. The message was short. It was also poignant, something I think El missed. The chaplain had been Trudy's pastor for ten years. I hadn't realized she'd been a church goer. There were so many things I hadn't known about her.

He finished up and introduced Trudy's oldest, Megan, who sat in the first row with a man I assumed was her husband and two adorable little girls. As Megan mounted the small stage, El looked at me. "He said he'd never heard of anything like that before—a reaction to the embalming fluid—but he got kind of excited. He wants us to get a hair sample to him. He says it'll be a great experiment for the class."

"A hair sample?"

"Yeah, for an analysis. It'll show any drugs that were in her system a month or so prior to her death. I might even get extra credit."

I squinted my eyes at him. "I don't think we should desecrate a corpse just so you can get extra credit."

He opened his mouth to argue, but clacked it shut when Megan stepped to the microphone. She didn't speak for almost a full minute. I could see she was struggling to compose herself. So was El. He squirmed in his seat like a second grader.

"My mom," she finally said, and launched into a touching, sometimes humorous, synopsis of Trudy's life. She did pretty well, until she got to the part about Trudy's swing dancing. "She was the youngest, healthiest, most active seventy-eight-year-old I've ever known. Which is why her death—" She choked up for a moment, cleared her throat, then went on. "Which is why her death was such a shock." A sob cut into the last word. Megan tipped her chin toward a man in the front row and went to her seat.

El leaned forward as soon as she left the platform. "That's not the only reason," he said as if there hadn't been a ten-minute break in our conversation. "What if we could find out what killed her?"

"What killed her was a heart attack," I whispered.

"Her daughter just said she was healthy. No heart problems."

"She was seventy-eight. Stuff happens when you're seventy-eight." I aimed my gaze at the podium to let him know I was done discussing it.

The man from the front row was Trudy's son, James. I'd seen photographs of him. She'd spoken more about him than she had her daughter. Not because she'd been more proud or had loved him more. She'd adored both her children. But because she'd worried about him more. James, in her words, was flying with Peter Pan. He didn't want to grow up.

"Maybe, maybe not," El said sotto voce. "It seems suspicious to me. I was in the hallway listening to the guests for a while. They were shocked by her death."

"Shhh."

El huffed, but he shushed.

James looked, if possible, even more stricken than his sister had. His eyes were red rimmed and puffy from crying. He held a limp sheet of notebook paper in his hand. My gaze traveled to his mother's face. I crossed my fingers. *Please Trudy, please. Don't make a scene.* I'd never said anything to Carlton about her escapades of the previous night.

In the light of a new day, I'd realized my panic had been excessive. My excuse was I'd never seen a corpse before, never mind touched one. And there I was alone with a body in an embalming room. My imagination had run amok. In my nervous state, it was no wonder I'd imagined jolts and knocked Trudy's head around.

James began with a tear-jerking story from his childhood. I felt waves of impatience rolling off El. I regretted getting him involved in all this. He was using my inexperience to make points with his forensics teacher. I planned to shut this down as soon as the service was over.

James struggled to get out the few words he'd prepared and left the stage. The pianist played something familiar. A hymn, but I didn't know which one. El leaned toward me again, about to speak, but I glared at him. Really, the man had no sense of propriety. When the song ended, the pastor invited everyone to a light luncheon in the community room. The mourners began to file out of the pews.

I started to rise, but El put a hand on my arm. "Wait." I stiffened, but he gave me a pleading-puppy look, and I stayed put. A minute. I'd give him a minute. No more.

He waited until everyone had left the chapel, took my arm and led me to the coffin. "I have a gut feeling about this."

He sounded so much like a detective from a cop show, I barked a laugh. El looked over his shoulder. "Lower your voice." I covered my mouth with a hand. "Laugh all you want, but I'm serious. From all accounts, this was a very healthy woman who died suddenly, and no one did an autopsy."

"That's because the doctor said she had a heart attack."

"But what caused the heart attack? Have you thought about that?"

I shook my head. "What do you think happened?" It was apparent I wouldn't get out of there until I heard what he had to say.

"Seniors die from taking prescription drugs the way they were told to take them all the time, and it's covered up. If we find out there are high levels of something in her system, we can report the doctor who overdosed her."

I thought about this for a long moment. Strange he should say this right after the conversation I'd overheard between Gran and Phil that morning.

"We'd be doing a service for the people of Liberty Grove," El said.

"Well . . ." I was beginning to weaken.

"We could stop a quack from hurting more people."

He had a point.

"And bring meaning to Trudy's senseless death."

I rolled my eyes.

Realizing he'd gone too far, he lightened his tone. "Besides, what's the harm in taking a sample?"

"Is it legal? What if we get in trouble?" I needed to know the ramifications.

"You're her hair stylist. If anyone has the right to cut Trudy's hair, it's you."

"Well," I said again.

"We can take the sample from the back of her head. No one will ever notice."

I eyed Trudy. She wasn't moving, and I wanted to keep it that way. "How are we going to do that?"

He pulled a pair of shears from his pocket. "I'll hold her head up. You snip."

I recoiled from the scissors. I'd had enough physical contact with the dead in the past twenty-four hours to last me a lifetime.

"You could hold her head, and I could cut," he offered.

That was worse. "Give me the scissors." I reached for them but stopped short.

A deep voice resonated through the hall and into the chapel. "Forty-five minutes, and we'll be graveside." El and I pivoted toward the door. I couldn't see him, but I recognized Carlton's bass rumble. "I'm going to close the casket now," he said to an invisible person.

El and I locked gazes. Relief and disappointment washed over me. I would have liked to know what caused Trudy's twitches if it were possible. But I was wary of touching her hair without gloves and hated to desecrate the hair-do.

We stepped away from the casket as Carlton entered the chapel. "She did a lovely job, didn't she?" he sang from the doorway.

El nodded and palmed the scissors. "She did."

"Have you thought about going to mortician school, Imogene? You've got the touch. I don't say that to just anyone."

I wasn't sure that was a compliment, but I said, "Thanks."

"I'm serious. We're hiring."

Not in a million years. "I'll think about it."

Carlton placed a hand on the casket. "Take your final look. I've got to close up."

El and I exchanged a glance. We were too late. I guessed I'd never know if Trudy's twitches were my fault, or from leftover sparks, or a chemical reaction, but I was at peace with it.

I watched her disappear as the lid lowered and shut with a final thump. That was it, then. Life in a box. Seventy-eight years of experiences, wins and losses, travels and homecomings, loved ones and enemies, all crated up and waiting for burial. None of us spoke. I wondered if El felt the same sense of finality, or if working here had made him callous.

A crackle of static broke the silence. Carlton pulled a walkie-talkie from his jacket pocket. "Yes," he said into it.

There was too much interference for me to understand the voice on the other end, but Carlton did. "Now?" He sounded irritated. "Can't you handle it?" He listened again, and a frown formed on his face. "All right. Be there in a minute." He pocketed the walkie-talkie and looked at El. "Lock up for me, will you? Don't want her falling out in transit." He spun and left the chapel without waiting for a response.

El watched him go, then turned to me with a smile. He held out the scissors. "Get as close to the scalp as you can."

7

TRUDY'S LAST DANCE

The sun disappeared, leaving behind a spectacular sky, purple clouds rimmed with gold, streaks of gray and rose. It was as if even the planet was saying goodbye to Trudy. I appreciated all this from the Santa Ana Freeway on my way to the Neutron Dance Hall.

The graveside ceremony had gone without a hitch. El and I cut a lock from Trudy's head—no sparks—and he closed and sealed the casket. To my great relief, she stayed put in transit. Her family and only a few of her closest friends followed the hearse across the acres of gravestones to her final resting place.

I didn't have to go. Harry had only requested I attend the service in the chapel, but after everything she and I had been through, I wanted to. I felt closer to Trudy in her death than I had when she was alive. El went with me. I'd like to think he'd formed an attachment to her, too.

After the burial, we went for a burger. As we ate, he told me more about his schooling. El was a true crusader. He was passionate about law enforcement because he saw it as a way to right the wrongs of the world. This was a surprise to me. I guess I've always associated cops with power-tripping megalomaniacs. Comes from being raised by an ex-hippie. Gran may be a Christian, but she's never lost her suspicion of the establishment.

There was a long line outside Neutron when I pulled into the parking lot. I had to park at the far end. As I walked to the entrance, I tried to shake off the somber mood I'd been in since we closed the lid on Trudy. It wasn't like we were family, or even that close. She'd been a client, a fun client, and someone I saw at dances on occasion.

Gran would say I was upset because I'd never dealt with my end-of-life beliefs. My position has always been *I don't know what happens, and I don't care.* That position seemed kind of empty now.

I'd felt, or imagined I'd felt, emotions emanating from Trudy's corpse. That did raise a few questions in my mind about the human spirit. Specifically, how long does it hang around after its owner kicks the bucket? My best guess was that it faded away slowly, like the sun at the end of the day. I'd caught the tail end of Trudy's sunset.

"Hi, May," I said to the woman at the front desk. May was an aging Hawaiian beauty who started at Neutron as a Hula teacher back in the day when people wanted to learn Hula. "Good turnout tonight."

"You bet," she said. "The regulars are all here. Nobody wants to miss Trudy's last dance."

The lobby was dark, lit only by light emanating from the ballroom it bordered. A crush of people stood or sat at high top tables waiting for the class in the big room to end. I crossed to a wall of cupboards across from the restrooms, took off my ballet slippers, shoved them into a cupboard, and padded in stocking feet to a chair. I watched the newbies in the ballroom step on each others' toes as I strapped on my red heels.

That had been me only four years ago. Chad had brought me here on our second date. He already knew how to do all the steps and was a model of patience. He was all compliments and encouragement in the early days, said I had natural talent. The only time I missed him was when I was at Neutron.

Pandemonium broke out as those leaving class and those entering for the open dance collided. I joined the throng. The bright lights used during instruction had been turned down low. But even in the dim light, I recognized most of the fifty or so people in the room, and they recognized each other. Greetings echoed off the mirrored walls. Neutron's dancers were a community.

This place was the best thing to come out of my relationship with Chad. It made dating him almost worth it. I chatted with the group around me until Big Bad Voodoo Daddy blared from the speakers.

Hank, a fifty-something divorcee, jigged across the floor in my direction, hand out. I took it, and he pulled me into a spin. He's a flirt, but he's a good dancer, so I put up with it. All thoughts of death and dying and the meaning of life were driven out of my head. Dancing was exactly what I'd needed.

By the third song, I was in a much better mood. I also decided I'd had enough of Hank. He was getting a little too touchy-feely. I excused myself and headed to the water cooler in the lobby. I poured a cold cup, turned to head back to the ballroom, and collided with a plaid shirt. Water sloshed from my glass and soaked the person in front of me.

I glanced up, ready to apologize, but the words died on my lips. Chad deserved to be doused. "Damn it, Imogene. Why don't you watch where you're going?"

I lifted the corners of my mouth, but I don't think my expression could have been confused for a smile. "Why Chad, what are you doing here?"

The terms of our separation had specifically stated he got Patty's Pub, our favorite post-dance hang out, and I got Neutron. The idea was to stay out of each other's orbits.

"Trudy," he said. "I came to pay my respects."

I snorted. He may have liked Trudy, but she didn't feel the same way about him. "He's trouble, Imogene. He'll make you miserable. I know the type." She'd said that so sincerely and so often, I was sure she'd once had a Chad in her life. I should have listened to her and dumped him sooner. But I'm strong-willed.

"Don't worry, we won't stay long. Just want to catch a couple of dances," Chad said. I checked out the "we" he was referring to. Standing a little behind him was a tall, skinny blond. She was the type that gave me fits when we were dating.

I could be blond, something Chad never let me forget. "Most chicks dye their hair blond. You're the only blond I know who dyes it black," he'd said often.

His statement was wrong on so many levels. First, you don't "dye" your hair blond. If your hair is dark, you have to bleach it. Take color out before you add any. Second, plenty of girls in my circle dye their hair black. The color goes well with straight cut bangs, retro clothes, and red lipstick. I added burgundy highlights to mine just to stand out from the crowd. The new color started as an experiment, but when I found out how important blond hair was to Chad, it sealed the deal. I switched from semi-permanent to permanent dye.

"Are you going to introduce me to your friend?" I said. Not that I was interested in meeting her, but I wanted him to know her presence didn't bother me. I couldn't care less who he dated. I was so over him.

He looked confused for a moment, then the lights clicked on. "Oh, McKenzie." He jerked a thumb over his shoulder. "Imogene. Imogene, McKenzie."

The music stopped, and a voice boomed through the speakers. Chad, McKenzie, and I headed into the ballroom and found a spot amid the listening crowd.

"A special lady left the planet this past week," a Neutron instructor said. "Gertrude Rosenblum was one of my favorite students. I love you all." A low chuckle crossed the room. "But Trudy was this teacher's pet."

She told us about Trudy's incredible aptitude for dance, her stamina, and her generosity with new students. She got a bit choked up once or twice but managed to get through it without tears. I heard a loud sniff on my right.

It was Doris Miller, Trudy's onetime best friend. Doris had changed out of her funeral black and looked perky in a red shift dress that almost hid her wide hips. Several strands of her salt and pepper hair had been dyed to match her outfit. I hadn't done that. She'd obviously cheated on me with another stylist.

"She was queen of the Lindy Hop," Doris said in my ear.

"She was." Should I mention that I'd seen Doris at the funeral today? I'd never made it over to say hello to her, Rita, or Norman. I'd been distracted, and I assumed I'd see them at Neutron that night.

"I still can't believe it," Doris said. "I can't believe she's gone."

I believed it, considering everything that had happened in the past twenty-four hours. But I agreed with Doris to be polite.

"Join us in a memorial dance in Gertrude Rosenblum's honor." The words blared through the speakers, and the music started. I glanced around the room looking for a partner. Hank-the-hands was already groping a brunette. I moved toward a guy about my age I recognized from classes, but someone grabbed my wrist from behind. Before I realized what was happening, I was pulled center floor by Chad.

I should have protested. Walked away. But Chad is a dream to dance with. We were partners for four years. In that time, I learned him the way a first chair violinist learns her violin. My body reacted instinctively to each movement of his shoulders. I knew what he was going to do before he did.

This was the reason I stayed with Chad long after I knew who he was. Off the dance floor Chad was a lying, two-timing, macho loser. And, worse, he was stupid. His idea of literature was *Popular Mechanics*. His favorite movie was *Smokey and the Bandit*. We have nothing in common. On the dance floor, we were soul partners. Problem was, most of life was spent off the dance floor.

This was my excuse for partnering with the creep for the Gertrude Rosenblum memorial Lindy Hop. When the music played, I was drawn to him like a magnet. But as soon as the last notes faded, I pulled away. I was managing my addiction—a dangerous game.

"One more," he said, his eyes bright. He felt the magic, too.

"Nope." I shook my head. "I promised the next dance to..." I spied the guy from classes standing alone near the sound booth, but couldn't remember his name. "Him." I sashayed across the room. "Next dance?" I said when I reached him. He looked surprised but took my hands.

He was a decent dancer, but it wasn't the same. No synchronicity. When the song ended, I thanked him and headed to the lobby. My heart was no longer in it.

I made myself a cup of mint tea and sat at a high-top table near the entrance of the ballroom where I could watch the couples rotate past. People of all ages, sizes, and shapes, spun and hopped and threw each other to the beat. Most were doing the West Coast Swing, but some were doing variations of East Coast. One pair Texas Two-Stepped by.

Doris emerged from the dancers and made a beeline to my table. I groaned. I wasn't in the mood for small talk.

I liked Doris, don't get me wrong. She was a generous lady. Maybe too generous. I often wondered how Trudy dealt with all the attention. Once Doris decided you were a friend, she attached herself like an overly helpful limpet.

She hefted her chubby frame onto a stool, pulled a tissue from her sleeve, and mopped her forehead. "I'm not getting any younger."

"None of us are." I felt silly as soon as the words left my lips. It's exactly what Phil would have said. Moving out of Gran's place was less want and more need. It wasn't healthy. While it was true I wasn't getting younger, what twenty-six-year-old says something like that when a seventy-year-old complains about their age? None. That's who.

"Trudy looked beautiful," she said and fanned herself with her tissue.

"Thank you."

"I think you're going to get a lot of business from today. I heard several of the girls talking about it at the luncheon."

I wondered if she meant immediate business, like while people were alive, or if I was going to have to wait for them to knock off. I didn't know how to ask without sounding skeevy, so I didn't.

"I, for one, am coming back." She fingered a strand of red hair and had the decency to look uncomfortable. "I switched to Gayle when she ran that holiday hair deal. But, as I told the girls today, you get what you pay for. You're much better."

"I'll try to fit you in." I had plenty of empty slots on my calendar, but I wanted to make her squirm.

"Did you see Rita today?" Doris switched topics.

Although they hung out in the same circles, there wasn't any love lost between Doris and Rita. They were polar opposites. Doris had been a nurse. When she retired, she moved to Liberty Grove and began taking care of her neighbors. Doris was short, dumpy, and had an excessively fleshy nose, which may explain why she never married.

Rita, on the other hand, was tall and lithe and carried herself with the grace of an aging film star, which she claimed to be. She'd been married at least twice, maybe three times, and was either a divorcee or a widow at the moment.

"I saw her in the back of the room, sitting with Dr. Norman. I saw you, too. Sorry I didn't make it over to say hello," I said.

Doris waved her hankie. "That's okay. I wasn't in a fit state to talk to anyone. Trudy's death didn't seem to bother Rita much, though."

I arched an eyebrow.

"Did you see her dress?"

I must have seen it, but it hadn't registered as unusual. I shook my head.

"Maybe I'm just old fashioned," Doris said. "I don't think it's appropriate to show that much cleavage at a funeral. She was laughing up a storm at the luncheon, too. Like she didn't have a care in the world. I think it bothered Phil."

"Phil? My Phil? I mean, Gran's Phil?" I hadn't seen him at the funeral.

"Yes, he walked out without eating a thing. Not that the service was about food. It wasn't a social occasion, was it? I don't think a funeral should be treated as one. But there are those who don't agree with me."

Bait in the water. Okay, I'd bite. "Who doesn't agree with you?"

She paused to take a sip of water. She wanted me to ask again. I obeyed. "I can't imagine anyone being that thoughtless. Who would be that thoughtless?"

She set her glass down and tightened her lips as if drawing back the bow string before letting the arrow fly. "I'll bet you can guess. Just look around." She gestured to the ballroom. "Who is missing?"

I wrinkled my brow as if I was thinking very hard, then widened my eyes in feigned surprise. "Rita and Dr. Norman?"

Doris nodded. "Yes. They met up with the Bunko group at the luncheon. Turns out there were some cancellations for tonight's game, so instead of coming to Trudy's farewell dance, they went to Bunko."

I tried to look scandalized, although I'm sure Trudy wouldn't have wanted anyone to miss out on Bunko because of her. She was a social butterfly who never let a party pass her by. She was also as kind and thoughtful as Rita was self-absorbed and as respectful of other's privacy as Doris was invasive. I'd always thought of her as the glue that bound that group together. Now that the glue was gone, it appeared to be falling apart.

I patted Doris's hand. "Thank God for friends like you," I said.

Doris dabbed at her eyes with the tissue. She'd gotten a lot of mileage out of that bit of paper. "I'm going to miss her." She sniffled.

"We all will." I glanced over Doris's shoulder, looking for an excuse to escape. The day had been stressful. I didn't have the energy to deal with any more Liberty Grove soap opera. My gaze thudded to a stop on Chad.

He was leaving the dance floor, Skinny-McKenzie in tow. His eyes locked on mine. Before I could tear mine away, he mouthed, "Next Friday. Open dance. Seven." Then he pulled McKenzie alongside him, threw his arm around her shoulders, and bent his head to hers. Well, that settled it. I wouldn't be here. He could stuff it if he thought he could order me around.

8

POST LIFE SERVICES

Six days after Trudy's funeral, Harry's Hair Stop was humming like a hive of happy honey bees. Every stylist's chair was filled with a customer but mine. I was perplexed. There had been so many compliments, I'd assumed I'd be booked from now until the end of the year. But although the shop was buzzing, my chair had been empty almost all week.

I wandered to the reservation desk to check the books. Harry was on the phone making an appointment for Maddy. I peered over his shoulder at the computer screen. Everybody's little boxes were filled with client names. Mine stood out from the rest, naked and empty. I had one, lone client at three and nothing until.

When Harry hung up, I said, "What's going on, Harry?"

"What do you mean, darling?" he said, typing and only giving me half his attention.

"What I mean is, we're busy. Really busy. I assume it has something to do with Trudy's funeral."

He glanced at me and smiled broadly. "It absolutely does. We've had five new customers call with the twenty percent off coupon code just this morning. I think they're passing it around Liberty Grove."

"Why don't I have appointments on the schedule, then?"

He rubbed his nose, a stalling gesture. There was something he didn't want to tell me.

"Harry." I stamped my foot.

"I've tried to book appointments for you." He made an apologetic pyramid with his eyebrows. "They don't want you."

"Why? Why wouldn't they want me? I'm the one who made Trudy beautiful."

"That's just it."

I waited for him to continue. He didn't. "What's just it?"

"They don't want the girl who does the dead people. Not while they're alive, anyway."

"But, but . . . I've only done one dead person." The words exploded from me. He lifted a shoulder in a halfhearted shrug.

"Did you tell them that?" I slammed a hand on the desk in frustration. "Did you tell them I've only done one dead person?"

"Calm down, Genie." He patted the air. "You're upsetting the customers." He was right. Several foiled and teased heads had turned in my direction.

I lowered my voice. "It's not like I'm some kind of corpse expert."

"I know that, but people can be..." He searched for the right word. "Superstitious. Especially at this age. They're so close to the grave, they don't want anything to reach out and pull them in."

I closed my eyes. I couldn't believe this. By taking the funeral job, I'd boosted business for Harry, but I'd sabotaged my own.

He put a hand on mine. "Look at it this way, people are dying over there every day. As word gets out about Trudy, you'll be so busy you won't know what hit you."

I spun away from him. Great. Abso-friggen-lutely great. I was the new corpse queen. I should redo my business cards, tag line: *Shuffle off this mortal coil in style. Beautify your goodbye with Imogene Lynch.* "Trudy," I whispered. "What the heck did you do to me?"

I walked to my station, pulled my purse from the cupboard under the mirror and threw it over my shoulder. I had to get out of there. I needed air.

"Where are you going?" Harry said as I marched out the front door.

"Over to the hospital. Thought I'd drum up some business." I shot the words over my shoulder.

"Genie—" I let the door slam behind me, cutting him off. Nothing he had to say would make me feel better. I was in a pickle, as Phil would say, and Harry couldn't help.

The only silver lining in my day, and it was an oxidized silver lining at best, was that when I'd called about the studio apartment on Monday to tell Peter Daniel's I'd take it, he'd told me his wife had rented it to someone else. I'd been disappointed, but now I realized that had been providential. The last thing I needed in the current circumstances was another bill to pay.

I got into my car, put the keys into the ignition, but before I started the engine, my phone rang. I looked at the screen. It was El. "Can we meet somewhere? I have news." He sounded excited.

"Why not? I've got nothing but time."
"Where do you want to go? My treat."
"How about Don's Diner on Moulton?"
"The place all the old people go?"
"They have good pie," I said.

Fifteen minutes later, I arrived at Don's. It was only eleven o'clock—too late for breakfast and too early for lunch—so there were plenty of tables.

I took a booth by the window and ordered a Diet Coke. It's terrible for you, I know, but I was drowning my sorrows.

El showed up just as I was sucking the last bit of soda from the glass. He was more casually dressed today than I'd ever seen him. He wore fitted jeans and a thin white t-shirt. My earlier assessment was correct. He was cut.

I tried not to look at his biceps as he sat and reminded myself he wasn't my type. Much too clean cut, much too military. He probably voted Republican.

Don't get me wrong, I wasn't a Democrat. I took my stand outside the ballot box. Gran said there hadn't been anybody worth voting for since Ronald Reagan, so, by the gods, I didn't vote. It was kind of a principle thing with me.

El shoved a paper under my nose. "We got the hair analysis back."

My eyes crossed as I tried to read the small print waving in front of my face. I snatched the page, held it still, and focused. It didn't do much good. I knew it was English, but—as Phil would say—it was Greek to me. "We have to plan our next steps," El said.

"Next steps?"

"Right. I think we need to get a hold of Gertrude Rosenblum's daughter."

"Daughter?" I said.

"Trudy's doctor won't talk to us."

"Doctor?" I realized how inane I sounded, repeating everything he said, but I didn't have a clue what he was talking about.

He looked thoughtful. "You make a good point. Maybe we should go straight to the police."

I was saved from saying *police* in the same questioning tone I'd used for *doctor* and *daughter* by our server. While El ordered a burger, I searched my brain for a way to ask what we were talking about without sounding like I didn't know what we were talking about.

"Hit me again." I held my glass out to the server. "So, about the police, just what would you say to them? I mean, if we decided to go that route."

"I'd tell them about the digitalis." He tapped the paper on the table between us. I squinted and sure enough, the word "digitalis" stood out in bold print. I opened my mouth to utter the word with a pensive expression on my face but had a sudden recollection of a conversation I'd had with Gran about Alfred

Rogers, her neighbor. He'd had a heart attack a year ago and had been put on digitalis, which Gran swore was poison.

"That's a heart medication," I said, proud of myself for being able to contribute more to the conversation than an African Gray.

"Exactly." El grinned at me. "We got him."

"We do?"

"Don't you see? It was just what we'd thought. Trudy was being over-medicated by a neglectful doctor. There shouldn't have been any digitalis in her system, never mind enough to show up at these levels."

"And we know this because . . ."

He threw himself back into the red vinyl upholstery. "Because her heart was as strong as a horse's, according to her daughter. Trudy didn't need heart medication."

I pondered this information. It did seem suspicious on the face of it, but maybe Trudy had a medical condition she didn't want anyone to know about. Some of my clientele made appointments just so they could tell me about their latest bunion surgery. Trudy wasn't one of them.

El started rattling off statistics: numbers, names, and percentages of medications that killed. He listed the most dangerous and the most commonly overused. It was a tsunami of information. I was relieved when his burger came and he had something else to keep his mouth busy.

"How do you know so much about this?" I said when half his burger had disappeared.

His expression turned somber. "My grandfather died from an overdose of prescription meds."

"I'm sorry." I didn't ask anymore, and he didn't offer anything. I could tell he didn't want to talk about it. His grief had an impact on me though.

My inclination, up to that point, had been to mind my own business. Trudy's death had done enough damage to my life already. Why stick my nose in any farther? I now realized, if there was a Doctor Death out there handing out dangerous medication like candy, I had an obligation to do what I could to stop him.

"So, daughter or police?" El said between bites. "What do you think?"

"Neither." I sucked up a cold mouthful of Diet Coke. El's face drooped like a disappointed bloodhound's. "I'll go to Neutron tonight."

The disappointment disappeared as I told him about Doris and her relationship with Trudy. If anyone knew what Trudy had been taking, ex-nurse and Nosy Parker Doris would be the one. Her business was knowing everybody else's.

El mopped up the last bit of ketchup on his plate with a French fry. "What time?"

"Open dance starts at seven tonight. She's always there on Fridays."

"Great, I don't have to be to work until ten." He beamed at me.

I drummed my fingers on the table. I'd assumed I'd go alone. What would the gang at Neutron think about El? It's not like they wouldn't notice him, not with his size. I could just imagine walking around all night explaining we were just friends while knowing smirks were thrown my way.

"Do you dance?" I asked.

"I can line dance," he said.

"It'll be couples dancing, not line dancing."

"I can fake it."

I doubted that. West Coast Swing wasn't something you faked. I could give him a lesson, I guessed. It wasn't like we were really going for the dancing. "Okay, want to meet there?"

"I could pick you up."

"No, I might stay awhile. You have to get to work." I typed the address into his phone while he paid the bill. It would be an interesting night. I'd planned to stay away from Neutron to teach Chad a lesson. Showing up with El might be just as good, maybe better.

9

ON MY TOES

El was leaning on the building next to the Neutron entrance when I pulled up. He hadn't changed clothes, but he'd exchanged sneakers for cowboy boots, which made him even taller. I'd put on a pair of heels, but he still dwarfed me.

"Looks like a fun spot." El signed in at the front desk, and May gave him a long, appraising look. She wiggled her eyebrows at me in appreciation. I shook my head so she'd know El and I were just friends. She winked, obviously not believing me. I led El away before he got wind of what we weren't talking about.

The lobby was crowded with dancers waiting for the class in the ballroom to end. The smell, kind of a cross between locker room and perfume counter, was familiar and comforting to me. I wondered if it would bother El. I glanced at him. His face wore its usual genial expression. "Do you see her?" he said when he caught my eye.

I searched the sea of faces and found Doris. She was tucked in a corner, leaning her elbows on a high-top table. "There." I jerked my head in her direction.

El took off, parting the press of people like Moses parting the Red Sea. I trotted in his wake. He let me slip in front of him when we reached the table.

She raised her gaze to mine and gave me a weak smile. She looked terrible. Her eyes were dark hollows, her skin pale, her hair unwashed. It looked like she hadn't slept in a week. "Doris." I almost gasped her name. "Are you ill?"

"No. I'm fine." Her voice was languid.

"You don't look fine."

"I haven't been sleeping well. I probably shouldn't have come. This place makes me miss Trudy even more." She pulled a tissue from her sleeve and dabbed at her nose. I eyed it with suspicion, but it looked fresh.

"You were friends with Trudy?" El said.

Doris started at the sound of his voice.

"This is my friend, El." He held out his hand, and she stared at it. After an awkward minute, she took it and shook.

"Did you know Trudy?" Doris said.

"They were . . . " I searched for the right words. "Recent acquaintances."

"She was a wonderful woman." Doris sighed. "I can't tell you how lonely life is without her."

"Odd how sudden her death was. She was so healthy," El said. My jaw tensed. He was about as subtle as a fire truck. Doris looked at him and furrowed her brow.

He opened his mouth. I intercepted. "How are Norman and Rita doing?"

"They're just fine." Doris's words were laced with sarcasm.

"I thought you three would be together, you know, finding solace in each other's company."

"Oh, they're finding solace in each other's company all right. They're just not interested in mine."

I didn't know what to say. The vitriol in her voice was startling. It turned out I didn't have to say anything. She was on a roll.

"Rita has Norman run her errands now, so she doesn't need me anymore. When I think of all I did for that woman."

"I'm—" I was going to sympathize.

She waved her tissue like a surrender flag. "No. Don't say a thing. I'm glad. Glad this happened." She clamped her jaw shut for a brief second. "Not glad Trudy died. I didn't mean that at all, but I'm glad Rita is showing her true colors. Now I know who she really is. I'm a giver, Imogene. You know that."

I nodded. I did know that. She was a giver. I also knew there was usually a ribbon attached to her gifts. Maybe Rita and Norman had figured that out, too. I spotted the couple standing near the entrance to the ballroom. Rita's lovely profile tipped up to face Norman. He gazed fondly down. They looked pretty cozy.

"I love to give, but I won't be taken." Doris sniffed.

"You were close to Trudy?" El said, bringing the conversation back to territory that interested him.

"The closest," she said.

"So you probably know—"

"The ballroom is open now," I said, interrupting El. Really, he needed to mellow out. Gossip was an art, especially with Doris's generation. Younger people often made the mistake of thinking seniors were childlike, or naïve, that their weakened physical condition extended to their cognitive abilities. Sometimes it was true, but most of the time it was the exact opposite.

Gran's friends had a wealth of life experiences I didn't. They knew things I couldn't because of my youth, and often understood my motives before I did. If they had even an inkling someone was underestimating them, or trying to manipulate them, the conversation would be over before it started.

El shot me an irritated glance. "Let's go dance." I dragged him toward the ballroom. I faced him when I found a spot on the floor. "You need to back off a bit, Bruiser." He looked confused. "If you offend Doris, you won't get anything from her. Barging in asking personal questions too soon will only make her suspicious. Then she'll clam up."

"I'm only trying to help the community. Seniors are so often victims of overzealous—"

"I know that. She doesn't. Let's go slow. Doris is hurting. Let me handle her."

El's jaw tightened into a stubborn line. He looked like he was about to argue, but Brian Setzer's Orchestra stopped him. The dancers around us started swinging with enthusiasm.

El grabbed me around the waist with confidence and began bopping to the beat. His head swiveled as he watched the throng spin by. A minute later, his cocky expression was replaced by one of confusion. So much for faking it.

"Here. Watch me," I yelled into his ear. I pulled him to my side and led him in a basic six count: a rock step followed by two triples. It took a few minutes, but he caught on. He was lighter on his feet than I expected, especially with those heavy cowboy boots.

Once he had the basic step down, I attempted to show him how to lead me into an inside turn. The first five or six went fine. I could tell El was enjoying himself. Maybe a bit too much. When the chorus of the song came around, he got so enthusiastic he yanked me into a spin without so much as a warning. I fell against him. He stumbled, and I felt crushing pain. Lightning bolts exploded behind my eyes.

"Sorry, Oh my gosh. Sorry," El said.

I couldn't speak, which was probably a good thing. He supported me to one of the benches along the wall. I sat and examined my toe. It amazed me that something so painful could look so normal. "I think it's broken."

El looked stricken. "I'm a clod. Let me get you some ice."

"Ask May. Front desk."

He ran off. I leaned my head against the wall and closed my eyes. Guess I wouldn't be dancing for a while, just one more thing wrong in my pitiful life. No clients. No apartment. No dancing. I melted into a puddle of self-pity.

A hand grabbed mine and yanked me to my feet. I squealed in pain and outrage. "Chad, what are you doing?"

"Let's dance, baby. This is our song." He did a few steps in place.

"I can't."

"Come on. Don't be like that. You want to. You know it."

I pulled my hand away, thudded onto my seat, and folded my arms across my chest.

"What's the matter with you?" He sounded angry, not concerned.

"I—"

"You come just to mess with me?"

"I—"

"This is why I broke up with you. You're always messing with my head."

Broke up with me? I broke up with him. I opened my mouth to say so, but he was on a rant. "You know we're good together, Imogene." The expression on my face must have cued him in that he needed to modify that statement. "Okay. Okay. I made a couple of mistakes."

Marlene, Christy, Chantelle, and those were only the ones whose names I could remember.

"They didn't mean anything. And, I apologized. You're a hard woman, Imogene. You know that?"

Not hard enough, but I was learning.

"You made mistakes too, you know."

I did. I went out with him. It was too bad I couldn't get in a word edgewise, as I had some great one-liners in my head.

He reached for my hand again, like somehow berating me was going to soften me up and put me in a dancing mood. I jerked it away. He made a grab and latched onto my forearm. We glared at each other.

"He bothering you?" A deep growl sounded behind Chad.

"It's none of your business," Chad said without turning.

"Imogene?" El said.

"Yeah. He's bothering me." Normally, I didn't go in for the damsel-in-distress routine. I'd rather fight my own battles, but I was in pain both physically and emotionally. Besides, if you have a friend who looks like the Incredible Hulk, you might as well take advantage of it.

Chad pivoted, and he came face to face with El's chest. He paused for a split second, then looked up the expanse of him. "Who're you?" I may have been imagining things, but it seemed Chad had shrunk a foot.

"I was going to ask the same question." The look El gave him reminded me of a golden retriever gone rogue. I wouldn't have messed with him.

"I'm a friend of Imogene's," Chad said with more bluster than necessary.

"Funny. She doesn't seem happy to see you."

"We're having a disagreement, okay? No big deal. Now, could you . . . " He waved toward the dance floor.

El looked at me, a question in his eyes. I gave him a quick nod. He handed me a baggy of ice. "I'll be back," he said like Schwarzenegger.

Chad watched his retreating back. "What the hell, you got a bodyguard now?"

I shrugged. "Just a friend." I put the ice on my toe and winced.

"What'd you do?"

"I think I broke it. I was trying to tell you that, but you didn't give me a chance."

Chad had the decency to look embarrassed. He sat next to me. "How long before you can dance again?"

"I don't know. I just did it." He stared at his hands. There was something up. I was under no illusions that he was concerned for my well-being. "Why?" I could hear the suspicion in my voice.

"There's a dance contest in LA at The Hop, end of May. I thought maybe . . ."

"Really?" I pivoted so I could look him square in the face. "You think you can come waltzing back into my life after everything that's happened?"

He raised an eyebrow. "Winners get cash."

That stopped me cold. Cash. I needed an infusion, especially with what was happening—or not happening—at work. Could I take the risk of letting Chad back into my life? He was like a barnacle on a boat bottom. Once he attached himself, the only way to get rid of him was to scrape him off. "How much?" I seemed to be asking that question a lot lately.

"First prize is five thousand. We'd split, fifty-fifty."

Twenty-five hundred wasn't going to change my life, but it would help. "I'll let you know," I said.

"Soon." He rose. "If you're gonna be a gimp, I've got to find somebody else." He disappeared into the crowd. What a jerk.

I scanned the dance floor for El. I wanted to go home. I didn't want to talk to Doris or anyone else tonight. It wasn't hard to find him. He towered over everybody in the room. He was dancing with someone, but I couldn't see who through the crowd. Whoever she was, she was a brave woman. Those cowboy boots were lethal.

He looked like he was catching on, though. Hopefully, being a bit more circumspect after our mishap. He leaned down to talk to his partner, then turned an ear toward her. I was impressed. He could already dance and carry on a conversation simultaneously. He had hidden chops.

The song ended, and El headed toward me. As he cleared the crowd, I almost jumped to my feet. Doris hung on his arm grinning like a lovesick calf.

10

EL'S BELLS

" I wish you'd listen to me. I'm the one who knows this crowd. I'm the one who understands how they think." My words came in panted breaths.

I hopped alongside El, my arms around his waist, taking some of the weight off my bad toe. He wanted to carry me, but that wasn't going to happen. "Not only could you have shut down Doris as a source of information—which matters more to you than me, by the way—you could have cost me a client. And believe you me . . . " Ugh, another of Phil's antique expressions flew out of my mouth. I noted I used them more when I was upset. "I can't afford to lose another client right now."

El didn't try to stop my flood of words. I guess he planned to let the river take him until I was done. When we reached my car, he leaned me against it and adopted a stoic look.

"Thanks to Greener Pastures and thanks to Trudy—not to speak ill of the dead—I'm financially screwed. Granted, I wasn't making money hand over fist before all this." Thank you, Phil, for another cliché. "But I had a somewhat steady income. Now I have nothing. Nada. You know how much I've made in the last five days?"

El shook his head.

"One hundred and thirty-five dollars after I paid Harry for the chair. That averages out to . . . " I paused to calculate in my head, but before I'd even realized I needed to divide the number by five, El said, "Twenty-seven dollars a day."

"Right. Not enough. That's how much. And now my toe is broken, which may have cost me another two-thousand five-hundred."

The stoic expression became concern. "I don't think they do very much for a broken toe. Just wrap is all. I can't see how it would cost that much."

"Not the doctor." I stared at the blacktop while I explained Chad's proposal about the dance competition.

El crossed his arms over his big chest. "I don't want to tell you what to do, but—"

"Then don't," I said.

"But," he ignored me. "I wouldn't trust that guy as far as I could throw him."

"Well, it's a moot point. I don't think I'll be dancing in any competitions now." I held up my injured appendage for effect. "Anyway, how would you know? You just met the guy."

"I know the type."

"What type is that?"

His face darkened. "He's a user, a con. He'll take advantage of anyone who'll let him." El was correct, of course, but it bothered me that he'd sized Chad up in four minutes when it had taken me four years. I changed the subject. "So what did Doris say?" It had looked like he'd won her over, the way she'd been mooning at him, even if I hated to admit it.

His expression cleared. "She said she didn't think Trudy had heart problems, at least she'd never mentioned it."

"But she wasn't sure?"

"No. And she didn't seem to want to talk about it. She's taking Trudy's death pretty hard."

"So we're back to square one. We don't know if Trudy was on digitalis, or not."

"Right," he said, much too cheerfully.

I stared at him. "Why do you look so happy then?"

"Because Doris told me something else."

I waited for him to fill me in, but he must have wanted me to beg for it. "What?" I finally said, annoyed.

"She told me that Megan, Trudy's daughter, will be at Trudy's old place all day tomorrow going through her mom's things. She's having an estate sale on Sunday."

"And this is good news because . . . " He stared at me without responding. "Don't tell me you want to go over there and question her grieving daughter?"

He uncrossed his arms so he could gesture with his hands. "If my mother was killed by prescription drugs, I'd want to know. Besides, I'll be subtle."

"Like you were with Doris?"

"Okay, when we first arrived, I was, maybe, a bit too direct. But I got her to open up when we were dancing."

"Yeah, how did you do that?"

He shrugged. "I used a method from my Interrogation Techniques course. I disarmed her with questions that had nothing to do with Trudy, then dropped the bomb."

My toe throbbed. I needed to get home and put my foot up. I pivoted and opened my car door. "Have fun at Trudy's tomorrow."

"You have to go with me."

I started the engine. "Nope. I'm busy tomorrow."

He leaned into my window. "I thought you didn't have any customers."

"I don't. I'm going to be busy figuring out how to get some."

"I need you. I can't get into Liberty Grove without a pass."

That was true. It was a gated community, and since most of the people manning the gates were people who lived inside them, they took their jobs very seriously. El wouldn't get in without my help. "I'll call and let the gate know you're coming," I said.

He got that pleading puppy look on his face again. I was beginning to hate that look. "I have no connection to Trudy or her family. You're the one who knew her." I didn't respond. "Tell you what, I'll help you get new customers if you go with me to talk to Trudy's daughter."

"How are you going to do that?"

"Don't you have coupon cards for Harry's?"

"Yeah. They're working great for everybody else at the salon." My voice was bitter.

"That's because you only gave them to people who knew you did Trudy. Write your name on a batch of them, and we'll hand them out to people who don't know anything about the funeral."

That wasn't a bad idea, except it meant walking. "My toe hurts."

"I'll go door to door for you."

I agreed to meet him at the grocery store parking lot at three o'clock the next day and headed home. Tonight, I'd have to risk parking inside Liberty Grove since I couldn't make my usual trek on foot. I hoped I didn't get a ticket, or worse, get towed, but there was nothing I could do about it.

I pulled into the lot behind Gran's, placed my visitor pass in the window, and limped up the path to her front door. The house was dark and quiet when I entered. Gran believed all that early to bed, early to rise stuff and always retired by ten. She must have taken Harley with her, because he wasn't there to greet me.

Using furniture to lean on, I made my way to the kitchen. I filled a zipper baggie with ice and grabbed a clean dish towel. I was about to hop from the room when I noticed a prescription bottle sitting on the counter.

This was such an unusual occurrence in Gran's house, a stab of anxiety shot through me. I picked it up. It was too dark to read the small print, so I carried it to the window over the sink. I rotated it until moonlight illuminated the label. To my relief, it was Phil's. He must have left it here.

Before I stepped from the window, I noticed the drug name, digoxin. I wondered if this was what Phil and Gran had fought about the other day. If so, it wasn't too bright of him to leave it here. It wouldn't surprise me a bit if Gran dumped it.

I turned to leave the kitchen and drove my toe into the edge of a cabinet. All thoughts of digoxin and Gran and Phil were drowned in a sea of pain. I would never dance with El again.

11
Humming Along

I danced in my dreams and woke with a start as a pair of giant cowboy boots galloped toward me. It was a rude awaking. I decided to wait until the hammering in my chest stopped before attempting to climb out of bed. Besides, I couldn't feel my foot but was sure, as soon as my toe brushed against the covers, I'd be in pain.

When my bladder became a bigger problem than my toe, I sat and pulled back the covers. My foot was black—black and ugly. I swung my legs over the side of the bed, placed it on the floor and applied pressure. A dull ache, but no sharp pain. That was promising.

By the time I made it to the bathroom, I found I could put my full weight on my foot with only mild discomfort. It must not have been broken after all—the only good news I'd had that week.

I put on a black sundress and a pair of sandals that gave my toe plenty of breathing room and headed downstairs. The clock in the kitchen said 10:30. I really had slept in, not that it mattered. I only had one appointment today, and that wasn't until the afternoon.

Gran was long gone, probably taking water boot camp, or yoga, or hiking the Aliso Creek trail with a friend. Her mornings were devoted to exercise. I didn't take after her in this. She always said it was a good thing I liked to dance because I didn't like to do anything else.

The coffeepot had turned itself off and what was left in it had a greasy, unappealing sheen, so I rinsed and refilled. Gran left a note on the counter telling me about the bagels and cream cheese she and Phil had saved for me. I smiled. This was her way of telling me to eat something. She knew full well I was capable of scouting through the fridge for sustenance.

We'd been having the battle of the breakfast ever since I was in high school and discovered coffee. In my mind, it was the perfect start to the day. Since I added cream and sugar, it covered all the essential food groups: carbs, fat, and caffeine.

Today, I'd make Gran happy. I was in no hurry to get to work and eating a bagel now would save me lunch money later. I had to be frugal.

I spread cream cheese on a blueberry bagel. While I ate, I opened my laptop, and typed "Help Needed" into the search engine. There wasn't much there: dog sitting, babysitting, and one ad for a marketing performer, which I assumed meant they were looking for someone to stand on the street and spin a giant arrow.

I closed my computer and chewed my lip. Maybe El was right. Maybe instead of looking for a new salon, I needed to look for new clients. If I turned it around, this entire episode could be viewed in a positive light. I'd needed more business before Trudy died. I just hadn't needed it badly enough to get out of my comfort zone and find it. Now I had no choice. I had to do it. The memory of the one corpse I'd done would die—no pun intended—sooner or later. And when my old clients returned, I'd be that much busier.

Another plus was I had El to help me. With his size, he was as attention-getting as an arrow-spinning performer and a lot better looking than most. I might not be attracted to him, but his clean-cut good looks had impressed Doris. The ladies of Liberty Grove would fall victim to his charms.

Feeling more optimistic, I headed into Harry's early so I could put together some marketing materials. When life handed you lemons . . . *Shut up, Phil.*

The day was beautiful, cool, and sunny. My car was right where I'd left it the night before, no ticket on the windshield. And Mr. Rogers was nowhere to be seen. It was going to be a good day. My luck was turning. I could feel it.

I was still buoyed when I left the salon to meet El. My one o'clock had been thrilled with her haircut and promised to give my card to the girls in her gardening club.

I found El sitting in his truck in the grocery store parking lot as planned. He drove a Ford F150, another reason we could never date. I didn't do country or western. He was too much of a cowboy for me. Speaking of which, I shot a nervous glance at his feet and exhaled with relief. He was wearing sneakers. I pulled alongside him. "Hop in."

I sailed through the Liberty Grove gate with a wave, proudly displaying my annual pass and wended my way through the tree-lined streets. Trudy's place was near Phil's in a newer section of the community. It was a single-level unit with a lovely, enclosed patio. The front door stood open, probably to capture the floral scented breeze. I knocked anyway.

Megan's eyes widened in surprise when she saw us. "I don't know if you remember me," I said.

"Of course. You were Mom's hairstylist. Imogene, right?"

"Right."

"You did a beautiful job for the funeral." Her voice grew thick. "Would you like to come in?" I could see the unspoken question on her face: *Why are you here?*

"Thanks. We won't take much of your time." As we crossed the threshold, a wave of sadness broke over me. Trudy's condo smelled of the lilac perfume she'd always worn. It was too sweet. I hadn't liked it when she'd filled my station at the salon with it, but now the faint whiff made me melancholy.

"I lent Trudy a book on swing dancing a couple of months ago, and I heard you were getting ready for an estate sale." I hadn't really lent Trudy a book, but knew she had several on the topic.

"All the books are in the back bedroom," Megan said, and led the way.

Trudy's house was an eclectic blend of old and new, bright colors against black and white, soft surfaces and hard shiny ones. It was as distinctive as the woman who'd lived here.

I followed Megan into the second bedroom. It was piled with boxes. Stacks of linens and towels hid the bed. A long table stood under the only window. Leaning against the panes was a framed hummingbird done in stained glass. Sunlight glittered through it and dappled the vases, pots, dishes, and trinkets covering the table's surface with color. A pen and stack of price stickers sat on the windowsill.

"The books are over there." She gestured to a set of shelves overflowing with volumes.

"That hummingbird is interesting," I said, and I meant it, although I think I noticed it because it didn't fit with the rest of Trudy's things. It had an amateurish appeal, a bit ill-proportioned, but there was something about it that attracted me.

"You can have it," Megan said. "A friend of Mom's made it for her. She put it in a window for a while, but it wasn't her."

"You don't mind?" I wasn't sure it was me, either, but I found my gaze returning to it.

"No, take it. I have enough stuff to get rid of."

I picked it up and set it with my purse.

We'd lost El somewhere between the front door and the bedroom. He must be poking around the rest of the house, looking for evidence. I knelt on the floor by the shelf and began searching for a likely book.

"It must be overwhelming," I said. "Going through your mom's things."

"It is. So many have memories attached. Like this." She held up a blue glass vase. "She used to put sunflowers in it whenever we had summer barbecues.

The yellow looked so pretty against the blue. I thought about keeping it, but then there's this one." She pointed to a clear glass globe. "Hydrangeas, when the bush out front was in bloom." She looked at me and held out her hands like she was pleading for understanding. "I can't keep everything."

"Of course you can't."

She turned to the table and began writing and attaching price stickers. "It makes me feel disloyal, selling off her things."

I wanted to broach the topic of Trudy's health, but didn't know how. I hoped Megan would bring it up herself, but she didn't. After several long, silent minutes, I finally said, "The memories are hard, but I bet you've had some surprises, too. When my mother died, I found a diary I had no idea she'd kept."

"Hm." Megan hummed. "No surprises yet. But my mom and I were pretty close."

"Speaking of surprises," I tried again. "I just found a prescription bottle at my Gran's place, and I didn't even know she was sick." It was one version of the truth.

"That must have been upsetting. Hope it's nothing serious."

"I think it's for digestive problems." I was shocked by how easily the lie tripped off my tongue. "But I haven't had a chance to ask her about it yet."

Megan placed two vases in a box on the floor. "Oh, well. I wouldn't get too upset. So many older people are on medications. Doctors are preemptive these days."

"They give out drugs like candy." I tried El's line to see if she'd bite. She shrugged, picked up a pen, and resumed writing stickers.

El popped his head in the door. "Nice place you've got here."

"Thanks. We'll be putting it on the market after the estate sale. If you see anything you can use, let me know."

"The rocker is really nice. How much are you asking for it?"

Megan followed him into the living room, and I returned to the book search. After thumbing through five volumes on swing dancing, I found two without inscriptions on the title page and chose the newest looking one. I rose, dusted off my black dress, picked up my things, and left the bedroom.

El stood by the fireplace, resting a forearm on the mantle. His eyebrows arched in concentration as he focused on Megan, who rocked in the rocker. "She was so healthy," she said. "Mom called me after her last check-up just to brag. The doctor had said she'd outlive her and her entire staff."

"She wasn't on any medications? That's amazing in this day and age," he said.

"No. Nothing. She took her multivitamin every day with a big glass of apple cider vinegar and water. That's it."

How had he done that? First Doris, now Megan. I threw out all kinds of bait, no bites. El showed her a naked hook, and she took it.

"Who's her doctor? Sounds like someone I'd like to go to," he said.

Megan laughed. "Doctor Foster? Oh, you don't want to go to her. She specializes in Geriatrics."

Something about that name was familiar. I'd heard it recently. Before I could shuffle through my memory to figure out where, Megan glanced at me over her shoulder. I held up the book. "Got it," I said.

She rose and looked at the volume in my hand. "That one? Huh. I thought Mom got that for herself from Amazon."

"She, ah, she was going to." I stumbled over my words. "But I told her I already had it and could lend it to her."

Megan eyed me with suspicion but didn't say any more about it. Why would she? She was trying to get rid of everything anyway. She turned to El, and her face softened. "So, do you want the chair?"

"Let me think on it," he said. "I'll let you know by tomorrow morning."

"The sale is tomorrow, so snooze you lose."

We moved toward the door, she and El leading, me trailing behind. "Now don't forget my offer," El said.

"That's so sweet of you." Megan beamed at him.

"Not at all. I know what it's like to lose someone close."

He turned his sad puppy gaze on her, and I thought she was going to melt into the carpet. "I might need you for some of the heavier things."

El's biceps twitched as he reached into his jean pocket and handed her a business card. "Call me. I mean it. I generally only work at night. Mornings are free." She took the card and thanked him again.

"Ready?" I said more sharply than I should have. All the gushing made me irritated. "Did you get what you needed?" I asked on the way to the car.

"Yup. If Trudy was on meds, she was hiding it. Why hide digoxin from anyone? It's not like heart problems are shameful."

I stopped walking. "Wait, what did you say?"

El stopped too. "I said it's not like heart problems—"

"No, not that. What was the drug?"

"Digoxin?"

"I thought Trudy had digitalis in her system?"

"Digoxin is the brand name for digitalis."

"I thought digoxin was for indigestion."

"No. Heart problems."

I resumed walking to the car with rapid steps. I didn't like this at all. Phil had a heart problem. And Phil was on the same drug that may have taken Trudy's life. I wanted to get home and talk to Gran.

El opened the car door. "What are you so upset about?"

As I drove, I told him about finding the bottle of pills the night before. "Did you know he had heart problems?" El said.

"No. I thought it was something to do with his stomach. Gran's always on him for eating too much and eating the wrong things."

"Heart disease comes from eating too much and eating the wrong things, too."

We didn't speak again until we pulled up to the curb in front of some of the most expensive homes in Liberty Grove. I was pretty sure no one in this neighborhood had come to the funeral.

"Did he know her?" El said.

"Who?"

"Trudy. Did Phil know Trudy?"

"Yeah. They were neighbors. Why?" He shrugged. "Wait. You don't think Phil had anything to do with Trudy's death? I thought we were looking for an over-zealous doctor."

"An officer has to keep an open mind." He recited that bit from a textbook, I could tell.

"To quote Phil, don't be too open-minded or all your brains will leak out." I turned off the ignition. "If you're going to start suspecting everyone in Liberty Grove who's on heart meds, you're going to have a long list of suspects."

"If, and I'm not saying this is the case, but if a doctor didn't prescribe it, how would she have gotten it?"

"She would have to have taken it by accident."

"Maybe, but how would she have gotten hold of it? She lived alone."

"I don't know." I threw up my hands in frustration. "Maybe we should go to the police?"

El huffed. "We don't have any evidence."

"The hair analysis," I said.

"It's not official and probably not legal. We can't prove where we got that hair from. It could belong to anyone."

Not legal? The words sent a jolt of electricity up my spine. "Wait a minute, you said if anyone had a right to cut Trudy's hair, it was me. You never said anything about it being illegal."

"I said cutting her hair wasn't illegal. I never said anything about testing it."

"We broke the law?" My voice rose several decibels.

"Illegal is probably the wrong word," he said in a comforting tone. "It just wasn't authorized. It wouldn't hold up in court."

I wasn't mollified. "What do we do then?"

"I'll see what I can find out about the doctor. If she's on the up and up, patients aren't dying at surprising rates, maybe we let it go. Don't do anything."

"But Trudy?"

"We may never know."

We sat for several minutes staring out the window. Then I handed a stack of Harry's coupons to El, and he exited the car. "Charm them," I hollered through the open window.

"I'll do my best."

A half hour later, El returned empty-handed.

"How'd it go?" I asked.

"Good. I was invited in for tea three times. Didn't go. Asked if I could help move a reclining chair. Did. Asked if I'd be at the salon when they came in for their appointment more times than I can count, and I said..." He broke off and grinned at me. "I'm there as often as I can be. If you become a regular, I'm sure I'll see you."

"Good answer," I said. "Free cut for that."

He ran a hand over his closely cropped hair. "I need one." I didn't think so, but I'd give it to him anyway. "Hate to end this productive afternoon, but I have to get going. Don't want to be late for work."

I drove him to his car, turned around, and headed through the gates of Liberty Grove again. The thought of parking inside two nights in a row made me a little sick to my stomach, but what was I going to do? My toe, although much less painful than it had been, wasn't up to the hike. El's marketing had better work. If I didn't get a place of my own soon, I was going to need Prozac. Then Gran would have a heart attack.

12

PENDING NUPTIALS

Saturday's optimism didn't make it to Monday morning. Phil must have noticed. As I left the house, he told me to keep my chin up and reminded me that today was the first day of the rest of my life. I've never understood why people found that comforting. Every day, even the days our cars breakdown, or we have the flu and puke in the toilet, or find out our boyfriends are cheating on us with tall, skinny blonds, they're all the first days of the rest of our lives. It seems to me, the expression is a reminder that life sucks sometimes.

Phil also admonished me to leave the past in the past—as if I could leave it anywhere else. But I'd accepted his clichéd encouragement in the spirit in which it was offered. Today would be the first day of my life post funeral gig. I planned to make a fresh start. I had two new clients on the books from El's door-to-door trek, and Doris was returning to my chair after lunch.

A cacophony of perfume swirled around my head as I made my way past the stylists' stations. I put my purse in the cupboard and pulled out a tray of sterile combs, brushes, and scissors. I organized my tools like a surgeon before an important operation. Nothing could go wrong with the new clients.

At nine-fifteen, Harry escorted a petite, attractive brunette to my station. "Imogene, this is Alicia." His eyes sparkled, and he winked at me over her head before returning to his desk.

Alicia, it turned out, was only fifty-two. She'd married into Liberty Grove, her husband being eight years her senior. She was young and funny and, hopefully, would be around for many years to come. I gave her highlights to hide the small amount of gray in her hair, an awesome cut, and a special conditioning treatment at no extra charge. She gave me a twenty percent tip, and asked after

El. I assured her he was in often, and she was sure to bump into him one of these days if she continued coming.

The second new client arrived at eleven-thirty. She wasn't quite as young as Alicia, but she was a healthy seventy-five with a great sense of humor who tipped fifteen percent of the bill. All in all, a good morning.

I ate a salad in the break room with my foot on a chair. Not even the ammonia odor of perm solution floating through the doorway or the throbbing of my toe could ruin my resolve to have, if not a good day, at least a productive one. I'd checked the schedule after my last job and found I had three more appointments for other days this week. El was a goldmine.

I wondered how he was doing, if he'd gone to Trudy's estate sale, and if he'd learned anything. I'd remembered where I'd heard Dr. Foster's name. She was Phil's doctor. I was anxious to hear what El had turned up on her.

I'd gotten myself so worked up about the idea that Phil was taking poison prescribed by a quack, I'd had a hard time sleeping. I hadn't talked to Gran about it as I'd planned either. She hadn't been home much on Sunday, and when she was, Phil was with her.

I couldn't figure out how to broach the topic with him around. How could I explain my interest in, or knowledge of, digoxin? *Well, Phil, you see, I took a hair sample from a corpse and it turns out . . .* That wasn't going to fly.

I cleaned my counter and my scissors and put out fresh combs and brushes. Right now, I needed to leave the investigation business to El and focus on my own, or I wouldn't have one. I was ready for Doris when she came marching through the salon.

The smile of greeting died on my face as soon as I saw her. Her expression was hard, her mouth a tight line, her shoulders rigid. She threw herself into my chair with a whoosh of air. Her eyes met mine in the mirror. "Have you heard?"

"Heard what?" *Lord, don't let it be another funeral.* I offered up a silent prayer in case Gran was right about the praying thing.

It wasn't a funeral. It was a wedding.

"Rita and Norman. Can you believe it?" Doris was spitting mad. "Trudy isn't even cold in her grave and those two are engaged. What're old farts like them getting married for anyway? It's not like they'll be having children."

I thought marriage was special at any age, but I didn't get a chance to say so. Doris's flood of words washed over me as I added color to her hair. "I always wondered if he had any real interest in Trudy. I warned her about him. He's one of those playboy doctors. Believe me, I know the type."

It was difficult for me to think of the distinguished Dr. Norman as a playboy. He did look a bit like an aging Derek Shepherd from *Grey's Anatomy*, but he had to be in his late seventies. And he wasn't a medical doctor.

He was a retired psychoanalyst who'd had a successful New York practice until his wife of thirty-eight years left him for an Italian half her age. He was devastated, according to Trudy, left his practice, and moved to California to be near his daughter. But once a hot doctor, always a hot doctor, I guessed.

"He and Rita were an item long before he took up with Trudy. Did you know that?" I hadn't. I hadn't even known he and Trudy were involved. "They were," she continued. "It was that stupid New Year's Eve party that changed everything."

The New Year's Eve party I did Trudy's hair and makeup for?

"You did her hair and makeup," Doris said, as if responding to my unspoken question. "You really have a way with hair, you know that?" She gazed at me in the mirror. "She looked beautiful that night. I know that caught his eye, but it was only the half of it."

It was time to rinse the dye from Doris's hair. She stopped talking as I leaned her head into the sink, and I had to wait to find out what the other half of it was. Funny, I'd wanted her to take a break, breathe. Her nonstop stream of angry words had been putting a damper on my attempt to have a positive outlook, but now I was curious.

When I finished rinsing her, I wrapped her hair in a towel and helped her sit up. It was as if I'd flipped a switch on a talking doll. She took up right where she'd left off without skipping a beat. "We were telling each other about our summer travel plans. Ed Mayer said he and Emma were going to France. They have a lot of money and like to make sure everyone knows it. Have you ever done Emma's hair?"

I shook my head, hoping Doris would get back to the point. "You should. She's rich," she said. I dragged a brush through her hair a bit too firmly.

"Ow! Anyway, Trudy said she was making a trip to Vermont. You should have seen Norman light up. He was all questions and smiles. Turned out both he and Trudy grew up there."

"Really?" I finally got a word in. That was curious.

"Yeah. Same town. Battleground, or Bratville, or someplace. Small world, huh?"

I finished combing out her hair, picked up the shears and began snipping.

"After that, Norman dropped Rita like a hot rock and took up with Trudy. They were inseparable. I'd go over for our Tuesday lunch date, and he'd be there. I'd stop by for coffee and backgammon, and he'd be there. She didn't even want to go to Costco with me anymore. Said Norman took her, and it was so convenient because he could carry her box. I'd always been good enough to carry her box before."

A dark look crossed Doris's features, and I wondered if it was anger or grief. Sometimes it's hard to tell the difference.

"We still had breakfast on Saturdays because that was Norman's golf morning, and Trudy didn't play. But that was it. I wouldn't have been surprised to hear wedding bells." She sighed. "Instead, it was the funeral organ."

I took advantage of the moment of silence to turn on the blow dryer and began curling Doris's hair with a round brush. The thought hit me once again that I knew more about Trudy now than I'd known when she was alive. Who knew there was so much drama in Liberty Grove? There was more romance and intrigue in these seniors' lives than there was in mine.

Living at Gran's had made me feel I'd become a little old lady trapped in a young woman's body. Doris made the Liberty Grove crowd sound like a bunch of teenagers trapped in aging bodies. If I stayed, some of their immaturity might rub off on me, then I'd be . . .

Doris was chomping at the bit. She launched back into her story as soon as I turned off the blow drier. "And now that playboy is with Rita again and planning a wedding that should have been Trudy's. Here I was feeling sorry for Rita. She'd been so upset when Trudy and Norman started spending time together. I can't believe she's taking him back."

I ushered Doris to the door. Her hair looked great, but neither of us mentioned it. She couldn't stop talking about the injustice of the Rita-Norman affair, and I was distracted by what I'd learned.

At the funeral, and since then, many people had mentioned how premature Trudy's death had been. I hadn't understood. Not really. After all, she'd been seventy-eight. This information changed everything. Hearing that she'd been in a relationship, in love, possibly planning to marry made the untimeliness of her death very real.

After Doris left, I swept her hair from the floor. What would I find if I sent it in for testing? Would it reveal poisons? Predict her untimely demise? Could someone have prevented Trudy's death if she'd had her hair tested sooner? I felt an almost parental urge to guard my seniors.

Was this feeling—this desire to protect the vulnerable—what drove El toward law enforcement? He spent a lot of time with those who'd passed on. He must see many bodies emptied of life too soon. That would get to you after a while. I'd only seen one, and it had gotten to me.

I put the broom away, washed my hands, and retrieved my purse from the cupboard. *Shake it off, Imogene.* I didn't work with the dead. I worked with the living, and I wouldn't be any good to anyone if I didn't stop dwelling on such depressing topics.

Harry was on the phone when I left the salon. He gave me a thumbs up then put up five fingers. I figured that meant I had five more appointments on the calendar. Good. Things were moving forward. I was looking ahead. Fresh start. Chin up and cheerio and all that jazz.

13
A PURLOINED LETTER

That night at dinner, Phil must have dumped a half bottle of ketchup on his slice of lentil loaf. Generally, he had other plans whenever Gran cooked up this gastric temptation. I wondered if his availability tonight had something to do with his recent doctor's appointment.

I was still searching for a way to bring up the topic without offending him. I must have opened my mouth to ask about the pills a half dozen times. What shut it was the thought that it was really none of my business. Phil wasn't my grandfather. He was my grandmother's boyfriend. Besides, I didn't want to embarrass him. His dietary habits were a source of tension between him and Gran. Here he was eating humble vegetarian loaf, so to speak. It didn't seem right to rub his nose in it.

If El would only call me with news of Dr. Foster, I'd have something concrete to say. I'd have facts and figures, objective data. But he hadn't, and I didn't.

There was a lull in the conversation at one point. In an attempt to bring up a neutral topic, I said, "I heard you were at Trudy's funeral. Why didn't you come say hi?"

Phil took a long time putting down his fork, dabbing at his mouth with a napkin, then arranging the napkin on his lap again. "You seemed busy," he finally said.

"I'm never too busy for you." I made my tone light. It appeared I'd touched a nerve.

He reached across the table and patted my hand. "You're a sweet child." His voice was solemn.

Gran rose. "Can I take that?" She scooped up my plate without waiting for a response and scurried into the kitchen. I wondered what was going on. They were acting strange tonight.

She returned a moment later and walked straight through the dining area into the living room. "Time for *Jeopardy*," she called over her shoulder. Phil and I followed.

It must have been the strain of the day and the awkwardness at dinner, but I got emotional about *Jeopardy*. One of the contestants was a lawyer, two categories were law related, and the Daily Double played right into his hands. It just didn't seem fair. The contestant I liked was a librarian and none of the categories represented literature, not one.

When the show was over, I took my cup into the kitchen and chucked it into the dishwasher with such force it broke. Gran stood in the doorway, arms crossed over her chest, with an odd expression on her face. "Is that studio apartment still available?"

I spun to face her. "Why?"

"Just wondering."

"I'll buy you a new mug."

Her eyes grew soft. "It's not the mug, sweetheart. It's you."

I knew it. I'd been worrying about this since I'd heard about Trudy and Norman. I was a third wheel. I knelt by the dishwasher and began picking ceramic shards out of its bottom. Not only wasn't Gran too old for romance, this could be her last chance for it. "Even if it was, I don't have the money," I said.

"I could lend you what you need."

I started to refuse. She'd offered me money before, and I'd turned it down. I wanted to support myself, not have to lean on my grandmother. I threw the bits of broken mug into the trash, straightened, and searched her eyes. What was she telling me? Did she want me to leave so badly she was willing to pay for it? Had I outstayed my welcome?

When I graduated from beauty school, I moved out of the home I'd lived in since my mother's death. I took a small apartment with a roommate that I found through an online ad. Gran put the house on the market. When it sold, she bought the Liberty Grove condo. She'd been concerned about the age restrictions, but I reassured her. I was an adult. It was time I started acting like one.

Unfortunately, the roommate situation, which began only tolerably well, took a dark turn after eight months. She got a boyfriend, a big, loud, hairy lout who moved into her room with her. He reminded me of a troll from one of my childhood fairy tale books.

I don't know which was worse, the fact that he ate all my food, monopolized the TV, or brought home other big, loud, hairy guys who were always making passes at me. Their primary forms of entertainment were ball games, attempting to belch the alphabet, and scratching unmentionable places. I wasn't interested in any of them.

Then one night, I walked into the only bathroom to find a naked troll-man asleep on the floor in a pool of vomit. I went straight to my room and packed. I was at Gran's door before the sun rose. That was three years ago, and I'd been living here ever since.

"I'm sorry, Gran. I'll figure it out."

Gran stepped toward me and took my hand. "Don't you be sorry. I love having you here. In fact, I feel selfish holding onto you. This isn't about me. It's about you."

That sounded backward. "Me?"

"I'm worried. I don't think it's good for you to spend all your time with us. You need to be with people your own age."

"I don't like people my own age." The words shocked me as they came out of my mouth. Was that true? I knew I had an affinity for older people, felt comfortable with them, but did I really dislike my own generation?

"That's the problem." She gave me a sad smile. "You work with seniors all day long, then come home to a couple of old folks at night."

"You and Phil aren't—"

She held up a hand and stopped my words. "We are, and you're not."

"But I love—"

"I know you love me, and I love you. Too much to let *Jeopardy* become so important to you."

She had a point. I didn't know any other twenty-somethings who even watched *Jeopardy*, never mind had strong opinions about it. "Sleep on it, Genie. I know you don't want to take money from me, but it's going to all be yours someday, anyway. Think of it as an advance."

I kissed her cheek and headed upstairs. I closed my bedroom door and flopped onto my bed. The muffled sounds of a television show slipped under the door. It was comforting. The soft lavender scent of Gran when I'd kissed her was comforting. Everything about living here was comforting.

However, Gran's words echoed my worst fear, the fear I'd never admitted to anyone until those words came blurting out of my mouth. What if my problem didn't stem from living with seniors? That was fixable. I could get an apartment, find a new job, make friends my own age.

What if it was just me? Some kind of weird DNA screw up. What if my biology hadn't advanced with the rest of mankind's but was stuck in the forties and fifties?

Even as a child, I'd known I was different. I liked old music, classic cars, and retro clothing. I wanted a vintage beach cruiser instead of a new bike. I watched *Twilight Zone* reruns instead of *Buffy the Vampire Slayer*.

I rolled onto my side and stared at the framed movie poster of *The Blob* on my wall. Not for the first time, it struck me how much Chad looked like Steve McQueen. I groaned. I'd even picked a retro guy. I was born in the wrong era.

I flipped onto my back and the ill-proportioned, stained-glass hummingbird I'd taken from Trudy's place caught my eye. Another groan escaped my lips. I was displaying DIY art made by one senior for another. Next thing you knew I'd be crocheting cozies for tissue boxes and toilet paper rolls.

No. I'd cling to the straw of hope Gran offered. If I made an effort, got my own place, started spending more time with people my age, I'd change. It would happen. Wouldn't it?

There was a house several girls from the beauty school shared. Every so often a bedroom came up. I'd never taken advantage of it because I was gun shy about roommates for obvious reasons. I also happened to know it was a party house. I didn't think I could take another bathroom incident. Maybe I should brave it now.

I lay there for several more minutes, debating whether I should call one of the girls or take Gran up on her offer for an advance, but came to no conclusion. I'd sleep on it, like she said. Maybe I'd wake tomorrow with the solution.

I got up and put on my pajamas. They were made from a vintage cotton print of daisies and honey bees. Girls my age didn't wear daisies and honey bees. I didn't think they even wore pajamas. If I moved into the party house, I'd have to get rid of them.

The book I'd taken from Trudy's sat on my dresser. I took it to bed, hoping it would free my mind from the troubled thoughts tumbling around inside it. *Fifties Dance Steps*, the cover said.

I wouldn't have to give up swing dancing, would I? There were plenty of young people at Neutron. I'd start hanging around with them. No more dancing with Hank-the-hands, even if he was only fifty-ish.

I cracked open the book. After three pages, I began to nod. It fell onto my chest with a thump. I jerked awake. I picked up the book to put it on the bedside table—I was obviously too tired to read—and a sheet of paper fluttered onto my pillow.

It was one of those printed Christmas letters people send to let everyone know what their family has been up to all year. Encircling the note there was a montage of photos: an older couple in plaid flannel shirts, bright-faced children bundled into ski clothes with poles in their hands, a house surrounded by flames of fall color. It must be from Trudy's family in Vermont. Doris had said she was planning a trip there this summer.

I was about to put the letter on top of the book when I noticed there was writing on the reverse side. Someone had penned a personal note. I hesitated. I felt strange reading it, like I was invading Trudy's privacy. Since her demise, Trudy's life had become like a book that, try as I might, I couldn't put down. I glanced at the page again. She was past caring, and I was so curious. I read the note.

Dear True,

It's been a cold December. I'm sorry we didn't come for Christmas, but Annie wanted to be with the grandkids. You know how that goes.

Got some strange news last month, don't know if it made it into the papers out there. Remember way back in ancient times when we were in high school and Mathew Palmer disappeared? I know you didn't know him. He was a few grades ahead of you, but thought you might recollect. People talked about it for years.

Anyway, a city couple bought the old Palmer house last summer. They decided to put in a fancy wine cellar and started digging up the basement. Guess what they found? Poor old Mathew.

Apparently, the cellar had been dirt until 1955, two years after he went missing. Someone must have killed him and buried his body in his own house. Can you imagine? His family searching and searching for him never knowing what happened, and there he was the whole time. It's a crying shame.

The town rumor mill thinks it was Mathew's father that did it—he had a drinking problem. He's been dead for years, how-some-ever, so there won't be any justice there. His sister is the only family member still living. She was in a dither over the news, as you can imagine. I think she's planning a small funeral. Most likely, I'll go. She was always a sweet girl.

I don't think the police can do naught about it now. The case is as cold as last night's potatoes. It bothers those of us who remember, I can tell you that. Hoppy, Sam, Buck, and the rest of the boys can't seem to talk about anything else. I had to stop going to Carla's for breakfast for a time. It was too dismal.

Speaking of, don't want to harp on about it, but thought you'd want to know. Give my love to Megan and James. We're looking forward to your trip east this summer.

Love,
Randall

I stared at the page for a long moment before folding it and placing it inside the swing dance book. The story was such a strange one. The idea Randall had expressed so eloquently haunted me—*His family searching and searching for him, never knowing what happened to him, and there he was the whole time.*

It reminded me of Trudy's hair analysis test. The digitalis had been there the whole time, but it was only because El insisted we go digging that we'd found it. What if those city folks hadn't dug up that basement? Mathew Palmer's sister would've gone to her grave not knowing what had happened to her brother.

I got out of bed, padded to my bookcase, and picked up a suspense story I'd gotten in a second-hand shop but never read—*The Cliff House.* It was about a real estate agent who finds a corpse in an ocean-front property she just listed. It was exactly what I needed to get my mind off things. A page-turner that bore no resemblance to my life.

My phone rang before I'd finished the first chapter. I looked at the screen. "Damn." The last thing I wanted to do was talk to Chad. I put the phone down, and it stopped ringing. A moment later, it started up again. It was apparent he wouldn't leave me alone until I talked to him.

I answered. "What?"

"Oh, that's nice. I haven't seen you in days and all you can say is, 'What?'"

"Sorry." I sighed. Why was I always apologizing to him when he was the one who had so much to apologize for? "It's been a long day."

"It's 9:15. You need to get out more." I didn't argue. "Which is why I'm calling. How's your leg?"

"It's my toe."

"How's your toe?"

I knew he wasn't asking because he cared, so I answered the real question. "I don't think I'm going to be able to dance in the contest."

"You might want to rethink that. I saw the list of contestants. We got this, Genie. We are better than everybody on that list."

I paused. If we won the contest, I might be able to afford an apartment somewhere without asking Gran for help. "Who's on it?"

Chad gave me the names, and I had to agree with him. We could beat all those people. The problem was, it would bring me into Chad's orbit again. I'd promised myself, and Gran, I was done with him.

I'd broken it off before—five times to be exact. I'd told myself six was the charm. However, I wouldn't be getting back together with him. Not romantically. This would be a business relationship only. I was in it to win it. I'd collect the cash and that would be that.

"I guess I could try," I said.

"Wednesday? There's open dance in the ballroom. We could start working on some choreography ideas."

"We're going to have to have a private room once we select music."

"Right. I'll talk to May. I think she likes me," Chad said.

He thought everybody liked him, every female anyway, but I thought he was right about May. Her eyelashes batted as fast as a hummingbird's wings when he was around. We worked out as many of the details as we could and hung up.

I tried to return to my novel but couldn't concentrate. I turned off the light and stared at the ceiling for a long time.

14

PROBLEMS OF THE HEART

I had a rough night and stopped to get something stronger than Gran's drip coffee on my way into work. Today I had three new clients, and El was coming in to get his promised haircut. I needed a double caffeine boost.

The salon was busy, and thank goodness, I was too. The after-effects of the funeral seemed to be wearing off. Nobody else had died. That was a positive. It seemed the clientele were beginning to realize I wasn't the Grim Reaper's younger sister.

My new clients were happy with their cuts, and I even convinced one to try a lovely shade of Kelly green on a strip of hair near her face. The color made her eyes pop. She walked out of Harry's with a new swing on her back porch, as Phil would say.

I was feeling pretty good, except my toe had begun to ache when I was blow-drying client number two. After limping through the third appointment, I headed to the break room to ice it. The ice in the old metal tray smelled suspicious, but I fished some out anyway and filled a baggie. I put my butt in one chair, my foot in another, and balanced the bag on my toe.

While I was lying in bed staring at the ceiling the night before, I'd done some calculations in my head. If I added what I had in the bank, half the contest prize money, and squirreled a bit more out of the new appointments I had on the schedule this week, I could almost afford first and last on a place in the same price range as the studio.

Problem was, I hadn't seen anything in that price range that didn't include roommates. I kept telling myself that as much as I didn't like the roommate idea, it could be for the best. Part of turning over a new leaf. Forced sociability.

Of course, this plan was predicated on my toe being able to withstand the Lindy Hop. Damned cowboy boots.

Maddy ducked into the break room. "Your two o'clock is here." She ducked out again. I moaned as my foot hit the floor. It always hurt the most right after I iced it.

El trotted through the salon with a happy, golden retriever grin on his face. He looked huge in this room full of small women. I wasn't the only one who'd noticed. Every foiled, wet, and teased head turned to watch him pass. Maddy almost lopped off a chunk of her client's hair. Stylist rule #1: Don't gawk and cut.

It took a few moments for him to wedge himself into my chair. It wasn't that his hips were wide. They weren't. I noted this in a clinical kind of way. His legs were too long. He looked like a circus clown riding a tiny bike, knees around his ears. I stepped on the foot pedal and raised the chair as high as it would go. It helped. A little. Then I had to stand on tiptoes, a painful process, to reach the top of his head.

"How's the toe," he said.

"Much better. I'm going dancing tomorrow night."

"Are you sure that's a good idea?" He frowned.

I picked up a clean smock and eyeballed it. No way it would fit across his shoulders. I threw it over him, blanket style. "If I'm going to enter that dance contest, I have to practice."

"So you're going to do it." His tone was disapproving.

"Yup," I said in a defiant one.

"What would your take of the prize money be?"

"Twenty-five hundred, if we win. Based on the competition, I think we have a good chance." I tried not to sound smug. I wasn't successful.

"I'll give you the money."

"What?" I shot him a glance in the mirror. "Why would you do that?"

"I hurt your foot. I should take responsibility for the losses incurred by the injury."

"There won't be any losses. I'm going to dance."

"I thought you didn't want anything to do with that guy. Your ex."

"It's not romantic. It's business."

"It can't be good for your toe."

I held up a hand like a traffic cop. "Discussion closed."

It was very heroic of him to want to give me the money, but there was no way I would take it. He hadn't committed a twenty-five-hundred-dollar offense. I was sure Phil had at least three clever expressions to cover why it was a bad idea to take money from El.

Neither of us said anything for a long moment. I set up my scissors and combs with extra care. He played with the hem of the smock.

I changed the subject. "Did you find out anything about Dr. Foster?"

"She seems fine. I checked all the doctor-rating sites. The only complaints against her are the kind everybody gets. The office is too busy. The staff are rude. That kind of thing. No medical malpractice suits. No unusual number of patient deaths."

"Good." I felt relief. Phil was in capable hands, whatever Gran thought. I was glad now I hadn't brought up his medication.

"I found out something else, though." He pivoted to look at me and almost lost an ear.

I placed a hand on either side of his head and directed it back to the mirror. "What's that?"

He swiveled around again. "It was crazy."

"You're going to lose a part of your anatomy if you keep doing that."

He faced forward. "I went to Trudy's estate sale to help Megan out on Sunday. She needed some of the heavy stuff moved."

I bet she did. "And?"

"And Rita and Norman were there."

"If you're going to tell me they're getting married, I already know."

He looked a little deflated. "Oh." Then he rallied. "There's more."

"What?"

"Did you know Rita has heart problems?"

"So does half of Liberty Grove."

"She got weak and shaky and had to sit in the shade for a bit. Megan got her water and Norman hovered."

"Sounds about right. She's a drama queen."

"I don't know. She looked pretty sick. Anyway, I walked over and asked if I could do anything to help. I sort of led them to believe I might be a paramedic."

I stopped cutting and stared at him in the mirror. "You're lucky you didn't have to do anything medical."

"I renew my CPR and First Aid certs every year. Greener Pastures makes me keep them current." That seemed strange considering the clientele, but I didn't say anything. "Norman told her she should get the strength of her medication checked, and Rita said it hadn't seemed to be working for the past couple of months."

His statement hung in the air like I was supposed to do something with it. I pushed his chin to his chest so I could get to his hairline.

"Interesting, don't you think?" he said in a muffled voice.

"Why is that interesting?" This conversation had started out well. My fears about a rogue doctor killing off Liberty Grove residents had been allayed. El had shown me his heroic side by offering to give me twenty-five hundred dollars. But now I was irritated. I didn't get what he was driving at, unless... No. Even El wouldn't go there.

He did.

"Maybe Rita's meds weren't working like they should have because she hadn't been taking them."

I put down my scissors, stepped in front of him, leaned on the counter, and looked into his eyes. They were very blue, which was entirely beside the point. "You're not saying you think Rita poisoned Trudy with her digitalis, are you?"

He shrugged. "I'm just saying it's a heck of a coincidence, and I don't like coincidences."

"It's not much of one," I said.

"What are you talking about? One woman with no heart problem dies with digitalis in her system. Her friend's heart medication suddenly stops working. That's a coincidence." His voice rose.

I shushed him and glanced around. He didn't understand the full reach and power of Harry's gossip ring. "As I said before, half of Liberty Grove is on some kind of medication for heart problems."

"Yes, but were all of them close friends with Trudy?" he said in a stage whisper.

I shrugged. "What do you think happened?"

He spread his hands wide. "Somehow Trudy took Rita's meds."

I was trying to be nice, supportive. I liked El, and—not to be mercenary—he was my cash cow. The way women fawned over him, he was the perfect spokesperson for *Hair by Imogene*. "I understood why you wanted to figure out if Trudy's death had been medical malpractice. You wanted to protect the larger community. We now know that's not the case. Trudy's doctor is a good doctor. If she prescribed digoxin for Trudy, she must have needed it."

"We don't know that she did prescribe it. No one knew Trudy was taking it. Not her daughter. Not her best friend, Doris. How do you explain that?"

"Some people are very private when it comes to their health. Maybe she didn't want to worry people."

"If she had AFib, people close to her would know. Doctors don't give out digoxin just because your heart races now and again. It's a serious drug. Plus, it's usually not prescribed alone. Trudy would have been taking a cocktail. Her daughter didn't find any prescription bottles in her condo."

"You asked her?" I knew he had a way with women, but that seemed pretty presumptuous, even for him.

He shifted under the smock. "Not in so many words. I told her about the list of medications my grandfather was on the year before he died, mentioned that one of his doctors believed his death was related to drug interactions."

He glanced at me with sadness in his eyes. "She said how grateful she'd been her mother hadn't had to take anything, but now she wondered if Trudy should have been on medication. She was upset with herself for not insisting her mother get more frequent checkups. We owe it to Megan to find out the truth about Trudy's death."

"That's a very touching story, but I think this is a mystery that isn't going to be solved. We can't go to the police with what we know. We can't ask Trudy's doctor. I don't know how we could explain to Megan what we did." I said all this as gently as I could. My effort was lost on El. He acted as though he didn't hear me.

His eyebrows drew together in a pensive knot. "There are only two possibilities: either she took digoxin by accident, or someone gave it to her."

I sighed. He was like a dog with a dried pig's ear. He wouldn't let go. "How could she take it by accident?"

"Maybe Trudy was at Rita's and popped a couple of pills thinking they were aspirin. They look pretty similar."

"Would a couple of pills kill someone?"

"If she took two every four hours for a day or two, maybe."

"I don't think Trudy was spending that much time at Rita's."

"I thought they were friends."

"They were, but Trudy stole Rita's man. Rita wasn't happy about it."

El lit up. "No kidding?"

"I wish I were. Apparently, Rita and Norman were an item for quite a while. Then on New Year's Eve, Norman found out he and Trudy grew up in the same town in Vermont. After that, he only had eyes for her. Dropped Rita like a hot rock, according to Doris."

Maddy walked past us to the break room in a much too leisurely fashion. I could almost see her ears twitching. The natives were getting suspicious. I walked behind my chair and began snipping El's hair.

"You don't think Rita could've slipped Trudy an overdose to clear the playing field, do you? Many a murder has been committed because of jealousy," he said.

I almost dropped my scissors. "No way. Rita may be a prima donna, but I can't see her taking things that far. Besides, if she had, would she have admitted she was having heart symptoms to Norman?"

"She wasn't well. It didn't seem like she had a lot of control over the matter."

"I can imagine Rita doing a lot of things, but killing someone? I don't think so." Even as the words left my lips, doubt entered my mind. Rita was my least favorite member of the threesome. She played the weak and vulnerable female well, but now and again a hard edge peeked through.

Albert Rogers came to Neutron once. He wasn't interested in dancing, however. He was interested in Rita. It was the only time I ever felt sorry for the guy. He'd gotten all dressed up in a suit and slicked back the little bit of hair he had. I watched him cross the floor to Rita's group of friends with a sinking feeling in my stomach.

He walked straight up to Rita and asked her to dance. I could tell from across the room that she turned him down. I couldn't hear what she said, but it couldn't have been too bad. He sat on a bench at the side of the room as if he planned to wait a while and ask again. When the next song started up, Rita jigged onto the floor with Norman. I saw the icy smile she gave Mr. Rogers as she swung past.

His face turned beet red. I was afraid he was going to have another heart attack. He'd had one the year before.

He left, and I never saw him there again. However, as cruel and thoughtless as Rita's behavior was, it was a long way from murder. Even sweet, kindhearted Trudy had stifled a laugh. No one liked Mr. Rogers much.

"I think we're taking the cart before the horse here anyway," I said and winced at the cliché.

"How so?"

"We don't even know what kind of heart medication Rita is on. Digoxin isn't the only one out there."

El looked stunned. "You're right. I don't know why I didn't think of that."

I preened, just a little. It was nice to be right for once, but my moment of victory was short-lived.

"How are we going to find out?" El said.

It was my turn to look stunned. "I have no idea."

"Who could we ask? Norman? Doris?"

I set down my scissors and picked up a comb. "Even if we find out Rita is on digoxin, so what? How does this change anything?"

"Detection 101: When you have a lead, follow it. You never know where you're going to end up."

That's exactly what I was afraid of. "What are you going to do?" I asked, not sure I wanted the answer.

He was saved from having to tell me by Harry. "Imogene, sweetheart, can you take a walk-in?" Harry's tone was deeper than usual, and he'd walked all the way to my station to talk to me instead of yelling across the salon. He looked different too. His hair had been teased and sprayed, and I could swear I saw eyeliner on his lids.

I must have been staring because he patted his head, then rubbed his nose. "Just checking to see if you're done with Mr. Brown." His lips parted to expose two rows of yellowed teeth.

Was he flirting? Had everybody in this salon lost their minds? I guessed I should be happy that all the members of the sixty-and-over club found El irresistible. He was great for marketing, but it was getting on my nerves.

"Yeah, we're done." I ripped the smock off El's chest.

His gaze slid to my face. "I have something else to tell you."

"I'll walk you to your car."

I felt a pack of hungry eyes on our backs as we exited the salon. "What's up?" I said when we were out of earshot.

"I don't know if you're going to be interested in this, but Amy Lee asked for you."

"For me?"

"Yeah. I guess she has a case that needs extra attention in the hair department. She's really busy right now and thought it would be up your alley."

I started to shake my head. My reputation was only just recovering from my last stint at Greener Pastures. I didn't want to jeopardize things.

El held up a hand. "I know what you're thinking, but there's no reason anyone would ever have to know you did the job." I narrowed my eyes. "It pays well."

Before I could answer, my phone rang. I fished it out of my sweater pocket.

"Imogene Lynch?" the voice on the other end said.

"Yes."

"This is Grace Daniels—the studio apartment on Elm St."

"Oh, hi." I felt a ripple of excitement.

"I know we told you the place was rented, but the tenant backed out of the lease. It's available, if you're still interested."

"I am," I said, and we made plans for me to stop by after work. I hung up and looked at El. "Pays well, huh? How much?"

15

Haunted Hair

After the walk-in, I cleaned my station and jogged to my car. I had enough time to shoot over to Elm Street and still make it to Greener Pastures by 5:30 if I hurried. Grace answered her front door on the first knock and ushered me into her home.

It was lovely, decorated in pale shades of blue and green with a mismatched assortment of furniture that somehow harmonized despite the variety of styles. It had the same beach-house vibe as the apartment, only on a larger, more luxurious scale.

A contract and pen sat on a coffee table in front of a distressed leather couch. Grace gestured to them. "Did you want to take another look at the place? Or, just . . . " Her words dwindled off.

I got the sense the question was a test. If I wanted to look again before I signed, it implied I didn't trust her. A vision of Mr. Rogers' suspicious prune of a face appeared in my mind. It wasn't fun living next door to someone who looked at life through legalistic, rigid lenses. I didn't want to be that person.

"No, I saw it the other night. It's just what I'm looking for. And I'm in a hurry anyway." I wrote my name on the signature line with a flourish. It was a good thing I'd agreed to do the job for Amy Lee. After handing over my deposit, I only had ten dollars in my checking account.

Fifteen minutes later, I drove through the gates of Greener Pastures. I parked behind the mortuary and entered through the side door that led to the stairwell I'd seen on my first visit.

I trotted straight downstairs. By avoiding the plush main floor, I avoided most of the shock over the sterility of the subterranean level. Going from parking lot to tile and steel wasn't as bad as going from thick carpets, draperies, and soft furnishings to the cold below.

When I came to the embalming room door, I paused. It was important to present a professional demeanor and rein in my nerves. The deceased weren't that different from the rest of us, I told myself. In fact, the rest of us would be them eventually. I filled my lungs, straightened my shoulders, pushed open the door, and jumped backward.

The sight that met my eyes was like a scene from Frankenstein. Lying on a table in the center of the room was a naked man, only his loins covered by a sheet. Tubes wove in and out of his unnaturally pale skin. In one bubbled a clear substance, in the other a viscous red-brown liquid. I was fairly sure the clear tube held embalming fluid. The reddish brown must be . . . I shuddered.

"Imogene Lynch?"

I tore my gaze from the table. Behind the body, in a white coat and rubber gloves, stood the mad scientist responsible for this monstrosity. She was a tiny Asian woman, gloved hands raised like a surgeon's. Her hair was pulled into a tight ponytail, her eyes accentuated by black-rimmed glasses.

"Yes." I choked out the word.

"Amy Lee. I'll be done in a minute. You sit." She gestured to a hard plastic chair not far from where she worked.

Her air was so authoritative, I didn't dare disobey. The thought crossed my mind that perhaps not obeying was how the poor man on the table ended up where he was.

I took my seat. After what seemed an eternity, the fluids in the tubes sputtered to a stop and Amy Lee withdrew them. I knew the victim was past feeling pain, but I averted my eyes anyway. I felt the pain for him.

Amy Lee wound up the tubes and placed them on the table that held the machine, covered the man with his sheet, and snapped off her gloves.

"You do hair and makeup." Her words sounded more like a command than a question, but I answered anyway.

"Yes, but usually for . . . Not for . . . You know."

She gave me a curt nod. "I have a job for you." She strode to a large door at the back of the room and opened it. Frost spilled out like escaping spirits. I had a sudden urge to do the same but sat rooted to the spot.

Amy Lee disappeared into the effluvium and reemerged a moment later, wheeling another sheet-covered table. She steered it to a place under a bright light and drew back the fabric.

I took in a sharp breath. The face that was revealed wasn't old. This was no Liberty Grove citizen moving on to their just reward. She was young. My age. In fact, she kind of looked like me.

I stepped closer to the gurney. Her hair was black with red highlights, like mine. Dark blond roots crowned her head. I couldn't see the color of her eyes, but I had an uncanny certainty they were blue—like mine. I was pale. She was marble white. A chill crept over me that had nothing to do with the temperature in the room.

"How did she die?" I almost whispered the question.

"Car accident," Amy Lee said. "I had to do a lot of reconstruction. See her ear, here." She donned another pair of gloves and pointed at the woman's right ear. At first glance, it looked the same as the left, but on closer inspection I saw a slender seam, a slight discoloration. "I made that from wax."

"It looks so real," I said.

Amy Lee's lips lifted in a half smile for a brief instant. "I used makeup to match her skin. I remolded her nose and built her jaw where it was crushed. See, here and here." She stroked the dead woman's face gently. "Today I will show you how to apply our cosmetics. You used your own before, but those don't work good most of the time."

I wasn't sure why she was showing me how to do this young woman's makeup, but I found myself bending closer to the body. I was fascinated by the transformation I could now see had taken place, shudders forgotten. Amy Lee opened a drawer, pulled out a box, and set it on a table near the gurney.

For the next half hour, she applied foundation to bring color into the bone white face, added a soft blush to the girl's cheeks. She created a paste with a few drops from a brown bottle and a lipstick the family had given her. She brushed the color onto dry lips. When she was done, the girl had come to life.

"She looks good," she said with satisfaction.

"Except for her hair," I said.

Amy Lee cut her eyes to me. "Can you fix it?"

"Sure." I reached out a hand to feel its texture. As my fingers closed over the lock, a flood of emotions coursed through me: grief, love, longing. I dropped the hair like it was on fire. The intensity of the emotions diminished, but an echo reverberated through my chest. It was happening again. Those feelings weren't mine any more than the rage I'd felt when I touched Trudy's hair had been mine. So whose were they? Amy Lee didn't look like she'd noticed a thing. She was as cool as she'd been when I'd arrived. There was only one other person in the room.

"Okay. Do it." Amy Lee pulled off her gloves and began cleaning up her tools.

"I didn't bring anything with me."

"The funeral is tomorrow. Two o'clock."

"I can come first thing in the morning."

"We need to dress her and put her upstairs by ten."

"I'll be here by 7:00." I stumbled out of the embalming room.

When I stepped outside, it was dark. El stood in front of the mortuary, an upturned spotlight casting eerie shadows on his face. "How did it go?"

"Fine," I lied. I'd connected with Belinda Simpson—that was dead girl's name—on a level I didn't understand. She was dead. She didn't exist any longer. Yet, making her beautiful for her funeral was now the most important thing in my world. When I thought about her family, a family I didn't know, a fist locked around my heart and squeezed until it hurt.

"Everything okay?" El was too perceptive.

"Yes. No. I don't know."

"What happened?"

"Nothing happened."

He nodded, his expression hard to decipher. "Why don't you come with me? I have to do my rounds."

I didn't know if I could explain my experience in the embalming room, or if I'd even try, but I needed El's solid presence.

We walked around the back of the building. Several golf carts were lined up next to a block wall. El started one, and I got in beside him. We putted away from the lights of the building.

"How do you do it?" I said. He waited for me to continue. "Face death every day."

"It's a part of life."

"Ever since I did Trudy's funeral, it's like I've been haunted. Not by a ghost. I don't believe in ghosts. I'm haunted by her life."

"I'm not sure what you mean."

I wasn't sure what I meant either. I did know one thing, however. When I was done with Belinda Simpson's hair tomorrow, I was going to return to the land of the living. I'd had enough of the dead. "I'm glad you looked into Dr. Foster. It's our responsibility to protect living people, but I think we need to forget about Trudy now."

"The hair sample—"

I flapped a hand in the air. "That was a mistake. It wasn't legal—"

"Authorized," he corrected me.

"Authorized, whatever. Trudy is gone. Buried. In her grave. We need to let her rest in peace."

"Aren't we doing that?"

We bounced over a speed bump, and I grabbed my seat cushion. "No. Every time we poke or pry, every time we come up with another theory, we're resurrecting her."

El glanced at me, and I saw a flicker of moonlight in his eyes. "What set this off?"

I pivoted in my seat to face him. "I don't have a lot of friends. I've never had a lot of friends."

"I can't believe that."

I stopped him. "I'm not looking for pity, just stating the facts. I've always been a loner. But now, it's like Trudy is with me everywhere I go. I even put my career at risk for her. And then that dead woman tonight. I feel closer to her than the girls I went through beauty school with."

"You care, that's all."

"I rarely care." The words came out more forcefully than I'd intended. "I mean, I care about Gran and Phil and Harry, but I'm not known for my compassion."

"You make it sound like caring about people is a bad thing."

"People, no. But corpses? I'm turning into a ghoul."

El stared straight ahead and worked his jaw muscle. "You think people who want justice for the dead are ghouls?"

"No, of course not. It makes sense for you. You're going into law enforcement. You work in a cemetery. I'm a hairstylist."

He didn't speak for a long time, and I began to regret opening up to him.

"So hairstylists can't be concerned about life and death issues?"

It was my turn to be quiet.

"It's difficult to work in the death industry," he said. "This job raises questions about the afterlife. It forces us to face our own mortality. I think what you did for Trudy was brave and kind, not ghoulish."

My cheeks grew warm. I was glad it was too dark for him to see I was blushing. That was one of the nicest things anyone had said to me in a long time. "Thank you," I said, my voice softening. "Most people don't see it that way."

"Why do you care what most people think?"

"Because most people pay the bills." My statement, although true, made me feel small and petty.

"You could work here. Carlton would hire you in a heartbeat. Even mortician's assistants make good money."

In a flash of imagination, I saw myself driving through the cemetery, walking down the cellar stairs, and opening the heavy metal door. Instead of the cheerful hum of voices, I'd be greeted with the hum of a refrigeration unit.

Instead of checking the schedule to see who I'd be working on that day, I'd open a door and wheel out a gurney. Instead of gossip, there would be silence. "No." I almost yelled. El shrank away from me.

He pulled into a small parking lot and turned off the engine. "I'm going to do a walkthrough. You should probably wait here. Your toe." He sounded hurt. I think I'd disappointed him. He'd thought I was a deeper, better person. I wasn't.

He got out of the golf cart, and I pulled my sweater around me. The warmth of the day was gone. The wind whipped up and tossed my hair into my face. I watched El move away from me, his shape growing indistinct. Soon he was only a shadow in a forest of glowing tombstones. A cold mist enveloped me.

"El," I called. The shadow stopped. "Wait up." I no longer wanted to be left alone. I caught up with him. He gave me a curious glance, but I avoided his eyes.

We crunched over a gravel path between aisles of graves. There was a full moon. I was able to read some of the inscriptions as we passed: *Timothy Carter - Beloved Husband and Father, Francine Carter - Beloved Wife and Mother, Edna Carter - Second Wife.* Second wife, I'd hate to go through eternity with that moniker.

Many of the graves were decorated with wilted flowers, but here and there, fresh flowers adorned a mound of dark earth. These must be the newer graves. Loved ones still left gifts they hadn't yet accepted the dead couldn't receive.

"Do you have to walk so fast?" My toe ached from the exertion.

El stopped and turned. "I have a schedule."

"Look, I know you're mad. I'm sorry."

"I'm not mad." His angry tone made him a liar.

"Right."

"I get it. You need to eat. You need to pay the rent."

"I do."

He began to walk, but slower this time. "When I was seven, my grandfather moved in with us. My grandma was gone, and my parents worked a lot. It was a good situation for everybody. Grandpa picked me up from school most days, and we'd spend the afternoons together."

I wondered what this had to do with our conversation but didn't ask. I liked hearing about his past. El, despite his guileless smile and easygoing ways, was an enigma to me.

"He loved mysteries. We read The Hardy Boys, all the Sherlock Holmes stories, Encyclopedia Brown. I decided I was going to be a detective when I grew up. But that's my thing. It isn't everybody's."

"I read a lot when I was a kid, too," I said. "Some mysteries, Boxcar Kids and Agatha Christie when I was in junior high, but I liked science fiction and fantasy best." We walked without speaking for several minutes.

El broke the silence. "Did you want to be an astronaut when you grew up?"

"Nope. I wanted to be an elf."

I saw the dark rectangle of the parking lot ahead of us and realized we'd made a loop. I was ready to end this awkward evening and picked up my pace. El took my hand and pulled me to a stop. I wondered why, until I saw where his eyes were focused.

There, behind a mound of roses and calla lilies, I read: *Gertrude Rosenblum - May she dance through eternity.* "Say goodbye, Imogene. Trudy won't bother you anymore."

"What are you going to do?" I forced the words past a growing lump in my throat.

"I don't know. I imagine you're right. This is a dead end—no pun intended—and digging around might cause more grief than it's worth. It just bugs the heck out of me that I'll never know why Trudy had digitalis in her hair sample."

"I hope you understand why I can't do this anymore."

"Who are you asking, me or Trudy?"

Honestly, I wasn't sure, but I said, "You."

"I do. We have to face reality. I'm not a detective—yet. And you're not an elf."

I squeezed his hand, then dropped it. "Your hair looks great." I made my tone light to dispel the mood and the surrounding darkness. We trudged toward the golf cart. A tickle crept up my spine, but I ignored it. We weren't being watched. Not by Trudy, not by anybody. At least, that's what I told myself.

16

ON THE BACK FOOT

Two days later, El stopped by Harry's to pick up discount cards. He'd called that morning and offered to take some around Liberty Grove. I was relieved. I'd hoped we could still be friends even though we weren't investigating buddies anymore. I'd thought I'd said all the right *it's not you, it's me* kinds of things, but you never know what's going to happen after a breakup.

I was between clients when he got there, and I was glad. My toe was killing me, so I perched in my chair with a magazine. The dance practice at Neutron hadn't been a success. I didn't want El to see me limp.

I could move forward. I could move backward. Spins were murder. Who ever heard of doing the Lindy Hop without spinning? To make matters worse, Chad wanted to throw me over his shoulder and launch me between his legs, movements that culminated in hard landings. My toe didn't like hard landings.

I danced for less than ten minutes before collapsing on a bench with tears in my eyes. Chad wasn't sympathetic—big surprise. He stormed off with his cell in hand scrolling through his contacts to find another partner.

I should have been glad to see him go—damn the money—and I would have been except for the apartment. I'd been counting on the twenty-five hundred to replenish my depleted checking account.

"Hey," El said as he crossed the salon.

"Hey, yourself," I said.

"I can't stay."

"That's okay. I have a two o'clock."

He seemed subdued. He took the cards from me and left, just like that. It was so unlike him I began to worry again, but my next client arrived and drove all thoughts of El from my mind. It was a foil weave that took over two hours.

When I was done, I said goodnight to Harry and headed out to my car. There were still several hours of daylight left. My plan was to head over to Elm Street. The apartment had been weighing on me all day.

After last night's botched dance practice, I decided to do the responsible thing—weasel my way out of the lease and get my nonrefundable deposit back. Part of that was the first month's rent, but I was pretty sure I wouldn't be able to cover the next.

Despite the new clients El had brought in, my business wasn't even close to what it had been before the Trudy debacle. It was going to take time to rebuild. Time I didn't have.

I turned onto Elm, drove up the block, and parked. Before I walked to the main house, I gazed up the white staircase by the garage to the red door at its top and sighed. The place was perfect.

I imagined myself welcoming a group of hip-looking friends through that door, jogging down those stairs and off on a neighborhood run with my dog at my heels. But I didn't have any hip-looking friends, or a dog. And I didn't run. However, somewhere deep inside, I believed I would if I lived here. This place could've changed my life—led me into a world of popularity, fitness, and prosperity. My Shangri-la. I sighed again. I had to do what I had to do.

I walked to the front door of the Daniels' home. They seemed like such nice people. I was sure when I explained my dilemma, they'd refund my deposit. I knocked and a long moment later Grace answered.

She didn't smile the way she had when I'd come by to sign the lease. In fact, she looked a bit annoyed. "You're not due for a couple of weeks."

"That's what I wanted to talk to you about."

"I hope you're not here to tell me you want out of the lease." She folded her arms over her chest. "Because if you are, you can forget it."

"Ah," was all I managed to say before she started talking again.

"You'd be the third person to do it in as many months. Like we told the last guy, we'll let you out of the lease, but you're not getting your deposit back. We have to pay the mortgage around here, you know. Every month that unit stays vacant, we lose money."

"I—"

"You probably found out about the Alzheimer's care home across the street. I'm sorry, but that's not a disclosure item, and there's nothing in the CC and R's against it."

"No, I—"

"They aren't a problem anyway. At least not much of one. We've only found two residents on our property since the place opened. One in the front yard, and we simply wrapped a towel around her and took her home. The man in the guest bathroom did give me a start, but if you keep your door locked, you'll be fine."

"Ah . . ." I tried again.

"Was it that Nosy Parker, Edna, who told you about the place? She's just trying to discourage you from renting our apartment. She voted against the addition, but the homeowners' association approved it. She's never gotten over it."

I shook my head.

"How did you find out, then?" Grace flapped a hand. "Oh, never mind. You don't have to tell me. Whatever you've heard, it's not that bad. The lady with nightmares died last month. There hasn't been any screaming since."

What was it with me and senior citizens? It wasn't that I didn't enjoy them, I did. I even had an affinity for them. I was sure I'd be a terrific one someday, if I lived that long. But, as Gran said, I needed to spend more time with people my own age, yet here I was moving into Senile Central.

Grace paused to breathe. "I'm used to seniors," I blurted out. "That's not a problem."

The smile from the day before returned to her face. "Good. Then why did you come by?"

Why did I? I couldn't ask for the refund now. That much was clear. "I, ah, I . . . " I was usually good at thinking on my feet, but my mind was a complete blank.

"If you want to measure for furniture, I can give you the key. So long as you promise to bring it back."

"Right. Furniture," I said. Good lord, I'd forgotten all about furniture. I'd been so overcome by desire, I hadn't stopped to think about all the expenses involved in moving. Not only did I have to come up with money for next month's rent, but I'd have to get something to sit on, as well.

Grace disappeared into her house without asking me if I'd like to come in. As I waited, I realized I hadn't brought a tape measure. I guessed I could pace off the room. A moment later, she reappeared and handed me a key chain. "Sometimes the door sticks. Just give it a kick."

I walked to the white staircase. As I climbed, I noticed the paint on the treads was not only worn, it was peeling. Two weeks ago, I'd thought it looked shabby chic. Today it just looked shabby.

The red door had a lot of black scuff marks at the bottom. A testimony to its stickiness, I guessed. I turned the key in the lock and pushed. It didn't budge. I kicked. The door flew open. I wondered if I'd have to enter my home like that all the time, or only when it was humid.

Was it humid today? I wasn't sure, but I gazed at the sky as if I'd be able to see the moisture. All I saw was sunshine.

When I entered the apartment, I saw light streaming through the grime on the front windows. It landed on some suspicious-looking stains on the carpeting. My gaze travelled across the living room. The dingy white walls were stained as well. At least everything matched.

I took another step inside, and the smell hit me. The one I'd associated with beach houses and vacations. I sneezed. It was mold. I was allergic to mold.

I wiped the counter with my sleeve before setting my purse on it, then surveyed the kitchenette. It was smaller than I'd remembered, but it did have that half-sized fridge, which was more than many apartments had.

I opened the appliance and was immediately sorry. No food would darken its door until the entire thing was scrubbed with bleach. I wondered if it was the source of the moldy funk in the air. I pivoted to where I'd thought the oven was, hoping it wasn't as filthy as the refrigerator.

It wasn't. Because it wasn't there.

What I'd imagined was an oven was actually a tilt-out trash cabinet. Where was the stove? I circled the abbreviated space with excruciating slowness. Tiny stainless-steel sink. Tiny green laminate countertop. Tiny cabinet at eye level and two tiny cabinets below. The unfortunate refrigerator. And, the trash cabinet.

No stove.

Which meant no group of cool friends invited over for dinner unless we got take out. How had I missed this basic fact? I hadn't thought to ask what the difference between a kitchen and a kitchenette was. Apparently, kitchenettes didn't have any way to cook food.

I wandered through the rest of the apartment in a daze. It didn't take long. There was only one room. The studio was bigger than my bedroom at Gran's. I had remembered that correctly. And I'd have my own bathroom instead of having to share. That was a plus.

Bathroom.

My blood ran cold.

Had I seen a bathroom? The colored lenses covering my eyes the first time I was here had blurred my vision and my memory. There were two doors on the far wall of what Peter had referred to as "the great room." I walked toward the closest, my heart beating a tattoo on my ribs.

I reached for the knob and, based on my experience with the refrigerator, prepared myself for anything. I hesitated but only for a moment. Better to get it over with, like a pelvic exam.

I yanked. It was a closet. A very small closet. I tried to imagine my entire wardrobe fitting within. I couldn't. Maybe Gran would let me store some things at her place.

I closed that door and padded to the next. I inhaled and held my breath just in case, then opened it. I definitely hadn't seen this the night I was here, because this I would have remembered.

It was a bathroom. Thank goodness. The only odor was old Tidy Bowl. Thank goodness, again.

It was small. No, let me rephrase. It was minuscule. Like it had been designed for a child's playhouse, but no one would do this to a child. Grace and Peter had made the bizarre decision to cover this microscopic space with wallpaper. Green vines climbed the walls at odd angles and grew over the ceiling like kudzu. Both the sink and the toilet were green. They blended so well with the vines I almost missed them.

The important thing, I told myself, was that they were there. And small wasn't terrible. It was a good weight-management incentive. I was fairly certain I wouldn't fit inside if I put on ten pounds. Also, small meant less to clean.

My personal pep-talk was interrupted by an uncomfortable thought. I reached across the space and twisted the crusted knob of the faucet. The pipes sputtered for a second, then a gush of orange water spewed forth. There was water. I felt silly checking, but I'd assumed there was a stove and look how that had turned out.

I did an about-face but was stopped by another thought. A toilet and a sink were good. I could pee and brush my teeth. But what about a shower? I spun and scanned the room.

Leaves and more leaves everywhere I looked. Despair closed around my heart. I was like a woman marooned on a jungle island surrounded by more jungle. How would I get clean? How would I wash my hair?

Then I noticed a ripple. It was a small ripple, barely visible, but it was there. My eyes followed it upward and found a metal rod decorated with green plastic rings. I leaned forward, grabbed the ripple and pulled.

The shower curtain slid back to reveal a green bathtub the size of the ones I'd seen at the dog groomer Gran took Harley to. Attached to a faucet caked with calcium deposit, was a lovely, mold-green, hand-held shower attachment.

17

NIGHTMARE ON ELM ST.

I left the apartment with a sinking heart. My desperation to move had blinded me to reality the night I'd toured it. I slogged up to Grace's front door and knocked. She had to have the place cleaned or I wouldn't move in. It was the only leverage I could think of. If the place was a pit, they couldn't expect me to take it. Could they?

The door opened, but instead of Grace standing there, it was a tall, skinny blond. A familiar tall, skinny blond. Her eyes widened in surprise when she saw me. "Aren't you Norma Gene, Chad's friend?" she said.

"Imogene," I said. "And you're McKenzie." She was Chad's new flame. The one I'd met at Neutron.

"What are you—" we both said at once. I let her have the floor.

"What are you doing here?" she asked.

I held up the key chain. "I'm renting the studio."

"Oh, Mom said she had a new tenant. I didn't know it was you."

Mom? Great. One more thing to add to no money, no stove, a disgusting refrigerator, a bathroom camouflaged for jungle combat, and a band of confused, wandering senior gypsies across the street—Chad's girlfriend was my landlord's daughter. "Small world," I said.

We stood looking at each other for an awkward moment, then she reached for the key. "When do you move in?"

"That's the thing," I said. "I can't move in until the place is cleaned."

McKenzie's eyebrows lifted, and her lips pursed. "Did you put down a deposit?"

"Yes, but—"

"I think the lease says you agree to take the place as is."

"Maybe, but when I signed it, I hadn't seen the inside of the refrigerator."

McKenzie shrugged as if to say tough luck. "I'll tell my parents."

"Can I talk to Grace?"

"She's not here."

"How about your dad?"

"He's not here, either."

"Well, let them know, would you? Either the place is cleaned, or I'll have to back out of the lease."

"You won't get your deposit back."

There was no point in arguing with McKenzie. She wasn't the decision maker. I nodded a goodbye and walked away. Her voice stopped me before I got to the street. "How's your toe?"

How did she know about my toe? I turned. "Getting better, thanks. How did you know I'd injured it?"

"Chad told me."

I must have looked confused, because she explained. "He told me you couldn't dance in the contest because you hurt your toe. He was upset about it."

"He was?"

"Yeah, but he's over it. I'm his partner now." She flashed me a smug smile. "He said he'd asked you first, for old times' sake and all that."

"For old times' sake?" I parroted. Chad had never done anything for old times', new times', anything's, or anybody's sake but his own in his life. Chad did things for Chad.

"He said it was all for the best." A hand fluttered to her mouth. "I mean, not that you got hurt or anything, but dancing with me instead."

I didn't know what to say, so I headed for my car. My cell rang as soon as I put on my seat belt. It was El.

"I need to talk to you," he said without preamble.

"What's up?"

"I, ah, stopped by Rita Tarkington's place to give her a discount coupon."

A mini-surge of adrenaline shot through me. I didn't like the hesitation in his voice. I plugged my phone into a headset and started the engine.

"I know you're out on the detecting thing, but I think you should know about this."

"Know about what?"

"Norman was at Rita's when I got there. She invited me in, but I could tell he wasn't happy about it. He acted nervous. Kept picking at his fingernails."

"Wait, don't tell me. That's a body language signal for guilt."

"Not necessarily, but he was definitely uncomfortable." El missed my sarcasm. "Anyway, I gave Rita the coupon and engaged in a little small talk about Neutron. I told them I'd talked you into taking line-dancing classes, by the way. We'll have to go, keep up our cover."

I had no intention of line dancing, or of ever dancing with El again, but I let it slide. Best to let him finish his story. I would be home in a few minutes. All I wanted to do when I got there was drown my sorrows in a clean tub that was big enough to stretch out in.

"I asked if I could have a glass of water and insisted on getting it myself. I figured a lot of people keep their medications in the kitchen on the counter so they don't forget to take them. Sure enough, there were three prescription bottles near the sink."

"I'm afraid to ask you what they were."

"I only saw one. Norman came in and threw me out before I had a chance to look at the others, but—"

"What!" I almost hit a tree. I straightened the wheel and swallowed the panic rising in my throat.

"Don't worry. I saw what I needed to see. She's on—"

"I don't care what she's on. Don't you realize what you've done?" I interpreted the silence on the other end of the line as guilt and heaped on. "You have ruined my career."

"I think you may be overreacting," he said.

"You have no idea how fast word travels in a place like Liberty Grove. I was just starting to overcome the grim-reaper label, and now the man who hands out my business cards is caught pawing through someone's stuff. Norman probably thought you were stealing."

"No. That's not what he thought."

"Then why did he throw you out?"

El coughed and cleared his throat like he was buying time. "He thought I was sniffing around to figure out who was most likely to, you know, to help your business."

"What are you talking about?"

"Who was most likely to peg out."

"Peg out!" I think I shrieked at that point.

"Yeah. He thought you wanted to . . . How did he say it? Cultivate clients for your post-life services while they were still alive."

A moan escaped my lips.

"Seriously, don't worry. He has absolutely no evidence to support that theory, and I told him so."

"You said that? That he had no evidence?"

"Of course. I defended you all the way. I told him I was just curious about the meds, because in my Crime Scene Investigation class we're taught to notice those kinds of things."

"You told him you were taking Crime Scene Investigation?"

"Yeah, but he threw me out anyway."

"What did he say when he threw you out?"

"That part wasn't great. He said to tell you if he saw your snooping boyfriend around Liberty Grove again, he'd give the gate a picture of me and tell them to call the police if I showed up."

I felt like someone had punched me in the gut. "What did you say?"

"I told him I wasn't your boyfriend."

I groaned again.

"I have good news, though. Rita is taking digoxin."

I hung up. My life had taken a terrible turn since I'd met El. The man was poison. It had been a tremendous mistake to put my business in his hands. He might be attractive to unsuspecting females, but he was the proverbial bull in a china shop. Well, he'd broken enough cups and saucers in mine.

Phil says life is three steps forward and two steps back. I disagree. It's more like a treadmill. A few days ago, I'd been on top of the world. I'd thought I'd discovered a gold mine in El. I had an easy twenty-five hundred dollars coming my way. And I'd put down a deposit on my dream home.

Today I had to do some fast-stepping to prevent the end of my career. McKenzie was going to get my prize money, and my dream home had become the nightmare on Elm Street. By my calculations, I hadn't made any progress at all.

18

UNINTENDED CONSEQUENCES

I entered Liberty Grove through gate three but, instead of turning left to go home, I made a right toward Rita's. Damage control was needed. I wasn't sure what I would say, but I'd come up with something.

Rita and Norman were at the center of a large senior social network. They knew almost everyone. I couldn't afford to alienate them.

I parked next to Rita's powder blue Caddy and walked up the path to her condo, practicing my opening lines. "Rita, Norman, what's this I heard about El?" No. Take control of the dialog. Don't start with a question.

"Rita, Norman, El called me. I'm so sorry about the misunderstanding." No. Don't make them wrong. Don't suggest El's behavior was acceptable, and they were too stupid to get it.

"Rita, Norman, El called me. I can't apologize enough for his behavior." That wasn't bad. I was throwing El under the bus, but he threw my business under the bus by going through Rita's private property, especially after I'd broken up our detecting team.

I knocked on the front door, and Norman answered. His eyebrows jutted into an angry line when he saw me. "I know you're upset," I said, and he didn't deny it. "Please let me come in. I need to speak to you and Rita."

He hesitated for a moment, then took a step backward so I could enter. Rita's home was like a fairy tale version of heaven—a firmament of powder blue dotted with cloud-like fuzzy white objects. Blue walls were decorated with gray and white photos in white frames. Furry white throw pillows were tossed onto a blue sofa. I crossed a white shag carpet to Rita, who reclined on a blue easy chair, feet propped on a white ottoman. Her eyes were closed, and the back of one hand rested on her brow in a theatrical pose.

"Rita," I said.

She fluttered the other hand in acknowledgment but didn't speak.

"That boyfriend of yours is a menace," Norman said.

"Rita, Norman—" I began my speech.

"What is wrong with him?" Norman lowered his voice. "Rita's heart can't take much more. Trudy's death shook her more than she likes to admit."

"I'm sure it did." I wasn't sure at all, but it didn't seem like a good time to say so.

"I miss her terribly," Rita said in a plaintive tone.

"You need to rest, darling." Norman looked at me and jerked his head toward the kitchen. "Imogene and I will make some tea." I followed him to the scene of the crime.

The kitchen was the reverse of the rest of the home—predominantly white with touches of powder blue here and there. White walls, cupboards, counter, and floor, with only the occasional blue dishtowel or potholder to give the eyes a break. I couldn't imagine cooking in the pristine space. Just thinking of what a pot of spaghetti sauce could do made me queasy, but who was I to criticize? At least this kitchen had a stove.

Norman put the kettle on and leaned against the counter. "I had a private practice in New York for many years. As you can imagine, Manhattan is a very competitive place. When I was a young psychiatrist, just starting out, I did some things I'm not entirely proud of today."

"I'm not sure what you're driving at." This wasn't going at all the way I'd envisioned.

"I'm saying I understand. You're an ambitious young woman who's trying to build a new business. I'm not sure the way you're going about it is wise."

"I'm not trying to build a new business. I'm just trying to hang on to my old one."

He shot me an unbelieving look.

I bristled. "I know how it appears—El poking around—but I had nothing to do with that. Honestly."

"Nothing to do with it?"

"No, nothing. I asked El to hand out coupons for me in exchange for free haircuts. That's it."

"It would be quite handy to know who had serious medical issues though, wouldn't it?"

"No. Of course not." My voice rose with exasperation. Dr. Norman gestured for me to lower it. He stepped into the doorway and peered around the dining area. Rita must not have heard me, because he resumed his position at the counter.

"It's Harry," I said.

"Harry?"

"The owner of the salon where I work. He's the one who wants to build the post-life services, not me."

"Harry hired El?"

"No. I did a trade with El, but only to hand out coupon cards, not to find out about people's health issues. Ever since Trudy's funeral, my business has tanked."

Norman's eyebrows shot up. "Tanked?"

"Yes. My clients are afraid of me. They think I'm a corpse specialist now, and if they use my services, they might turn into one."

The kettle began to sing. Dr. Norman reached over and turned it off. "How does that make you feel?"

"Terrible." My throat grew tight. "It's depressing, you know?"

He nodded. I don't know what came over me then. I blame his eyes, the way he looked at me as if I was the only person in the world. The dam broke. I told him about the drop-off in clientele, about my broken toe, about the apartment, all of it.

"I love my Gran, but if I live there much longer, I'm afraid I'm going to turn in an old lady before I'm thirty. I got upset about *Jeopardy* the other night. *Jeopardy*."

"Sounds like you're going through some deep emotional issues." He reached for a powder blue box of tissues on the counter and handed it to me.

I took one and blew my nose. "Is that weird?"

"Weird isn't the word I'd use." He oozed warmth and sympathy. I choked up again.

"I don't know what to do. I can't dance. I don't want to borrow money from my grandmother. El can't market for me anymore. Not after this."

"Tell me more about your friendship with El," Norman said in a creamy voice.

"I met him when I went to do Trudy." I sniffled.

"And you hit it off?"

"We—" I bit my tongue so hard I almost yelped. A red flag waved behind my eyes. A warning bell went off in my mind. Norman's smooth questions and empathetic eyes suddenly spelled danger. The story about the hair sample had been in my mouth, ready to pop out like a bubblegum bubble.

"Yes?" he prompted.

"We hit it off," I said without emotion. "Then he offered to take the coupons around Liberty Grove for me."

"And you said yes?"

"Right." I was on to him now. He wasn't getting any more out of me.

Norman reached into a cupboard and took three blue and white mugs from it. "Why El?" he said with studied casualness.

I widened my eyes, hoping he'd understand my body language. He widened his and plopped tea bags into the mugs.

I folded my arms in defiance. "Women like him." Okay, so I was objectifying El. I wasn't proud of it, but I saw it as a necessary evil.

"How do you feel about that?"

I shrugged. "It comes in handy."

Apparently, Norman sensed I was done spilling my guts. He poured steaming water into the cups, put them on a tray and headed to the living room. I followed.

Rita opened her eyes and bestowed a wan smile at Norman as he placed the tray on the glass coffee table. "You are so good to me," she purred. He patted her hand.

"Rita," I said. "I want to apologize for El. I don't know what came over him. His behavior was unacceptable, and I told him so."

She shimmied into an upright position and took the cup Norman offered. "You need to be more careful about who represents you, darling. I learned that the hard way. My first agent was a disaster."

She blew in her cup and took a tentative sip. "You may be too young to remember, but there was a movie, *Deadly Fling*, that came out in the eighties. Lynn Forward played the lead." She looked at me over the rim of her mug, a question in her eyes.

"I've seen it," I said. I knew where she was going with this. Everyone who'd known her for longer than ten minutes had heard the story. I was here to make Rita happy, however, so I'd listen to it again.

"Well, I was a shoo-in for that part, but my agent blew it. Lynn got it, and the rest is history. Her career sky-rocketed after that. And mine, well, mine . . . "

Before she could launch into an hour-long discourse on the ups and downs of her Hollywood career—which, according to Gran, consisted of a series of TV commercials for an over-the-counter diarrhea medication and a spot as a murder victim on a detective show—I interrupted. "Congratulations, by the way."

I knew if I wanted to shift topics, I had to keep things about her. It worked. "For what?" She played innocent, but I could tell by the smile she hid behind her cup, she knew what I was talking about.

"I heard you two were planning to tie the knot," I said.

"Now, where did you hear that rumor?" She batted her eyes and feigned innocence.

"Are you kidding? I work in a hair salon—the birthplace of rumors."

Rita put out a pale, blue-veined hand. Norman stepped to her side and took it. "It's true," she said.

"We weren't going to make an official announcement until after the wedding," Norman said. "It's going to be a small affair, just our families and closest friends. We don't want any hurt feelings."

Rita gazed at him, her face filled with adoration. He returned her look, although it didn't have the raw longing of hers. The aging film star and the distinguished psychiatrist, they made a handsome couple.

"I'll do your hair and make-up. Without charge. To make up for El's behavior." The words blurted from my lips before they'd formed fully in my brain. I was shocked when I heard them, but it was impossible to take them back.

"What a lovely offer." Rita beamed.

"I could use a trim." Dr. Norman ran a hand through his white mane.

After we firmed up the date, I trotted to my car in a daze. What had just happened? I'd planned to go in, apologize for El, distance myself from his actions, and leave.

Instead, I'd told Dr. Norman my life story and agreed to do an entire wedding. For free. The week before I was scheduled to move into a new apartment. An apartment I didn't have the money for. El had struck again. I had to get the man out of my life.

19

ATTACK OF THE KILLER CHORKIE

The next morning, I stepped out of Gran's apartment into a cloud. The fog was so dense, I could only see four or five feet in any direction. Cold, damp tendrils pressed around me as if they were trying to warm themselves with my body heat. I drew my long, black sweater tighter around me and picked up my pace.

I'd had five appointments on Wednesday, four on Thursday, but only three today. My new leads were evaporating like this fog would once the sun came out. I had hoped to have El canvas a different Liberty Grove neighborhood every week until I could establish enough regulars to keep me busy. Unfortunately, that income stream was gone, poisoned, fouled.

If it wasn't for the apartment, I could weather the storm. But unless Grace let me out of the lease, I was committed. They say love is blind. In the soft glow of candlelight, during the heat of passion, it's true. When you wake up in the morning, however, it's a whole different story. The problem with that studio was I'd moved from dating to engaged during the bewitching hours.

Something black shot into my cone of sight and launched itself at my ankle. Pain shot up my leg. I kicked, trying to detach the dark tangle of hair. It arced through the air, but held on by its teeth.

"Rikki-Tikki, bad boy. You stop that." A voice came out of the gloom.

I kicked harder. "Get this thing off me."

Mr. Rogers loomed into view. When he saw me, a wicked grin spread across his face. "Rikki-Tikki doesn't like outsiders."

I could feel blood oozing down my ankle into my shoe. "Stop him."

"He's just defending the neighborhood. Aren't you, Rikki?"

I gave one especially violent kick and Rikki-Tikki, the Chorkie—Chihuahua-Yorkie mix—from hell lost his grip and spun into a tree trunk. He squealed and lay still on the grass.

"What have you done?" Mr. Rogers ran to his dog's side. In the seconds he took to get there, Rikki-Tikki stood and shook himself. I knew he'd be okay. It takes more than a tree trunk to annihilate the living dead. You need a silver bullet, or a stake through the heart.

"Keep that thing on a leash," I said, but not forcefully. I had no weight to push around when it came to following Liberty Grove's rules.

"I've kept my mouth shut about you for your grandmother's sake, because she's a lovely woman. But if you ever touch my poor Rikki again . . . "

I limped away, my foot squelching in the rapidly cooling blood that filled my shoe. My toe had been recovering nicely, and now I had an ankle injury. I wondered if I'd ever dance again. Mr. Rogers was one nasty piece of work. If there was a murderer loose in Liberty Grove, he'd be my first pick of suspects. Him and his little bloodsucking mongrel.

I arrived at the salon with only minutes to spare. My first appointment was an early one. Harry was at the reception desk sipping a cup of coffee. "What happened to you?" he said as soon as he caught sight of my ankle.

"I was attacked by a miniature vampire."

"Well, clean yourself up. Don't want you scaring away any more business."

He was such a support. "Don't worry about me, Harry. I'm sure my blood volume will return to normal without a transfusion." I clomped toward the bathroom. "Thanks for your concern," I shot over my shoulder. If I'd scared away business, it was nobody's fault but his.

I closeted myself in the loo, slipped off my sandal, and put my foot on the sink. It was a bloody mess. I rinsed it under the tap. The wound was smaller than I'd thought, but a dark bruise spread out from the tiny puncture wounds. My ankle was swollen and sore.

Maybe I was a jinx, cursed, bad juju. Why else was all this happening to me? I'd had rough patches before, but nothing like this. Things seemed to be crumbling around me.

My life had started out okay. I had a great mother. My father wasn't around very much, but it wasn't because he didn't want to be. He was a Marine.

Mom was the quintessential military wife. She was tough and gutsy and made the best of the times he was away. I didn't know him well, but she talked about him every day. He lived in my imagination like the princes from the Andrew Lang *Coloured Fairy Tale* books I devoured. Whenever he came home on leave, it was like Christmas, Easter, and my birthday all rolled into one.

Three weeks after I turned eleven, we got the terrible news. He'd been killed in Afghanistan in a Jeep accident. He wasn't even in battle, just a stupid accident. A year later, my mother was diagnosed with breast cancer. She was dead before she reached the ripe old age of forty. That was the worst time in my life.

Gran had moved us in with her when my mother fell ill, and I stayed after Mom died. Gran became mother and father and friend and confidante. She soothed the pain and made things good again. And they had been, until now.

I cleaned the blood out of my shoe with paper towels, put it on, and gimped to my station with all the dignity I could muster right before client number one arrived. As I combed and clipped and recommended anti-aging foundations, I pondered my options.

I'd flirted with the idea of giving the guy I'd been in classes at Neutron with a call. I was pretty sure his name was Alex, but May would know. He was a good dancer and not as prone to throwing his partners around as Chad was. I'd thought maybe he and I could give McKenzie and Chad a run for their money in the contest. My toe had been feeling so much better. Thanks to Count Chorkula, that was no longer possible. I was pretty sure my ankle would take at least a week to heal. Since we weren't an experienced team, that wouldn't leave us enough time to prepare.

Client number one left, and my phone rang. It was Grace. "My daughter told me you wanted to talk."

I walked into the break room. There were ears everywhere. I didn't want Gran to hear I might be moving out from someone else. "The apartment really needs a thorough cleaning before I can move in," I said.

"You approved the condition of the unit when you signed the lease."

"I didn't see all the dirt. It was night. The lighting was poor."

"You approved it."

"I never saw the inside of the refrigerator."

"It wasn't locked."

"I could call the Board of Health." This was an idle threat. I was fairly certain the Board of Health only came out for businesses and places open to the public, but it was all I could think of.

"It isn't a restaurant." Grace didn't sound worried.

"I'll report you to the anti-slum lord association."

"There's no such thing."

"Okay, I don't know its name, but I bet there's a state agency that puts corrupt landlords out of business."

There was a long pause on the other end of the line. "I'll tell you what." I held my breath, hoping she'd let me out of the lease. "The place could use a little bit of sprucing up. I'll give you two free weeks. You can have the key now. You can come and go and get the place ready before you move in. I'll even throw in the cleaning products."

"Wait a minute, you're—"

She cut me off. "Two free weeks is equivalent to at least five-hundred dollars. I could get in a cleaning crew for much less than that. I'm doing you a favor."

"You wouldn't get the five-hundred either way."

"Take it or leave it. It's my final offer."

I stomped my foot in frustration. Big mistake. When the black dots cleared from behind my eyes, I saw client number two hobbling to my chair in heels much too high for her eighty-five years. "Fine," I said and hung up.

Number two got a shorter cut than she'd asked for, but it wasn't my fault. Every time someone came into the salon, her head spun toward the front door. It's impossible to do precision work on a moving target.

I finally put two and two together—the high heels and the expectant attitude—and realized she was hoping for a glimpse of El. I mentioned he was out of town in a nonchalant kind of way, and she held still for the rest of the cut. My quick thinking may have saved her an ear.

Of course, El would turn me into a liar. Just as number two opened her wallet to give me a tip, who should come waltzing across the floor? Her eyes batted, her mouth gaped, and her wallet shut. El beamed at her and acted like she was his long-lost cousin.

They chatted about the price of hummus at Mother's Market, her overweight Himalayan, and how her hair made her look twenty years younger. He swore she didn't look a day over fifty. She tittered and said that would make her seventy. And he said, don't tell me you're older than that. I tapped my foot, crossed my arms, and huffed until El got the hint and walked her to the front door.

By the time he returned, I only had ten minutes until my third appointment. "What do you want?" I said.

He looked hurt. "I've been doing some investigating. There's something I think you need to know."

I glanced around me. Every female eye in the place, and Harry's two male ones, were locked onto El. "Come with me." I grabbed his arm and pulled him into the break room.

"But—"

"After that stunt you pulled at Rita's, I'm afraid to be seen with you."

"But—"

"I had to promise to do Rita and Norman's wedding. For nothing. No pay. Why? Because I had to compensate for your poor judgment. I appreciate what you did for me, handing out the cards, getting the new clients you've gotten for me. But, we're done."

"I—"

"I have two weeks to get my pit of an apartment ready and figure out how to pay for it. What I don't have is time to clean up after you." I turned to leave. El grabbed my hand.

"I'm sorry. I really am. But I found out something you need to know." I glared at his hand, willing him to release mine. He didn't. "Rita was blackballed by the movie industry for harassing another actor in the eighties."

My indignation leaked out like air from a punctured tire. "What?"

"When I was over there yesterday, she told me she'd been an actress. That she'd been up for a role, but it was stolen from her by Lynn—"

"Lynn Forward. *Deadly Fling*. I know."

"Work was dead last night, so I spent some time researching. She did audition for the part, but as far as I could see, she was never a serious contender."

No surprise there.

"It embittered her. I found an interview in a gossip rag where Lynn Forward talks about an envious actor who'd sent her threatening messages after she got the *Deadly Fling* role. She said, although it was a terrible experience, it worked for her good. The woman inspired her interpretation of the character."

"How do you know the other actor was Rita?"

"I don't for sure, but Rita lost her agent at the same time. From all appearances, he fired her. After that, all she could get were TV commercials."

"Right, the diarrhea medicine."

"Oh." He grimaced.

"As interesting as this is, I don't know what it has to do with me." I hoped he wasn't trying to rope me into the detective business again.

El's eyes grew soft and misty. "I want you to stay away from her. I'm trying to keep you safe."

A chill ran over me. Nothing with El ever went the way it should. His desire to keep me safe made me feel more vulnerable than ever.

20

BATTLING MICROBES

When I left Harry's, I went straight to Target and bought a big bucket of cleaning supplies. I didn't trust Grace to provide what I'd need. Then I drove to Elm, got the key from Grace, and walked up the rickety stairs to my new place.

I turned the key and kicked the door open. The morning fog had burned off, leaving behind a hazy film that made me feel like I was looking at the world through a dirty window. Since the window in the apartment actually was dirty, the effect was doubled. The dim lighting softened the unit's depressing edges. The place wasn't as bad when you couldn't see it very well.

Tackling the worst first seemed the best strategy. I set down my bags on the counter that separated the kitchenette and the great room—the only room. I took the pair of industrial strength rubber gloves I'd bought and snapped them on. Then I cut three slashes in a large garbage bag, stuck my head through one, and threaded my arms through the other two. A painter's mask and safety goggles completed my hazmat suit. I grabbed a bottle of spray bleach, a brush, and a sponge and walked into the kitchenette.

My stomach tightened into a knot as I approached the refrigerator. I held my breath, threw open the door, and jumped backwards. Nothing ran out. Holding my bottle of bleach in front of me like a shield, I advanced.

About a half hour into my battle with the mold, I heard a knock. "Come in," I yelled.

El filled the doorway. "Nice outfit."

I humphed. It was fine for him to mock me. He wasn't the one facing microbes of unknown origin. His silent gaze traveled the room.

"I know it needs work," I said, embarrassment making me sweat under my plastic poncho. "I got two free weeks though. That's worth, like, five hundred dollars." The only acknowledgment that he'd heard what I'd said was a nod. "I think it'll look a lot better with a fresh coat of paint and a good cleaning."

He came in, shut the door behind him, and walked to the counter. I was glad he didn't come into the kitchenette. I was claustrophobic enough in my garbage bag.

"There's no stove," he said.

I felt my cheeks flame. It had taken me two visits to the apartment to notice there was no stove. He saw it immediately. He was studying to be a detective, I told myself. It didn't make me feel any better. "I'm going to get a toaster oven and a microwave."

He looked skeptical. "Where are you going to put them?"

I waved a hand toward the two-by-two foot counter space next to the sink. He nodded again.

I stuck my head into the fridge and began scrubbing. "Thanks for stopping by."

"Is there a bathroom?" he asked.

I almost said no. I could already feel his nonverbal disapproval. "It's over there." I pointed a gloved finger at the door.

I heard him cross the room and scrubbed harder. A minute later, he was at the front door. "I'll be back." He disappeared.

I sat on my haunches, pushed the hair from my face with the back of a gloved hand and exhaled. The inside of the fridge was now a not-too-terrible shade of off yellow. All the black, green, and purple patches were gone. Once it dried, it would be safe for food habitation. I pivoted on my butt, opened one of the bottom cupboards, and sighed. It was filthy inside.

By the time El returned, I'd cleaned the scum and crumbs from the cupboards—thankful there were only three—and was cutting shelf paper to line them. He kicked the door open and dropped an armload of things into the center of the room. I saw paint trays, rollers, a pole, a tarp, brushes and two gallons of paint. "What's that?" I said.

"Paint," he said, and I rolled my eyes. "If you don't like the color, I'll get something else."

He popped open one of the cans. Inside was a creamy puddle of straw-colored paint that exuded clean and cozy. I must have "ooh-ed" because the lines in El's forehead smoothed. "I can do a first coat tonight before work."

I hesitated. I'd told myself El was a problem that needed elimination, kind of like the refrigerator mold. But the dark mood that had hovered over me for the past twenty-four hours lifted when I looked into that paint can. "You don't have to do that," I said.

"I think I do."

He didn't say it, but I knew he was trying to make up for the problem he'd caused with Rita and Norman. "Thank you," I said.

Two hours later, we sat on beach chairs that had magically appeared after one of El's trips outside, nibbling pizza and sipping beer. "Rita had motive, method, and opportunity," El said. We'd picked up the conversation from the salon.

"Motive and method I get. I'm not so sure about the opportunity, though. Rita and Trudy weren't on the best of terms."

"She could have done it in one visit. Just switched out the aspirin in a bottle for her digitalis."

I swallowed before I answered. I knew we shouldn't be talking about this, but it seemed a hypothetical kind of conversation. Besides, he'd just turned down my offer of reimbursement for the paint and pizza. "That's kind of dangerous, isn't it? How could she guarantee Trudy would take them? Or that someone else wouldn't?"

"It's not a perfect murder. The point is, she could have done it."

"I guess so. She didn't murder Lynn Forward, though. She harassed her."

"I found another article in which Lynn Forward said she was afraid for her life on one occasion. She said the actor in question flipped out and began threatening her one night after filming. If it hadn't been for a grip who showed up when he heard the commotion, she wasn't sure what would've happened."

"Even if Rita did have killer tendencies in her younger years, it doesn't prove she did Trudy in."

"Right. So how do we prove it?"

I shifted in my seat. Darn him. I'd told him I didn't want to be part of his investigation team, but he wouldn't leave it alone. He was like a cute dog you'd forgotten had a humping problem until he did it again.

"El." I said his name so sharply, he locked eyes with me. "This obsession of yours is . . . It's ruining everything."

His jaw tightened into a stubborn line.

"I shouldn't have let you talk me into taking the hair sample. If we'd never done it, we, like everyone else in the world, would believe Trudy died of natural causes."

"Now we know she didn't," he said between gritted teeth.

I stood and dumped the rest of my pizza into a trash bag. "We don't know that. What we know is, she had digitalis in her system. We don't know if it was enough to kill her. We don't know if she took it knowingly, or someone slipped it to her. We don't know much."

We cleaned up our dinner and paint supplies in silence. There wasn't anything else to say. El believed Trudy was murdered, and it was our responsibility to get enough evidence to take to the police. I wasn't sure what I believed. I only knew I didn't want to be involved in anything else that smacked of death, dying, or murder.

"Ready?" I said, after I'd stowed the last two pieces of pizza in the fridge.

"Yup." El shrugged on his jacket.

"Hello?" McKenzie stepped into the room. "I saw lights. Oh, nice." She looked at the straw-colored walls, then she looked at El. I wasn't sure which she was referring to. "I'm McKenzie," she said and batted her eyelashes. It was El.

"El," he said and stuck out a hand. She took it, never removing her eyes from his face.

"Nice to meet you," she said in a breathless voice.

El struck again. I didn't get it. Sure, he was big and handsome, and had pretty good muscles. Okay, he had great muscles. But he wasn't interesting. He was a bucket of vanilla ice cream—tasty and comforting, not exciting.

"We were just leaving," I said.

"Are you a friend of Norma Jean's?" McKenzie asked.

El looked confused. "Imogene," I said.

"Oh, right." She giggled. "Imogene's?" Nobody could accuse her of being overly intelligent.

"No, he's my dentist," I mumbled under my breath.

El furrowed his brow. McKenzie widened her eyes. "Really?"

"El's a friend. He's helping me get the apartment ready."

"I love the paint color," she said.

"Thanks," El said.

"Did you choose it?"

"I did."

"It's so nice. What is it? I have a bedroom that needs to be repainted."

"Straw."

"What brand?"

While the two of them chatted about paint, I made a final tour of the place, tossing trash and looking for my things. It didn't take long. "I hate to break this up, but I need to go home and get some sleep."

We trudged down the stairs single file. El and I headed toward the street, and McKenzie turned toward the big house. As we reached our cars, she called out to El. "So, where is your office? I need a teeth cleaning."

21
RELATIVE PROBLEMS

I woke on Saturday morning with a headache, probably from all the paint and cleaning fluid fumes. Thank goodness my first hair appointment wasn't until after lunch. I stumbled downstairs, hoping Gran had left some coffee in the pot. If it was cold, I'd nuke it. I needed caffeine and needed it now.

The scent of freshly brewed coffee and the sizzle of bacon greeted me as soon as I hit the landing. I wandered into the kitchen to see Gran standing at the stove.

"What are you doing here?" I said.

"I live here."

"I mean, why aren't you out running a marathon or something?"

"I was tired."

I eyed her. She was too focused on her frying pan. It seemed like she was avoiding my gaze. I meandered to the coffeepot, poured myself a cup, doctored it with cream and sugar and sat on a counter stool. "Where's Phil?"

Gran shrugged. "At his place probably."

I sipped my coffee. What was going on? The only morning Gran wasn't up and out at the crack of oh-dark-thirty was Saturday when Phil brought bagels. Phil wasn't here, and neither were the bagels.

She dropped slices of bacon onto a plate covered in paper towels and poured beaten eggs into another frying pan. She never made big breakfasts either. Worry niggled at me. "Gran?"

"Hmmm?" Even her hum sounded too nonchalant.

"What's going on?"

"Does something have to be going on for me to want to spend a little time with my granddaughter?"

"No, but—"

She turned, walked around the counter, and put her arms around me. "I love you, sweetheart."

My apprehension escalated. Gran was only demonstrative in a crisis. I gave her a little shove and held her at arm's length. "What is going on?" I repeated.

Her lips formed a thin line. She looked like she was fighting tears. "Phil asked me to marry him."

Relief cascaded over me. "That's great. Wow. When?"

"We haven't set a date. There's no hurry. So don't you worry."

"Me?"

She looked deep into my eyes. "You are more important to me than this marriage."

"Thanks," I said. "I appreciate that, but I don't see what one has to do with the other." As the words exited my mouth, I had the uncomfortable feeling that I did. This must be the reason Gran had been acting so strange lately. She didn't want me to feel rejected, tossed out.

"You'll always have a place with me, and Phil knows that."

The sentiment was sweet, but I couldn't imagine living with Phil. I had enough problems with clichés as it was. Besides, they needed their space to start a new life together.

"I got an apartment." I blurted out the news. I'd been planning to tell her after I got the place looking half-way decent. She'd have a fit if she saw it now. Even with El's paint job, there was a lot of work left to be done.

Her hand flew to her heart. "You did?"

"Yeah, the studio."

"Oh, thank God. I'm so glad. After our conversation about the *Jeopardy* incident, I told Phil I couldn't, wouldn't, ask you to move out. Either he took both of us, or he didn't get either of us."

It was my turn to get emotional. I swallowed the lump in my throat and said, "That's crazy, Gran. I'm an adult. Your child-rearing days are over."

"Just for the record, Phil didn't hesitate. He said it was a bargain—two for the price of one. He'd lucked out."

"That's very nice of him, but it's a moot point. I have a place of my own now."

"I thought you didn't have the money? If you need . . . " Gran sniffed the air. "Shoot." She ran to the stove.

I was saved from having to admit I was short on cash, a lot of cash, by burned eggs. I was still holding out for a miracle. Still hoping I wouldn't have to borrow from Gran. Especially now. Weddings weren't cheap.

"Where will you live?" I said, changing the subject.

Gran lifted the pan from the heat. "Here. At least that's the plan. Phil is going to put his place on the market." I moved to the dining room table, and she set a plate of bacon and slightly brown scrambled eggs in front of me. "When do you move into your new apartment?" she asked.

"Two weeks."

She carried over another plate for herself and sat across from me. "That's so soon."

"Yeah. I was there last night."

She widened her eyes. "Doing what?"

"Cleaning, painting, you know. Getting it ready."

"Those are the landlord's responsibilities, aren't they?" There was a hint of mama-bear growl in her voice.

I forked a bite of egg into my mouth and took my time chewing. After I swallowed, I adjusted my face to read excited and happy and said, "We worked out a deal. I'm getting two free weeks in payment for doing the work myself."

"Honey, you're busy. I could have—"

"I wanted to. This way, I can fix the place the way I want it."

"Well, I can't wait to see it. Do you have time after breakfast?"

A knock sounded at the door, giving me time to come up with an excuse to keep Gran away from the apartment. "I'll get it." I rushed from the table.

El stood in the doorway.

"Genie, who's at the door?" Gran called. A moment later, she stood beside me. "And who is this?"

"This is—"

"El," El said and stuck out a hand. "I'm so happy to meet you. Imogene says such wonderful things about you."

Gran beamed at him. "Genie, aren't you going to invite your friend in?"

"Ah." I backed out of the doorway.

"We were just having breakfast. Can I fix you a plate?" Gran bustled toward the kitchen.

"I don't want to intrude," El said.

"No intrusion at all. I was wondering what I was going to do with all this extra food." Gran's tone was bright and breathless. "Coffee?"

"Please, but I can get it."

"No. No. You sit down with Genie."

We both obeyed. I glared at him over the table. I knew what was going through Gran's mind. She'd been trying to fix me up with all her friends' grandsons for the past two years. One of her greatest goals in life was marrying me off to someone besides Chad.

Gran placed an enormous plate of bacon and eggs and a mug of coffee in front of El. "I'm at a disadvantage here. You seem to know all about me, but I don't know anything about you." She shot me a glance and sat.

"There's not much to tell," El said and began chowing down like he hadn't eaten for a week. I guessed it took a lot of calories to keep a man of his size going.

"Where did you and Genie meet?"

"We met when I did Trudy's funeral," I said, so El wouldn't have to talk with his mouth full. "El works at Greener Pastures as the night watchman."

"Oh." A small frown crossed Gran's features. I think she'd been hoping for a doctor, or lawyer, or at least an accountant.

El took a slug of coffee. "I'm studying for a career in law enforcement. My ultimate goal is to make detective."

I saw the struggle behind Gran's eyes. Being an ex-hippie, the cops weren't her favorite people on the planet. However, she had matured enough to move into a guarded gate community, something I'd always considered ironic. After a long moment, her face cleared, and she made a declaration. "That's a needed profession."

"I think so," El said.

"So, why'd you come by?" I said, a bit more abruptly than I'd intended. Having him in the same room with Gran made me nervous, although I wasn't sure why.

El mopped up the last of the bacon grease on his plate with a piece of toast. "I was talking to Carlton this morning on my way out. It seems we just got in a slew of new business. Flu season. Amy Lee is overwhelmed. Can't get everybody done in time. I mentioned your name, and he bit. He wants to hire you."

A patter of trepidation ran up and down my spine like a field mouse. "Me?"

"Yeah. He's paying seventy-five an hour."

"Oh."

"It isn't a permanent position or anything, but I did the math. At two hours per client, it would only take ten to get you the cash you need for the next two months' rent. We've got five of them sitting there right now."

Gran's coffee mug came down with a thump and a splash. "Genie." Her voice was stern. "I thought you had the rent for your apartment all worked out."

"I—"

"She would have, Ms. Lynch," El interrupted.

"Darnell," Gran snapped. "I'm Imogene's maternal grandmother."

"Well, she would have, Ms. Darnell. Except I stomped on her toe, so I feel responsible."

"Her toe? What does her toe have to do with anything?"

I could hear the train a-coming. The alarm bells were singing. The horn was screaming, but I couldn't lower the safety arm quickly enough.

"She was going to dance in a competition with . . . " El searched for a name.

"Chad?" Gran's voice rose.

"Right, Chad." El gave her a benign smile.

Gran froze. I dropped my head into my hands.

"Chad?" Her voice was like velvet. Too smooth. Scary smooth. "I thought you were done with Chad. You told me you never wanted to see Chad again, which was too soon for me. Genie, I'm, I'm at a loss for words."

If only that were true. "It was just a contest," I mumbled into my hands.

"That's the way it starts. After the first time you broke up, he lured you back with a special two-for-one deal on advanced Western Swing lessons. The second time, it was Salsa in the Park. We've talked about this. Imogene Amanda Lynch, you're an addict, and addicts have to stay away from their drug of choice."

El must have realized he'd lit the fuse on a stick of dynamite and did his best to blow it out. "It was all because of the funeral, Ms. Darnell. Her business started drying up, and she didn't want to lose the apartment. You didn't see her face when she said yes to Chad. I was there. I can tell you, she didn't look happy about it."

I shot him a grateful glance from between my fingers.

"What do you mean, her business started drying up? What did the funeral have to do with her business?"

"She did such a good job on Trudy, her clients started to look at her as a specialist. They weren't too excited about needing her expertise, if you get what I'm saying."

Gran's mouth opened, but she didn't say anything. El continued. "Then Chad came along and told her they could earn a quick twenty-five hundred just by dancing in this one contest."

He pleaded my case for me. Maybe it was his way with women, or maybe it was just the strangeness of the story, but Gran settled down and listened. He told her about how he stepped on my toe, then got the idea to hand out cards for me. About how my business started picking up, and how I signed the lease on the apartment. But then he screwed things up again.

It was El's turn to stare at his hands. "I don't know what I was thinking, but I went into Rita Tarkington's kitchen and started snooping around. Norman Fielding came in, caught me and threw me out. Now I can't help Imogene with her business anymore, and I feel terrible about it." He looked at me. "So I really hope you'll take the job at Greener Pastures."

When he finished, Gran gawked at him for a long moment. She finally closed her mouth and turned her gaze on me. "There's something else. Something you two aren't telling me."

Gran always knew when I was holding back. Once when I was fifteen, I told her I was going to the mall with a group of girls, then sneaked over to Tommy Drysdale's house. He'd never been interested in me before his parents went out of town, but I was too stupid to realize what was going on. I'd thought he'd developed the kind of feelings for me I'd had for him all school year. The making out turned to groping, and the groping got way too pushy and persistent. I'd escaped with my virginity intact, but only just.

All the way home I'd rehearsed my story about the mall, from the shops we'd visited to the flavor of ice cream I'd eaten. I never made it to the Rocky Road. I was sobbing on Gran's chest in under ten minutes. With Gran, the truth was inevitable.

"Trudy twitched," I said, and between El and me, the entire story came out. When we were done, Gran got up and went into the kitchen. She returned a moment later with the coffeepot and the bottle of whiskey she kept above the refrigerator for medicinal purposes.

After pouring each of us a cup and a shot, she sat. "You know, Rita was questioned in conjunction with a murder back in the eighties."

I slammed back in my chair. Whatever I'd expected Gran to say after hearing about the hair analysis, the Trudy-Norman-Rita love triangle, and Rita's heart problems, it wasn't that.

"I read about it in the papers. Of course, I didn't know Rita back then, but it was such a Hollywood kind of story, it got a lot of press. When she moved into Liberty Grove, everybody was talking about it. Made quite the stir." Gran sipped her coffee and made a face. I don't think she liked whiskey.

"The diarrhea bit was kind of a big deal as far as TV commercials went. Whoever got the part would star in a series of ads. They'd be the face of the product." She paused. It was an unfortunate choice of words, but neither El nor I so much as grinned. "The job went to another actor, but she died before filming started. Rita was the understudy. She got the role."

"How did the other actor die?" I was afraid to ask.

"Apparently she'd been poisoned with the medicine she was hired to promote. Rita was the obvious suspect. They took her in for questioning, but they couldn't make anything stick."

I sat there for a long moment trying to absorb what Gran had just told me. It didn't compute. The silly, weak woman I knew, a murderer? I couldn't believe it. So many things I couldn't believe had happened lately. Anything was possible. "We should tell the police," I said.

"I don't think they'd do anything about it," El said. "Sure, it looks suspicious to you and me, but we know Trudy had a potentially poisonous drug she didn't need in her system."

"Couldn't you tell the police about the hair analysis?" Gran asked.

"We could, but like I told Imogene, it wasn't authorized. I'm not sure they'd consider what we have strong enough evidence to exhume a body the ME has already declared dead of natural causes. It would be an embarrassment for them."

Gran set her mug down. "My guess is Trudy's twitches were her way of telling you she wanted justice." El and I stared at her, neither of us knowing how to respond. "So, what are we going to do about it?"

"We?" I leaped from my chair. "*We* don't do anything. We aren't the police. We don't carry guns. We aren't authorized to do diddly-squat. And, we already have one possible murder victim on our hands. We don't need another." I glared at Gran. "It's bad enough trying to keep El out of trouble, but at least he's big enough to protect himself. *You.*" I wagged a finger at her. "You are staying out of this."

Gran shrugged. "I was using the royal we."

El cleared his throat. "For what it's worth, I agree with Imogene. If Rita has done the things we suspect, she's a dangerous woman. You both need to steer clear."

"Thank you," I said.

El put his fork and knife on his plate. "I hate to eat and run, but I've got to get going. What do I tell Carlton? If you're not interested in the work, he's going to call another mortuary."

Gran spoke before I could. "I'm lending her the money she needs. If doing one dead body did so much damage to her business, I can imagine what ten of them would do."

"No one would need to know," El said. "We don't usually advertise who does the hair and makeup. That was Harry's idea."

"Still, I don't like the thought of Imogene spending time with . . . those people."

"Those people?" El's voice took on a defensive edge. "You mean the deceased?"

"Right. I'm not speaking ill of them or anything."

El furrowed his brow. "Next thing you're going to tell me is some of your best friends are dead."

"Well at my age, it would be strange if they weren't."

"Ms. Lynch—"

"Darnel," Gran reminded him.

"Ms. Darnel," El corrected himself. "I don't want to be disrespectful, but I feel duty bound to fight societal prejudice whenever I see it."

I began waving my hands in the air, trying to extinguish the flames of this dispute before one or the other of them said something they'd regret. Neither Gran nor El knew how to back down.

Gran leaned forward. "I'm sure many of them are fine people, *were* fine people, but society isn't fair. I don't want my granddaughter to suffer because of her involvement with them."

"They don't cause as many problems as her usual clientele do, that's for sure."

Gran put a hand on top of El's. "I appreciate what you're trying to do for Genie. However, I think I know what's best for her."

"Wait," I said. The look of surprise on Gran's face was mirrored on El's. I think they'd forgotten I was there. "I'm an adult. I can make my own decisions." I turned my gaze on Gran. "I don't want your money." Then I locked eyes with El. "Tell Carlton I'll think about it."

I spun on my heel and marched upstairs to get ready for my afternoon appointment.

22

DOUBLE INDEMNITY

I never made it to the apartment on Saturday. After work, I went to a movie at Clubhouse Two with Gran and Phil. They were showing *Double Indemnity* with Fred MacMurray and Barbara Stanwyck. It was one of my favorites, but I couldn't concentrate. My gaze roamed the gray-haired crowd, and I was struck again by the fact I was always the youngest person in the room.

I had to make enough money to keep the apartment, whatever it took. *Even if that meant doing the odd job for Greener Pastures?* The question blared through my brain. Why not? Why was I so opposed to the idea? El had promised me no one would need to know.

I squirmed in my seat. I'd been trying to avoid the truth ever since he'd told me about the opportunity. If I was going to be honest, I was worried about the strange reaction I'd had to Belinda Simpson's corpse. And, of course, Trudy's twitches.

How much of what had occurred was reality and how much my imagination? Trudy's body had moved. I hadn't dreamed that up. El had seen her arms hanging down from her gurney. He'd fixed them. But had I put my own spin on that?

I was the one who'd decided it appeared she was pleading for help. El had given me a perfectly rational explanation for Trudy's movements. I'd allowed my imagination to go wild. Had I scared myself so much that, when I walked into the embalming room the second time, I had a preconceived bias? Had I subconsciously expected something to happen when I touched Belinda Simpson's hair, so something did happen?

There'd been no witness on this occasion. Amy Lee didn't see a thing, because there was nothing to see. Granted, I'd had gloves on, but the next morning when I'd dyed Belinda's roots, I'd felt nothing but hair when I touched her.

If I passed up good money, money I needed, what would that say about me? If I didn't jump on the offer from Greener Pastures, it would be because of cowardice. I'd have to admit I was superstitious. Me, clear-headed, logical, I'll-believe-it-if-I-see-it Imogene.

A thump and a whoosh of air from the back of the room disrupted my internal scolding. I glanced over my shoulder to see Rita and Norman enter the room. They made their way down the center aisle and peered over the dark rows looking for seats. They found two directly across the aisle from us.

Their whispers, jostling, and creaking chairs pulled Phil's attention away from the screen. I watched his reaction with confusion. His eyes narrowed. His jaw tensed. He returned his gaze to the movie in only a matter of seconds, but hostility surrounded him like static electricity on a dry day. I could feel the crackle, but I didn't understand it. They'd made a commotion, yet his reaction seemed an overreaction.

This was the end of *Double Indemnity* for me. For the next hour, another thriller played through my mind, one that hit much closer to home. Not all of Phil's odd behavior of late could be attributed to his upcoming nuptials.

He'd had a strange reaction to Trudy's death. He'd slunk in and out of her funeral as if he was guilty of something. He had a prescription for digoxin. He aimed animosity like a shotgun at Norman and Rita at this very moment. He had something against the three of them, that was obvious. An ugly thought tiptoed into my mind. Had that something provoked him to murder?

Dark thoughts still stumbled through my mental pathways when I kicked open the red door and dropped my parcels on the kitchen counter the next day. The walls glowed gold in the late morning sun. I soaked in some comfort from them. The color El had chosen was perfect. It brought life to the room just as Amy Lee's pots of color had brought life to Belinda Simpson's still face.

I stood with hands on my hips and surveyed my domain. The carpet was an eyesore. Large blotches, like patches of eczema, ran from the front door to the bathroom. Dirt was ground into the traffic patterns. I could rent a shampooer and clean it, but I had the sinking feeling the stains were there to stay. The flat nap would never pop back.

I heard the groan of wood. That was one thing good about the rickety staircase, no one could sneak up on me. I turned to see El duck through the doorway. "Hi," I said. I couldn't keep the surprise from my voice. He showed up at the most unexpected moments.

"Thought I'd do a second coat on the walls," he said.

I glanced around. "They look great to me."

He began laying a drop cloth over the hideous wall-to-wall. "They need a second coat."

"Don't know if that drop cloth is necessary. The carpet can't get much worse."

"I didn't want to say anything."

"I don't think I can get Grace to replace it."

He straightened and gazed around the room. "Why don't you rip it out?"

"What, and live with particle board?"

"We could paint it."

"People do that?"

"Why not?" El pried the lid off a paint can. "Did you decide what to do about Carlton's offer?"

"I'm going to take it."

A look of relief crossed his face. "Good."

I put a clean liner in a paint pan and set it on the floor. He tipped the can and a thick stream of gold cascaded out. "You don't seem very happy about it. You look like your dog just died."

"I'm okay."

"My Interrogation Techniques class had an entire section on body language. It was once believed that a full ninety-three percent of communication was nonverbal. We now know that's not the case. However, body language shouldn't be taken lightly. Based on the slope of your shoulders, the downturn at the edges of your mouth, and the furrows in your forehead, I can tell you aren't fine at all. You're depressed, worried, or both."

It was no use trying to hide things from El. He was like Gran. He saw into your soul. "It's Phil and Gran," I said. He raised an eyebrow. "Well, Phil really. Gran told me they're getting married."

El put a roller in the tray and coated it with straw-colored paint. "Is that bad news?"

"No," I said, but it didn't sound convincing. "It's just, I wonder if he's good for her."

"I thought you liked Phil."

"I do."

"But?"

"Okay, this is ridiculous. You're going to laugh at me."

"Not me."

"I feel like he's hiding something." I told El about how white Phil became when I told him about Trudy's death. His funny reaction when I asked why he didn't say hello at her funeral. "Then last night, Rita and Norman came into a movie late, and he was visibly shaken."

"You put these things together with the fact he's taking digoxin, and you think maybe he had something to do with Trudy's death?"

I pushed at the drop cloth with the toe of my shoe. "Stupid, right?"

"Not stupid, but I don't think he did it."

I grabbed a roller and started to work on the other side of the room. "Why? Because you're sure Rita did?"

"No, I'm keeping an open mind, but you have to admit, she's a good suspect—already accused of one murder." I didn't say anything. He went on. "She also had means and motive, which is more than Phil has."

"He had means," I said. "He has a prescription for digoxin, and he was Trudy's neighbor. He could have popped by for a cup of sugar and switched her aspirin bottle."

"You were the one who said if we suspected everyone on heart meds in Liberty Grove, we'd have to suspect half the community."

I shrugged.

"Okay, say I give you that. What about motive?"

"I don't know, but I would have sworn Rita didn't have any reason to kill Trudy until two weeks ago. Phil is acting funny. He sneaked into Trudy's funeral. Didn't stop to say hi to me. It seemed like he didn't want anyone to notice him. Don't murderers go to the funerals of their victims a lot of the time?"

"Sometimes, but why would he act upset when Rita and Norman came into the movie? What does that have to do with anything?"

"Maybe he thinks they suspect him? Maybe Trudy, Rita, and Norman were all in on something together, and he's angry at all of them?"

"So you think Norman and Rita are next?"

"No." I dropped my roller into the pan and buried my face in my hands. "I don't know what to think. I'm just afraid for Gran."

A moment later, strong arms encircled my shoulders. El pulled me to his chest. I stiffened for a moment, but only for a moment. Then I burst into tears.

Five minutes later, I swiped at my eyes with a tissue. Embarrassment burned through me. I hadn't let anyone see me cry since my mom died. Except for that time with Dr. Norman, but that was an anomaly, and I was pretty sure he hypnotized me.

"You okay?" El gazed at me, concern crinkling the corners of his eyes.

"Yeah." My voice sounded angry.

El's was gentle. "You've been under a lot of pressure. It's okay to let off steam once in a while."

I picked up my paint roller and turned my back to him. "Sorry I brought the whole thing up. I told you it was stupid."

"No, Imogene. It's not stupid. Sometimes a good detective has to go with his, or her, gut. If your gut is telling you there's something going on with Phil, it's worth looking into."

I wiped my nose on my sleeve. "You think?"

"Yeah. Sure. I'll see what I can find out."

I turned. "Thanks."

We finished the second coat in silence, then started tearing up the moldy carpeting.

"So what do you think of Amy Lee?" El asked. I was grateful to him for changing the subject.

"She's a little scary," I said.

"She's much nicer than she seems—soft heart under the hard exterior and all that."

"I guess you have to have a crust to do the work she does." I yanked at a stubborn bit of rug.

"It can be difficult. Especially when you see people cheated out of years of life they should have had."

I yanked harder. "The girl I worked on last week was only twenty-six."

"Car accident, right?"

"Right." I put all my weight into the carpet this time. It broke free, and I landed on my butt.

"You okay?" El moved toward me, but I waved him away.

"I'm fine." It crossed my mind that I was going from one dependent relationship to another. I was leaving Gran's house, but it seemed I was relying on El more and more. I didn't like that. He was a good guy. A great guy. That didn't alter the fact that I wanted to be self-sufficient.

"That's sad, but it's not what gets to me." El resumed our conversation. "What gets to me are the people whose lives are stolen."

"Like Trudy." I hated to bring her up again. Trudy was always the elephant in the room with us.

El stood, walked to the window, and stretched his back. I couldn't see his features. He was a silhouette against the dying light. I hadn't realized we'd worked so long.

"I don't know what to do about it," he said. "But it drives me crazy. I know she didn't die of natural causes. I'm pretty sure Rita did it, but I can't prove it anymore than the police could prove Rita poisoned that actor forty years ago. It looks like she's going to get away with murder. Twice."

I didn't know what to say to make him feel better. He was right. If she was murdered, Trudy's death was an injustice, just as the diarrhea commercial actor's was. He was also right that we couldn't prove it. He had to figure out how to let it go. We both did.

I flipped on the overhead lights. Despite the piles of carpet and padding that filled the corners of the room, it looked twice as big and twice as clean. "You're a genius," I said. "It looks better already."

A smile cracked the somber expression on his face. "It does."

I grabbed the closest pile. "Let's get this stuff out of here." We couldn't talk as we passed each other on the stairs, and it gave me a chance to think. His upset added to the injury of doing Rita's wedding party gratis. I saw how much it bothered him, but there was nothing I could do about it now. I was committed. When we were done, I locked the red door, and we walked to our cars.

"You coming in to Greener Pastures tomorrow?" he said.

"No. I'm going Tuesday. Tomorrow I have work at Harry's then . . . " I let my words trail off.

"Rita's?" He guessed.

"Yeah. I'm bringing over a book of up-dos, so she can pick one for the wedding."

El looked at the sky and shook his head. "Because of me. A woman who probably deserves to spend the rest of her life in prison is taking advantage of you. You, the woman I—" His words didn't trail off. They stopped abruptly.

The woman he what? The woman he was friends with? The woman he wanted to help out? The woman he felt sorry for? How did El feel about me?

"I gotta get to work," he said.

I stood on the curb and watched him drive up Elm Street. He really was a good guy. The kind of guy I'd encourage one of my girlfriends to date if I had any girlfriends. He was the complete opposite of Chad. Too bad he wasn't my type.

23

BLOODY HEAVEN

Monday's weather didn't match my mood. On my way into Harry's that morning, the sun shone. The birds chirped. A gentle breeze blew. And I was in a damp fog funk because I had to go to Rita's after my nine o'clock.

At 10:08 I swung my red patent leather purse over my shoulder and headed toward the door. "What do I have tomorrow?" I asked Harry before exiting.

Harry pulled up the schedule on the computer and scrolled. "You have a two o'clock, wash and cut."

"That's it?" My heart sank.

Harry patted my arm. "Genie, Genie, Genie, it's always darkest before the storm."

I think he meant *before the dawn*, but based on the turn my life had taken, this seemed more accurate.

The bell on the front door jangled, and Doris walked in. When she saw me, she skidded to a stop. "I didn't think you were in today."

"I'm on my way out." What was she doing here? She was my client, but we didn't have an appointment. I wanted to ask her, but it didn't seem polite.

Harry glanced at Doris. "Maddy is just finishing up. Have a seat."

She was cheating on me. Again. I glared at her, my jaw clenched. She waved a coupon card in the air. "Maddy ran a forty percent off deal. I couldn't resist." At least she had the decency to look sheepish.

"Humph," I said.

"Don't look at me like that. It's your fault. All the stylists are doing it since you started. I have five coupons at home. I won't have to pay full price for the rest of the year."

Great. El and I had created a monster. We'd single handedly turned Harry's Hair Stop patrons into discount harlots. No faithfulness. No scruples. Willing to sell themselves to the lowest bidder. Phil always said a rising tide raises all boats. I guess a low tide shipwrecks them all too. Now, not only had I lost most of my clientele, but if they did come back, they'd expect me to work for nothing.

Speaking of nothing, Doris brought up the current bane of my existence. "I heard you were doing the bridal party for Rita's wedding. What kind of deal did you have to give her to get that job?"

"Wedding *party?*" Acid swirled into my stomach. I'd planned to give Norman a cut and fix Rita up for the big day. Did that constitute a party?

"Yeah. Her cousin is flying down from San Francisco, and two friends are coming in from the Mid-West. I think it's ridiculous for a woman her age to have a maid-of-honor and bridesmaids, but nobody asked me."

"She told me this was going to be a small affair, just close friends and family." My voice sounded strangled.

"Are you kidding? Rita can't resist the limelight. It's probably why she's been married three times. Weddings are the only shows she gets to star in."

A ripple riffled across the pool of bile in my stomach. "Does she expect me to cut all the groomsmen too?"

Doris shrugged. "I guess so. She said the wedding party. Best man and groomsmen are part of the wedding party."

The mortuary gig was looking better and better. I'd make a decent wage, and El was right; the dead didn't make demands. I just had to get over the shudders when I was around them.

"At least you got an invite to the reception," Doris continued. "You did get an invite, didn't you?"

"Not yet," I said.

"They went out a couple of weeks ago."

"I guess I'm not invited then. I haven't seen anything in the mail."

"Me, either." Doris pinched her lips into a knot. "That man is the most closefisted person I've ever met."

"Who? Norman?"

"Yes, Norman. He's the one who's trying to keep the wedding so small. He's a skinflint. Doesn't want to spend any more than he has to."

"I thought he was a successful New York psychiatrist. He should have money, shouldn't he?"

"Oh, he's got it all right. He just doesn't like to spend it. When he and Trudy were together, she complained that all he wanted to do was stay home. Never took her out to dinner, to the movies, to parties. He even started cutting back on Neutron dances. She wasn't happy about it."

"Maybe he's an introvert." I was too busy worrying about my own financial status to worry about Norman's.

"He's no introvert. When he and Rita were dating the first time, they were at the hub of the Liberty Grove social wheel. They knew everyone."

I moved toward the door. "I'll see you later."

Doris didn't seem to hear. "Rita and I spent a lot of time together after he broke things off with her. I don't think either of us liked the other that much, but she was lonely because she didn't have Norman. I was lonely because I didn't have Trudy, and Rita's ticker isn't good. Did you know that?" I gave Doris a quick nod.

"I guess you can take the woman out of the nurse's uniform, but you can't take the nurse out of the woman. I felt sorry for her." She snorted. "Fat lot of good it did me. Here it is, an even bigger social event than Trudy's funeral, and I'm not invited."

I didn't know what to say. *If you don't like them, why would you want to go,* was on the tip of my tongue. I kept it to myself. Doris was one of those people who seemed happiest when she had something to complain about. I patted her shoulder and left.

My mood darkened, if that were possible, on the drive to Rita's. Poor, sweet, full-of-fun Trudy may have lost her life because she dated the wrong man. Now I was on my way to help the woman who might be her murderer look beautiful for the wedding that should have been Trudy's. It made me feel sick.

I parked at the curb, hefted a stack of hair style magazines from the back seat of my car, and dragged myself up the walkway. I raised a hand to knock on the front door, but it was open. It pushed farther ajar as I gave it a polite tap. "Rita?" The only response was a strangled sob. I stepped inside, heart skipping in my chest. "Rita?"

The celestial color scheme of the condo had been tainted. Hellish splashes of red were painted on the white carpet. Sprays of maroon feathers decorated the glass coffee table. My gaze traveled from the shaggy, no-longer-white ottoman where a pair of slippered feet rested, to damp pools of purpling blood on the blue easy chair, to Rita's startled face.

Her lips were parted in surprise, her eyes wide and glassy. In the center of her blue silk blouse was an artistic stain, deep crimson graduating to pale mauve. In the center of the stain was a white-handled letter opener. "Rita," I whispered. I knew by the emptiness in her eyes and the coagulating blood on her chest, she couldn't hear me. She was gone.

Another sob broke the stillness. The magazines fell from my hands with a swoosh and thud. My head snapped toward the sound. There in the kitchen doorway stood Norman, a pink-tinged dishtowel in his wet hands.

Run. The word rocketed around my skull. Rita was past help. If Norman had killed her, I could be next. He seemed transfixed, however, almost catatonic.

Besides, I was only feet from the door. I'd be outside before he made it into the living room.

Keeping my eyes on him, I fished my phone out of my purse and dialed 911. When the dispatcher answered, I said, "There's been a murder." Norman groaned, sank to the floor, and buried his face in the dishtowel.

We stayed that way for what seemed an eternity. Norman cried softly into the rag. I searched the room for hints of what had happened. El was rubbing off on me.

The obvious answer was that Norman and Rita had a tiff, and he stabbed her. It appeared she'd been opening wedding RSVPs. The floor was littered with red polka-dotted papers. A pile of unopened envelopes lay on the chair near her body. Could they have argued over the guest list?

I took a hesitant step closer. A lone postcard lay on the floor as if dropped from her lifeless fingers. Through splotches of blood I read, *Mr. and Mrs. Brandywine will be attending the wedding of Norman Fielding and Rita Tarkington.* The number "two" was written on the guest line. The box for chicken was checked. I didn't know who Mr. and Mrs. Brandywine were, but I doubted they were the cause of her murder.

Other than the papers strewn about, the blood spatters everywhere, and the corpse, the room looked as it usually did. There were no signs of a home invasion. Not that I was an expert, but I did watch *Forensic Case Files*. I knew, when a home was broken into, furniture was tossed, pictures were knocked from walls, books torn from shelves. Rita wouldn't be reclining in her chair if there had been stranger danger. She'd have jumped up, tried to run.

The look of surprise on her face and her composed posture told me whoever had done this was someone she knew and trusted. Someone she'd allowed to get close. Someone who could stand by her with a letter opener in their hand without setting off her interior alarm bells. The most telling thing was Rita's hair. Her chignon was undisturbed. If she'd struggled, the bun would have been the first thing to go.

I eyed Norman with suspicion and backed toward the door. The distant whine of sirens soon grew louder than his sobs. I heard the screech of brakes, the slam of car doors, the thud of boots. "We're in here," I called when the boots reached the door.

Two almost identical uniformed officers entered. Both were average height and build, and both had almost the same shade of dark brown hair. The only difference I noted was one man's hair was perfectly straight and the other's had a natural wave.

They moved closer to Rita. Wavy Hair put two fingers on her carotid and shook his head. "She's gone," he said to his partner. I could have told him that.

Straight Hair lifted a walkie-talkie from his lapel and spoke into it. More sirens sounded in the distance. Wavy Hair helped Norman to his feet and led him outside, avoiding the pools of blood on the carpet. I followed in their footsteps.

Soon there was a flurry of activity on Rita's small cul-de-sac. Uniformed and plain clothes officials came and went through her front door. Neighbors wandered outside and stood with arms folded over chests and watched the action.

Wavy Hair put Norman into the back seat of a squad car, then walked over to me with a pad and pen. "Name?"

"Imogene Lynch."

"What's your connection to the dead woman?"

"I'm her hairstylist." I explained that I'd come to go over wedding plans and walked in on the scene they'd found. After asking me the same questions several times in several different ways, he took my contact information and told me I could go. "We'll be in touch," he said.

"What about Norman?" I said.

"We'll take his statement at the station."

I walked to my car in a kind of daze. I hadn't wanted to do Norman and Rita's wedding, but I never thought I'd be released from my promise like this. I pulled away from the curb and drove aimlessly. Fifteen minutes later, I found myself turning onto Elm Street.

As unfinished and messy as it was, there was no place like home when you were shaken up. I threw my shoulder into the red door, then gave it a kick. I tossed my bag on the plywood floor and sank into one of the camping chairs. The warm, gold walls surrounded me like a hug.

My mind whirled. Why would Norman kill the woman he loved? I couldn't imagine. He'd seemed so solicitous the night I went there to apologize for El, so adoring. What could have happened between them that would cause him to pick up a letter opener and stab her to death?

My gaze wandered to where my cell phone poked out from my open purse. El. I wanted, no needed, to talk to him. I grabbed it, thumbed in his number, then paused before hitting the call button.

It was only eleven-thirty in the morning. He'd probably be sound asleep. He'd told me he usually slept from six to one or two in the afternoon. I chewed my bottom lip. He'd want to hear about this as soon as possible, wouldn't he? I mean, he wouldn't want to sleep through Rita's murder. He was a murder kind of guy. It was an event worth losing a bit of sleep over, wasn't it? Maybe I was rationalizing because I wanted to hear his voice. I hit CALL.

24

KILLER COINCIDENCES

El answered on the third ring, his voice thick with sleep. "Imogene? What's up?"

"Sorry to wake you, but I have news. Big news." He yawned loudly. "Rita is dead," I said.

There was silence for a long moment, then he said, "What?"

"Rita is dead."

"Her heart?"

"Kind of. I mean, I'm sure getting stabbed with a letter opener didn't do it any good."

Now I had his attention. "She was murdered?" All the sleep was gone from his voice.

"Yes. I went over there this morning to talk wedding hair, and when I got there, the front door was open. I walked in, and there she was. Dead in her easy chair, blood everywhere."

"Are you okay?"

That was sweet. Chad would never have asked how I was if I'd told him I'd found a dead body. His first question would have been, *Is there a reward?* Followed by, *The police don't think I had anything to do with it, do they?*

"I'm getting kind of used to dead people." I tried to squelch the pride in my voice, but it was true. I was beginning to get over my shudders around the post-life crowd. "The blood was upsetting, but I soldiered on. You'd have been proud of me. I didn't let the mess stop me from looking for clues."

"You're not telling me you hung around? That could have been dangerous, Imogene. The murderer might still have been there. He, or she, could have been watching you." El's voice rose.

"Oh, he was. At least I assume he did it. He'd just washed the blood off his hands."

"What?" El yelled through the phone. "Who?"

"Calm down," I said. "Norman was standing in the kitchen. I was only a few feet from the front door. I could've sprinted to my car and locked the doors before he made it to the front yard. Besides he was in shock."

"Can you start from the beginning and tell me, step by step, what happened?"

So I did. When I reached the part where Wavy Hair put Norman in the back seat of the squad car, El interrupted. "Do the police think he did it?"

"I don't know. I guess so. Isn't it always the significant other?"

"An estimated fifty percent of the time, murders are domestic in nature—a husband, wife, boyfriend, or girlfriend. Eighty percent of the time, the victim knew their killer. But it isn't a given. An officer shouldn't assume—"

"Should keep an open mind," I said.

"Right. There is always that twenty percent chance the perp was a stranger."

"Well, I'm not sure how open-minded these officers were. They didn't handcuff Norman, but otherwise it looked like an arrest to me. The cop even put a hand on top of Norman's head as he guided him into the backseat of the car. They always do that when they arrest people." Another factoid I'd picked up on *Forensic Case Files*, or maybe it was *CSI*.

"Where are you?" El switched topics.

"At the apartment. Why?"

"I'll be there in twenty minutes." He hung up.

He didn't need to come over. What would it accomplish? However, if I was going to be honest with myself, I was glad. Finding Rita was creepy. Standing there in her bloody living room listening to Norman's sobs was even creepier. A dose of El's rock solid presence would do me good.

I kept myself busy by washing and drying the few dishes I'd bought and arranging them in a cupboard. I'd just opened a box of new silverware when I heard El's heavy tread on the stairs. A moment later, he entered carrying a white paper bag and two cups of coffee. "Breakfast," he said.

It was noon, but I hadn't eaten yet, so breakfast was okay by me. I put two plates on the counter. El added two plastic containers of cream cheese, one plain, one jalapeño. The bag was filled with half a dozen bagels. They looked good.

"Here's what I'm thinking," El said after powering down a half bagel. "If Norman killed Rita, he must have killed Trudy. How likely is it there are two murderers in the same Liberty Grove social circle?"

I pondered his logic. "Why would he kill Trudy?"

"Why would he kill Rita?"

"Maybe he's like Bluebeard. He has a compulsion to kill women he gets involved with."

"Then why didn't he kill Rita the first time around? Why wait?"

I shrugged. "Maybe Trudy was his first, and it gave him a taste for blood."

El finished his bagel and reached for a second. "He's a psychiatrist, right?"

I nodded.

"He'd have access to drugs. He could have slipped some to Trudy, but I'm still hung up on the triangle. Why date Rita for a year or more, break it off, date Trudy for two months, kill her, then go back to Rita?"

"When you say it like that, it doesn't sound like he ever really cared for Trudy. It sounds like he only wanted to get close enough to get rid of her. Rita was his girl all along," I said.

"But why? If it was financial, he'd have married Trudy before killing her. If he's a psycho, he'd have to be a pretty clever one to hide it for so long. He's in his late seventies, isn't he?"

"Yes," I said.

"Assuming he's guilty, it would have to be something about Trudy herself that motivated him."

"Doris said they got together at the New Year's party. Norman and Trudy discovered they both came from the same small town in Vermont, and that was that. Norman dropped Rita like a hot rock—those were Doris's exact words."

El looked at the ceiling, chewed, then swallowed. "Why would finding out you were from the same town make you want to murder a person? Unless you believed they knew a deep, dark secret from your past."

I sat bolt upright. "The letter," I said, spewing bagel crumbs. El raised his eyebrows. "I found a letter in Trudy's book, the one I took that day we went to her place. I was going to return it to Megan, but I got side-tracked. It was from Trudy's brother in Vermont."

I grabbed a napkin and began wiping crumbs from my shirt. "A new couple in town were remodeling the old house they'd just purchased and unearthed the body of a boy who'd gone missing years and years before. He'd been killed, then buried in the basement of his parent's house. Trudy and her brother had known him from school."

"If Norman had something to do with it—"

"He might have killed Trudy to keep her from putting two and two together." I finished his thought.

"If Rita figured out he'd killed Trudy—"

"He'd have to shut her up."

We locked eyes for a long moment. "That's a lot of supposing and not a lot of facts," El said.

"How do we get facts?" I was shocked as the words came from my mouth. When had I rejoined our detecting team? I wasn't sure, but I was back in. All in.

"Do you still have the letter?"

"It's at Gran's."

"Can I borrow it?"

"Sure. Want me to bring it to Greener Pastures? Rita doesn't need me anymore, so I thought I'd go in and get up to snuff on the workload."

We finished up breakfast and headed toward the door. El planned to catch a few more hours of sleep. I was going to Gran's to get the letter and change into jeans. That was another nice thing about working at Greener Pastures. I didn't have to dress up for the clients.

I paused in the doorway and scanned the room. "I'd been thinking about painting the floor a deep red, but after this morning, I don't know."

"Battleship gray," El said. "I already bought the paint."

"You what?" I felt a ripple of irritation. It was nice of El to spend his money on my place, but I wished he'd ask my opinion about the decorating choices.

"Maybe I should have checked with you, but I figured color wasn't your thing."

"What do you mean, color isn't my thing?" I bristled.

He gestured to my outfit, a black, off the shoulder peasant blouse atop black capri pants. I lifted my purse. "Red," I said.

"There are other colors."

I thrust my arm in his face so he could see my tattoo. "Blue. Red polka-dots."

"We could paint the floor blue, but it'd make your place look like the Swedish flag. And polka-dots would be scary if you had too much to drink."

I shut the door. "Gray is good." I was tired of his being right all the time. Well, most of the time. He hadn't been right about Rita. He'd been sure she was the murderer. Now she was dead. I found that comforting in a perverse kind of way.

As I drove to Gran's, the scene I'd encountered that morning played through my mind—Norman's agonized sobs, his collapse to the floor, his grief-stricken face. I had a hard time imagining him as Rita's killer.

So you think Norman and Rita are next? El's question of yesterday rang in my inner ear. What if someone else had just gotten rid of two birds with one stone—offed Rita and framed Norman? Wasn't that the kind of thing Phil would think of? He ran his life on clichés.

I hated myself for the disloyal thought, but Gran's safety was more important than loyalty to a man I'd only known for a few years. I'd lost my father. I'd lost my mother. I wouldn't lose Gran.

What could Phil's motive possibly be? Why would he want Trudy and Rita dead and Norman out of the way? I couldn't imagine, but I was going to have to start thinking like El, do some poking around, find out everything I could about Phil.

25

WELCOME TO THE TWILIGHT ZONE

I spent an hour looking up Phil on the Internet, then headed to Greener Pastures with Trudy's letter. I'd ask El what, if anything, he'd found out about Phil when I saw him.

I didn't discover much, not for free anyway. There were several websites claiming they could tell me everything there was to know about Phil if I'd fork over ten dollars. Not that I minded spending the money; it was just that I didn't believe their hype. They looked like scams. El must have access to sites I didn't know about.

Amy Lee was in the embalming room when I arrived. "I thought you were coming tomorrow," she said by way of greeting.

"I had time today."

"Good. Come here."

Amy Lee bent over the body of an older gentleman. The tag on his gurney read, *Ed Kluger.* I watched her set his features. This was a gruesome process that included filling sunken eye sockets with cotton, gluing them closed and inserting a dental form into his mouth.

I felt queasy by the time she was finished. When she moved toward the embalming equipment, I moved toward the door. I wasn't going to watch that again. I told her I needed coffee and left. This mortuary gig was getting easier to handle, but I had my limits.

I found El before I found the coffee. He was in the guardroom on the main level, checking the grounds via security cameras. I handed him Trudy's letter. His face clouded as he read it. "His poor family," he said. "They walked over his grave for years never knowing he was there."

"It's a terrible thought."

He set the letter next to the computer. "How's it going downstairs?"

"Okay. I watched Amy Lee set a man's features, but I bailed when she started the embalming bit."

"That's hard to get used to."

"I hope I never have to. Want coffee?" I asked.

"No, thanks. Just had some."

I hovered around his desk, feeling awkward. I wanted to ask if he'd had time to research Phil, but the monitors were distracting him. Besides, Norman had been arrested, so he may have decided it was a moot point. He finally looked at me, a question in his eyes.

"Did you ever look into Phil?" I said in a rush.

"No. I haven't had time. Now that Rita is dead . . . "

"Could you?"

"You really think it's still necessary? It seems pretty likely the police have their man."

"I don't think we should assume. An officer has to keep an open mind." I gave him what I hoped was a winning smile.

He dropped his chin to his chest. "Using my own words against me."

"Not against you, but I'm still worried about Gran. About Phil."

He paused. I could see the argument going on in his mind. He hated to say no to me. He still felt guilty about the turn my business had taken since all this had started. On the other hand, he thought researching Phil was a waste of time. "Tell you what. If I have time after I look into this," he tapped the letter, "I'll run Phil's name through a couple of databases."

"Thanks," I said. I turned to exit his small office.

"Come see me before you leave. I take my lunch break around six."

I found the coffee, poured myself a cup, and took it downstairs. Amy Lee was done embalming by the time I got there. After she cleaned up her equipment, she turned the body over to me and left for the day.

"Welcome to the Twilight Zone," I whispered to Ed Kluger and was thankful he didn't whisper back. I was also thankful that when I combed his salt and pepper hair away from his peaceful face, both of us remained peaceful. In fact, I felt extraordinarily peaceful. I hummed while I snapped on gloves.

As I applied Ed's makeup, the waves of serenity that had wafted over me waned. I discovered something I didn't like about the embalming room. It was very easy to lose track of time here.

Actually, I found there were several things I didn't like about the embalming room: It was too cold, too quiet, and too creepy. *And* it was easy to lose track of time here. There were no windows. It was like working in a vault. A timeless vault that opened onto the maw of eternity.

I looked at my cell phone. It was six o'clock. I'd gotten so wrapped up in Ed's cosmetic work the time had flown by. I covered him with a sheet and wheeled him into the freezer.

Walking into the large refrigerator was another thing I didn't like about the embalming room. I steered past the draped bodies that lined the walls, guided Ed into his spot, and hurried toward the exit. The idea that someone was on my tail shot through me. A bubble of adrenaline burst in my chest. I ran out and slammed the heavy door shut behind me. I'd seen one too many zombie movies. If I continued to work here, I was going to have to change my viewing habits.

I cleaned up the cosmetics, put the brushes into disinfectant solution, washed my hands with the same, and jogged upstairs. The soft surfaces of the main floor helped take the edge off the freezer's chill.

El wasn't in his office now. He must have left for his rounds. It was dusk by the time I reached the parking lot. I decided to get in my car and drive around until I found his golf cart.

It was parked near the Happily Ever After section of the cemetery, but he wasn't in it. I exited my car and walked to the edge of the lot. I could wait here, or I could walk around and try to find him. My stomach growled. The last thing I'd eaten was a bagel. I wanted dinner, and I didn't feel like waiting.

My toe had healed and there was only a little stiffness in the dog-bit ankle, so I felt fine as I trudged between the gravestones. After a couple of minutes, I reached the top of a hill and scanned the horizon for El. The evening was balmy. Crickets chirped. Frogs sang. An owl hooted somewhere nearby. It wasn't so bad here. I was beginning to see why El liked his job.

He got to be outdoors. He had time to study. There wasn't any drama, at least not until I came along. Trudy and I had disrupted his quiet life. I wondered if he was sorry.

A shadow moved behind an oak tree up ahead. I strode toward it. The cemetery was closed for the night, so I figured it must be him. However, when I rounded the tree there was no one there. A breeze sailed past me, but no branches quivered in the cold marble orchard.

I hugged myself. Which way? He could be anywhere. I patted my sweater pocket looking for my phone. Not there. I'd left it in my purse in the car.

I paused, considering my options. I could go back the way I'd come or follow the path to the left. I was fairly sure it would wind around and lead me to the parking lot again. If I hadn't found him by the time I reached my car, I'd call.

Daylight was fading fast. The sky had become the deep magenta of Amy Lee's embalming tubes and Rita's carpet. The tombstones reflected the hue. I picked up my pace.

A few minutes later, I began to get nervous. By my calculations, I should be in the parking lot. I wasn't.

I broke into a jog despite the residual stiffness of the Chorkie-injured ankle. I craved electric light like a pregnant woman desires pickles and ice cream.

My foot, the one attached to the ankle the dog bit, hit something hard. I went down. Tears sprang to my eyes as I sat in the grass nursing my injured appendage. I choked back several words Gran didn't approve of.

Many minutes later, the throbbing subsided. I blinked away the tears and took a calming breath. The best thing about pain is the relief that comes when it stops.

I put a hand on a nearby headstone, planning to use it to heft myself up. My gaze traveled past wilted calla lilies and dead roses and fell on the inscription. *Gertrude Rosenblum - May she dance through eternity.*

I froze. How had I ended up here? I'd started out in an entirely different section of the grounds. Certainly, I'd wandered, but not this far. I couldn't have.

For a crazy minute, I thought Gran was right. Trudy sought justice. She'd drawn me like a flame draws insects. She'd called to me from her grave, and a part of me I didn't believe existed had responded. "What do you want?" I whispered the words.

"Imogene." I heard my name as if from far away.

"Trudy?" I said.

"What are you doing?" Her voice sounded deeper than I remembered.

A moment later, muscular arms raised me to my feet. "Are you okay?"

I laughed with relief and embarrassment. It had been El, not Trudy. "I twisted my ankle," I said.

"Then why are you laughing?"

"Happy to see you, is all."

He gave me a puzzled look. "You shouldn't walk around here in the dark. Visit Trudy in the daytime."

I didn't bother telling him I hadn't intended to visit Trudy.

"Where are you parked?" he asked.

"In the Happily Ever After lot. I was looking for you." I leaned on his shoulder as we hobbled toward the car. "Did you find out anything about Norman?"

"I did. In the archives of the Brattleboro paper," he said. "Turns out Norman and Mathew Palmer, the boy who went missing in 1953, were best friends. They were supposed to go fishing the day Mathew disappeared. Norman said he went to the house, but no one was home. Everyone assumed Mathew went on his own and got lost in the woods."

"Can they tell how he died?"

"Looks like head trauma, but it's been sixty-five years."

I stopped limping and faced him. "I bet that's the reason Norman started hanging out with Trudy. He probably wanted to know what she knew."

"Which would lead one to believe he killed Mathew, either accidentally or purposefully, and buried him in his parents' basement."

"I can't imagine living with that on my conscience for all those years."

"That's because you have one." El nudged me in the direction of the parking lot. "*If* Norman killed that boy and *if* Trudy told him about the letter she received, would it be enough motivation for him to kill her?"

"Don't you think the Vermont police would've resurrected the investigation and called Norman in on their own?" I asked.

"Maybe, but it's a cold, cold case. I'm sure they questioned Norman when Mathew disappeared and were satisfied by what he told them then. Why go after a man of his standing now? Especially if you have to track him all the way across the country."

"Justice?"

"Yeah, well, justice costs money. Vermont isn't the wealthiest state in the nation. Everybody's working on a budget."

I stopped hobbling to catch my breath. "So, he just gets away with it?"

El stopped with me. "We're assuming he did it. He might not have. He might just have wanted to touch base with someone from home after hearing the terrible news."

"That's a huge coincidence. Trudy, Norman's girlfriend, dies right after the body of Norman's best boyhood friend is discovered."

"When you put it like that."

We started walking again. Neither of us spoke until we reached my car. "So, what do we do?" I asked.

His eyes shone in the rising moonlight. "I think we have to take the letter to the police."

"The letter doesn't have anything to do with Rita."

He sighed. "I guess we bring them the hair analysis, as well. They have a murder on their hands, probably two. We can't withhold evidence."

My legs went weak with relief. I hadn't realized how heavily the responsibility of Trudy's death had weighed on me until this moment. "Good. When do we go?"

"Tomorrow morning. Is six okay?"

I wasn't a morning person, but I'd get up early for this. "Can you pick me up at Gran's?"

"I can do this by myself. You don't have to go."

"I do. You and I have been in this together from the beginning."

I got in the car and slammed the door. Before I left the lot, I rolled down the window. "Did you find out anything about Phil?"

"No. I ran his name, but nothing turned up. I don't think you have anything to worry about, Imogene."

I drove home in a somber mood. I should be glad this whole thing was almost over. The police had Norman in custody, and he wouldn't be able to hurt anyone else. But I couldn't shake the feeling Trudy was still restless.

26

CORPSE CAFFEINE

Six is a ridiculous time of day, but I was dressed, caffeinated, and standing out front by the time El drove up. I clambered into his Ford.

His hair was a tiny bit longer than when we'd first met and ever-so-slightly mussed. He wore a worn fleece-lined denim jacket that matched his eyes. The resigned expression on his face made me want to hug him. Maybe the jacket-eye thing made me want to hug him, too.

"Did you bring all the paperwork?" I said.

He nodded. He was quiet on the way to the station. I wondered if this was not only the end of our amateur investigation but also the end of our friendship. What would we talk about if there was no more mystery? Murder was the only thing we had in common.

The surrounding establishments were still dark, so the police station shone like a beacon. From the parking lot, it looked warm and welcoming, kind of like the gingerbread cottage in Hansel and Gretel. And we all know what happened there.

El and I were doing the right thing. Something we should probably have done weeks ago, which only made my rule-following anxiety greater. What if there was a law about sending in a deceased person's hair sample without the family's permission? What if they found out I stole Trudy's book?

Gran didn't like cops because she was a rebel at heart. Me, I didn't like them because they made me nervous. Now here I was about to walk into a police station and voluntarily tell them about all the rules I'd recently broken.

Wavy Hair was at the front desk. His name tag said *Officer Dulac*. He screwed up his forehead when he saw me, like he was trying to remember who I was. "Can I help you?"

El set a hand on the counter. "We've come across some information that may have a bearing on the Rita Tarkington murder."

Recognition dawned on Dulac's face. "The investigator isn't in yet, but I could take a statement. Hang on a sec."

We waited while Dulac picked up the phone. A moment later, another uniformed officer ambled to the desk and Dulac rose. "This way," he said.

We followed him down a short corridor into a small room with industrial blue carpeting and a conference table. He sat across from us, placed a tablet on the table, and looked at us expectantly.

El cleared his throat and pulled out Trudy's letter. Dulac read it with seemingly little interest, then gave us a curious look.

"Norman Fielding was best friends with Mathew Palmer." El slid a printout of an old newspaper story onto the table.

Dulac read that, humphed and typed on his tablet. "So you think this ties into the Tarkington murder?"

"I'd better start at the beginning," El said, and handed the hair analysis report to the officer.

Dulac looked baffled, and a little irritated. "Who's Gertrude Rosenblum?"

"She used to date Norman," I said.

"She didn't have a bad heart," El said.

Dulac eyed us each without expression. "I appreciate your coming in. We'll contact the Brattleboro department and see if they have anything for us." He pushed back his chair.

"We haven't told you everything," El said.

Dulac stifled a yawn. "Do you want coffee?" He didn't wait for an answer. He stood and left the room.

"We're not handling this very well," I said *sotto voce*, sure we were being observed through two-way glass. I didn't see any glass, but it had to be there somewhere. It was in all the cop shows.

A bead of sweat broke out on El's upper lip. "I'm better at interrogation."

Dulac returned with three paper cups and slumped into his chair. "Okay."

I eyed the beverages with suspicion. Did paper pick up prints? I decided I needed more caffeine too much to worry about it and sipped. I was sorry I did. The coffee was terrible.

El told Dulac the entire story, even about the twitching corpse. I wasn't happy about that, but Dulac seemed to appreciate it. He said, "Corpse caffeine," three different times and laughed every time he said it.

When we got to the hair analysis, he perked up. "You're taking Forensic Science?" he asked El.

"Yeah. It's a great class," El said.

"I've been thinking about taking some online classes myself. Don't want to be wearing this forever." He tugged on his lapel.

"Hey, I wish I was wearing the uniform."

Dulac nodded in sympathy. "It's hard to get into the department these days, with all the cutbacks. But it sounds like you'll have a leg up. Taking those—"

"Excuse me," I said. "Could we get back to the point?"

They each gave me a blank look, then El said, "Oh, right." He returned to the story. When he got to the part about how he'd used what he'd learned in his Interrogation Techniques class to get information out of Megan and Doris, Dulac stopped him again.

"I studied that at the Academy, but a refresher would be a good thing."

"I highly recommend it," El said.

"What's the name of the school again?" Dulac waited with fingers poised over the keyboard.

"The Palmer Institute."

"Guys," I said. I'd finished the crappy coffee and was eager to leave and get a good cup.

El's cheeks colored. "Anyway, nobody knew anything about Trudy taking digitalis, about a heart problem, nothing." He told Dulac about the Trudy, Rita, Norman love triangle and finished up with the insight we'd had in the cemetery. "We got motive out the wazoo," he said.

Dulac nodded. "So Norman kills this Trudy woman to keep her quiet about Vermont. Rita gets wind of it somehow, so he has to off her too."

"That's what I think," El said.

Dulac walked us to the front office. "I'll inform Detective Sherman when he gets in. I'm sure he'll want to talk to you."

Hearing that sent a tingle of anxiety through me. Dulac didn't act like the hair analysis was a problem, but he was distracted because El was taking a Forensic Science course. The detective might not be. We weren't out of the woods yet.

"You have my number," El said.

"I do."

El held the door open for me. Chad never held a door for me in his life. Not that I was comparing the two of them. El and I weren't dating or anything.

Before the door closed, Dulac called out. "Hey, you want to get a beer sometime? When all this is over."

For a nanosecond, I thought he was asking me out. Before I could let him down gently, El said, "Sure. Great."

Dulac grinned. "I'll be in touch."

How did El do it? The guy was a human magnet.

"Where to?" he said when we got in the truck.

"Gran's."

Ten minutes later, he dropped me at the curb. "See you soon."

I nodded. "Maybe sooner than we think if that detective wants to talk to us today."

"Keep your phone on." He drove off.

Maybe I wouldn't. I could use a day that had nothing to do with the dead.

27

CAT FIGHT

The Orange County Register was in the driveway. I carried it into the condo. The door thumped to a close behind me and muted the sounds of the outside world. Inside was dim, cool, and peaceful. The only sound, the ticking of the big grandfather clock in the living room. Gran must be sleeping in, an unusual occurrence.

I walked into the kitchen and set up a pot of coffee. Harley thumped his tail from his doggy bed but didn't get up. While the coffee dripped, I put a piece of toast in the toaster and pulled a jar of peanut butter from the fridge.

I planned to get a single-serve coffee maker for the apartment. I was too impatient to wait for coffee to drip. Besides, there was only one of me.

Only one of me. That sounded strange. I'd never lived alone before. I'd lived with Gran since Mom died, except for that one brief foray into the unfortunate roommate situation. The desire to have my own place had been a fixture in my heart for so long, I wasn't sure how I'd feel without it. A niggle of worry whispered in my mind. Would I like living alone? Would I be lonely? Would I get nervous at night?

I could get a cat. I was really more of a dog person, but I couldn't see leaving a dog in that tiny space all day. Might not be fair to a cat either. Maybe a betta fish.

By the time I resolved my pet dilemma, the coffee was done. I poured a cup, spread my toast with peanut butter, and took my breakfast to the dining room table.

I leafed through the paper, looking for something about Norman and Rita. I found a short piece in the Local News section. It didn't say much. The headline read "Murder in Liberty Grove," and mentioned there was a person of interest but didn't give his name.

Gran meandered down the stairs as I licked the last of the peanut butter off my fingers. She wore jeans and a flannel shirt—cozy and comfortable. Just like her. A stab of homesickness hit me, and I hadn't even moved out yet.

"What are you doing up so early?" she said.

"El and I went to the police station this morning." I hadn't told Gran everything, but I had told her we were going to take the analysis of Trudy's hair sample to the cops now that there was a second death.

Concern creased her features. "How did that go?"

"Better than I expected. The officer crushed on El."

"He's pretty crush-able." Gran disappeared into the kitchen but kept talking. "I like him, Genie." I pulled a face and was glad she couldn't see it. "And I think he likes you."

"Me?" I heard the surprise in my voice. "We're just friends."

Gran reemerged with a cup of coffee in her hand. "You sure?"

"Of course, I'm sure."

"All the work he's done on your new place? Seems like more than friendship to me."

I waved away her words. "He just wanted to rope me into his investigation. Now that it's over, I'll probably never see him over there again."

"We'll see," Gran said in the knowing voice she used whenever she thought I was wrong.

"What are you up to today?" I changed the subject.

"I'm headed over to Phil's. He's packing and sorting. Said I'd help. Want to come?"

I was exhausted, and I had plans, but I wasn't sending Gran to Phil's on her own. El hadn't found anything on him, and there was a ton of evidence against Norman. But there was an itch inside me that didn't scratch. "Sure. I'll come for a bit."

We saddled up Harley and walked into the morning sun. The day was going to be a warm one. Mr. Rogers was out digging in his garden. His face cracked into a crooked grin when he saw us. He might not like me very much, but he did like Gran.

"Suzanne." He stood and bowed his head, an almost deferential gesture.

"Hi there, Al. How's the garden coming along?" Gran said.

"Fine, fine." He bobbed and nodded.

There was an awkward silence, and Gran waggled her fingers. "Well, see you later."

"Ahem." He cleared his throat. "I heard a rumor."

Gran stopped walking. Harley's droopy eyes drooped even more. "I heard you and Phil were tying the knot." He sounded as if he hoped it wasn't true.

"We are." Gran's voice was light and cheerful.

Mr. Rogers scowled. "I wish you all the best."

"Thank you."

I waited until we'd rounded the path and were out of earshot. "Speaking of crushing."

"What?" Gran looked at me with wide, innocent eyes.

"You know what."

"I don't."

"Mr. Rogers. He's got a thing for you."

"Al? You're crazy. He's always been in love with Rita." She disagreed with me in word only. The small smile hiding in the corners of her mouth admitted I was right.

"This place is one big soap opera," I said. Gran pshaw-ed. "It is. My love life is a desert in comparison, and I'm only twenty-six."

"Oh, well. That's you."

"What's that supposed to mean?"

She didn't answer until Phil's place came into view. "You don't know how special you are. That's what that means."

It was my turn to pshaw.

Phil erupted onto his walkway with a black plastic garbage bag in each hand. He stopped short when he saw us. "My two favorite ladies." He set the bags on the sidewalk and kissed us each on the cheek. I couldn't help but tense. "There's a coffee cake in the fridge, Entenmann's. Help yourselves." He retrieved his bags and headed toward the dumpster on the street.

Gran, Harley, and I stepped inside. Phil's place had never been warm and cozy, but today it was stark. He'd removed all the pictures from the walls and the books from the shelves. The only things on his coffee table were a roll of masking tape and a felt pen. He'd been busy.

"Wow." I looked around me. "I thought you guys were taking your time on the marriage thing. Looks like Phil is moving out tomorrow."

"Now that you have a place, we thought we'd move the date up a bit."

I meant to say good, but what popped out of my mouth was, "Marry in haste, repent at leisure."

Gran looked at me in surprise. Before I could explain my statement, Phil came banging through the front door. A fat gray tabby slipped in behind him.

Harley lunged.

Gran dropped his leash.

The cat screamed.

And the race was on. The cat leaped onto the back of the couch, launched itself onto a bookshelf, slid off the other side, landed on the floor with a thump, and flew into the bedroom. Harley followed, paws sliding on the wood flooring.

The noises from the other room were appalling, screeches and bays and scrabbling claws. Phil pulled himself together first. He used a word I'd never heard him use before and darted into the bedroom.

Gran ran after him. That seemed an adequate number of people to handle one dog and one cat, so I waited in the living room. There were more thuds, barks, and curses. After a loud minute, Phil emerged the victor. His little bit of hair stuck up from his head in tufts, bloody scratches crisscrossed his arms, but the growling feline dangled from his hand by the scruff of its neck. Phil traversed the living room, deposited the animal outside, and shut the door.

Gran and Harley peeked around the corner. Phil glared at the dog. Harley gave him a halfhearted wag. "Whose cat was that?" Gran said.

"Trudy's."

"Trudy's?" I said with surprise. "I thought Megan was going to take her cat."

"She was, but she couldn't catch the damn thing. Doris said she'd feed it until Megan could come down again."

"Harley's sorry for scaring it. Aren't you, boy?" Gran scratched his head.

"Maybe Harley did me a favor and scared him off for good. That cat is always sneaking in. Drives me nuts."

"How sad. He's probably looking for Trudy," Gran said.

"Naw. He did that when Trudy was alive. We had some pretty sharp words over it." Phil's face became solemn. "I never told you, because I'm not proud of myself. Last words Trudy and I ever spoke to each other weren't very nice. I feel badly about that."

My cheeks flushed. Could that be all it was? The reason he'd paled when he'd heard about Trudy's death? The reason he'd slid in and out of her funeral so quietly?

"Well," he looked up and gave us a sad smile. "No use crying over spilled milk. It is what it is. I can only hope Trudy is looking down from that big retirement city in the sky with forgiveness."

"I'm sure she is." Gran patted his cheek. "How about a piece of that coffee cake?"

After coffee and cake, Gran and I started packing up Phil's dishes while he tore apart the pantry. The conversation turned to the upcoming nuptials, and the mood brightened. I felt better about the wedding since I'd learned the tension between Phil and Trudy was over nothing more serious than a cat. I was still concerned about his reaction to Rita and Norman. It didn't make Phil a murderer, but I was curious.

It was hard to stay worried with the cheerful banter going on around me. Gran planned to wear lettuce green for the wedding and wanted daisies in her hair instead of a veil. Once a flower child, always a flower child. Phil was going to wear a white suit, the white loafers I hated, and a daisy in his lapel.

They were going to marry under one of the oldest trees in Southern California, a tremendous oak planted on the bank of Oso Creek. You could fit a hundred people in its shade.

Just as I wrapped the last saucer in newspaper and wedged it into a box, there was a knock at the door. "Come in," Phil hollered.

Doris poked her head into the kitchen a moment later. "Are you moving?"

"What's it look like?" Phil answered with a growl.

"I had no idea." The shocked expression on her face lent credibility to her words.

"Phil and I pushed the date of the wedding up a bit," Gran said.

"What's the hurry?"

"We're not getting any younger." Phil's usual cheerful demeanor had disappeared. His tone of voice bordered on rude.

Gran shot him a disapproving glance. "Genie found a place. She's moving out in a week, so we thought, why not?"

"Oh." Doris entered the kitchen fully, and I noted with satisfaction that Maddy's choice of hair color was a poor one for Doris's skin tone. "Have you sold this place yet?"

"Nope," Phil said.

"Homes that are occupied sell faster."

"That's a risk I'm willing to take."

There was a long, tense silence while Phil stacked canned goods into a box. I thought about mentioning Doris's hair, but couldn't figure out how to do it diplomatically.

When the pantry was empty, Phil turned to Doris. "So what can I do you for, Doris?" Tension crackled in his voice. The behavior was so unlike him, I stared.

"I just stopped by to see if you'd seen Fred."

"Fred is the cat," Gran said to me by way of explanation.

"He was here," Phil said.

Doris brightened. "Recently?"

"Yup."

"Do you know where he went?"

"Nope."

She stared at him for a long moment, as if expecting more information. "I'd better go find him, then." She spun on her heel and left.

I eyed Gran. "What on earth was that about?" She put a finger to her lips, but it was too late. Phil had heard me.

"I can't stand that nosy biddy. That's what that was about."

"She's been a little intrusive." Gran's voice was subdued.

"A little? She sticks her nose into everyone's business."

"Now, Phil, I think she means well."

"She's a witch."

My head snapped back and forth between them like I was watching a tennis match. I had no idea there was so much acrimony between Phil and Doris. She wasn't a very faithful client, but other than that, she always seemed nice enough to me.

"That's harsh," Gran said.

"It's not harsh," Phil said. "She's got the evil eye, that one. Whenever she gets even a whiff that someone is sick, she hunts them down like a hound from hell."

"She used to be a nurse. She probably—"

"Doctor Kevorkian's nurse."

Gran grimaced. "Phil."

He slammed a can of tuna onto the counter so hard I jumped. "Every single person she's taken under her wing has kicked the bucket."

"That's like saying a hospice worker is a jinx because her patients die." Gran adopted a soothing tone. "Doris steps in when she hears someone is unwell because she wants to be helpful. It's inevitable some of those people die, especially in an old age community."

"What about Trudy? All she had was hay fever. Doris starts taking care of her, and she croaks." Phil dropped the tuna into the box. "She's bad luck, Suzanne. I don't want her hanging around me. Ever since she saw my heart medicine on the counter, I can't get rid of her."

Was that why Phil started keeping his meds at Grans? Gran put her hands on her hips. "I can't believe how superstitious you are."

"If it quacks like a duck . . . That's all I'm saying."

I realized my mouth hung open. I shut it with a clack, then spoke without thinking. "It wasn't Doris's fault Trudy died."

They both looked at me. I wasn't supposed to say anything, but Norman was already under suspicion for Rita's death. They'd find out about his past connection to Trudy soon enough. "The police are pretty sure Norman did it," I said.

"Norman?" They said the name in concert.

"Why would he kill her?" Gran said.

"Norman liked Trudy," Phil said.

"I found a letter." I launched into the story, and when I was done, Gran and Phil just stared at me.

Gran lowered herself into a chair. "How horrible. That poor boy. His poor family."

"I never liked the guy," Phil said.

I eyed him, wondering if he was about to give me a clue about his behavior at Club House Two.

"Not because you thought he was a killer," Gran said.

He shrugged. "No."

"Why don't you like him?" I asked.

"It was that thing with Al Rogers," Phil said.

"Mr. Rogers?" I was in the dark.

"Don't say another word." Gran used the same tone she used to use with me when I was a kid. Phil clammed up. I wondered if I'd ever find out why he didn't like Norman, but I guessed it didn't matter. If Gran knew about it, it couldn't have anything to do with murder.

28

A NEW CUSTOMER

The next day, I got a call from Detective Sherman. He wanted El and me to come in when I was done at Harry's. My gut wriggled as I drove to the station. It was illogical. I wasn't the criminal here. I was helping the police. But the butterflies batted their wings anyway.

El was leaning on the building when I got there. "Ready to do this again?" he said.

"I'm a little nervous."

"What are you nervous about?"

I exhaled. "The hair sample."

El shook his head. "I'm pretty sure what we did wasn't illegal."

I flinched when he said the word *illegal*. "I wish you were one-hundred percent sure."

"Dulac didn't have a problem with it."

"Dulac has a crush on you."

El furrowed his brow. "Do you think so?"

"He asked you out."

"Yeah, for a beer. It's a guy thing."

I could tell by the look on his face he thought I was saying Dulac was gay. "Maybe he wants to show you how to use his handcuffs," I said. The concern on El's face turned to horror. I was enjoying this. For once, I had one over on him. "He's pretty cute."

El stared at his shoes for a long moment. "I didn't mean to lead him on. I don't want to hurt his feelings." He looked into my eyes. "What do I say?"

The hilarity of the moment burst like an overfull water balloon. El was nice. Too nice. You couldn't even tease him. "Don't worry about it. It was just a guy thing. Dulac isn't gay." I opened the door to the station.

Detective Sherman, middle-aged, wiry, dark-haired and unremarkable, met us in the lobby and led us to the same interview room we'd sat in before. We told him the same story we'd told before. We drank cups of the same crappy coffee we'd had before.

I tensed when El got to the part about the hair sample, but Sherman didn't even raise an eyebrow. There was a lesson in that. I was very good at worrying about things I didn't need to worry about.

"You two have been a big help," he said when we finished. "Not that I endorse the amateur sleuth thing."

El looked sheepish. "That was my fault, detective. I got carried away."

"I understand. I was the same myself. Always looking for mysteries to solve, but I didn't come across any murders until I got hired on by the Sheriff's department. I'd have thought I was in hog heaven if I had."

Murder? Hog heaven? I'd never understand the mind of a law enforcement professional. I pushed back my chair, assuming we were done, but El spoke up. "Can I ask you a question?"

"Not sure I can answer, but fire away," Sherman said.

"How did that boy, Mathew Palmer, die?"

"Norman Fielding claimed it was an accident, and the coroner corroborated his story. It seems the boys got into a fight over Norman's new fishing rod. Mathew grabbed it and wouldn't give it back. There was a skirmish. Mathew fell and struck his head on an ax that was lying near the woodpile."

"So Norman buries him?" I couldn't keep the incredulity from my voice.

The detective's face grew solemn. "That's a sad thing. Turns out Norman's father was abusive. Used to beat the boy regularly. Norman was terrified of him, terrified what he'd do if he found out about Mathew. There are still hospital records—microfiche—and some old folks left that say Norman wasn't lying about that."

"So will the Vermont authorities prosecute?" El said.

Sherman shrugged. "Got to prosecute the current crime first."

"I guess you can't talk about that?" I said.

"You guessed right. I can say he pleaded not guilty at his bail hearing." That's all Detective Sherman would say on the topic.

When El and I stood in the parking lot again, he said, "So that's it, then."

"I guess," I said.

"You don't look convinced."

"Norman said he didn't do it."

El looked away, took a deep breath, then looked back. "That's what they all say."

"But—"

"If Norman didn't do it, who did?" It was the first time I'd ever heard exasperation in El's voice.

"I don't know. I was at Phil's yesterday and—"

He laughed. "You don't still think it was Phil?"

"No, but—"

"Listen, I get it. It's like I told Detective Sherman, once you get bitten by the investigation bug, it's hard to beat. We've got to let it go now. We've turned everything over to the professionals. They'll take it from here."

It was my turn to get frustrated. He was the one who'd started this. When I wanted to talk to the cops, he'd disagreed. Now that he was in with the in-crowd at the station, he didn't want to make waves? Was that it?

"Imogene." His voice took on an overly sympathetic tone. "I'm not trying to stick my nose where it doesn't belong, but I think you're having a hard time sharing your Gran."

He sounded so superior I couldn't speak without growling. I didn't appreciate being psychoanalyzed. Not by El. What did he know? I spun toward my car.

"We're getting in a new customer for you at work tomorrow," he called after me. I kept walking. "It's Rita."

A breeze blew up. The hairs on my arms rose. I didn't like that idea at all. I turned to look at him. "So soon?"

"The ME released the body."

"Why me?"

"You were requested."

"By who?"

He frowned. "That's the weird thing. Doris is making all the arrangements."

"Doris?"

"Rita never had any children, and her only close relative is a sister with Alzheimer's. Doris has power of attorney."

"I didn't think those two even liked each other."

"I guess they were closer than we thought."

All the way home, Phil's words about Doris ran through my mind. He'd called her a witch. Said she had the evil eye. Accused her of being involved with everyone who'd died in Liberty Grove. Of course, that was hyperbole. Too many people died in Liberty Grove every week for any one person to have known them all, but how many had she befriended? And why?

Could it be she wormed her way into the homes of the ill and elderly in the hopes they'd leave her something when they died? Or put her in charge of their affairs, like Rita did? It had been done before. Only recently I'd read about a private care home owner who'd killed her charges, buried their bodies in the garden and continued to collect their Social Security checks.

I wasn't saying Doris killed Trudy and Rita, but something about the fact that she had power of attorney in Rita's affairs didn't sit right. I wanted to know more, but I couldn't talk to El about it. He'd made that crystal clear.

By the time I pulled into Liberty Grove, I had a plan. El might be the king of online investigation, but I had resources he didn't. I worked in a hair salon.

29

GOSSIP GRIST

I got to Harry's forty-five minutes early the next morning. Even Harry wasn't there yet. I heard clatter coming from the break room. It had to be Maddy. She was always first in, and Maddy was the one I wanted to talk to. I wandered through the empty salon and poked my head into the break room. "Hey."

Maddy jumped, hand to her heart. "Imogene. Don't sneak up on a girl like that."

Maddy wasn't as old as most of our clients, but no one would call her a girl despite the leopard print leggings and platform shoes. "Sorry," I said. "Wasn't trying to scare you."

"What are you doing here so early? Your first appointment isn't until nine."

That irritated me. Maddy kept better track of my appointments than I did. I knew it was because she saw me as a threat. I was, by far, Harry's youngest stylist, and I also had my cosmetology license. When I'd come on board, my business had built quickly. I took some of her clients without meaning to. Doris had originally been Maddy's.

Why Maddy was still worried about it was beyond me. She had four times as many clients as I did at the moment, and she had Doris again. Which was why I wanted to talk to her. I sidled up to the coffee machine and slid in a pod.

"I felt like company," I said in as sad a voice as I could muster. Maddy stared at me, suspicion in her eyes. She and I weren't very chummy. "Gran left for her exercise class and ever since Rita . . . " I let my words trail off.

Maddy's face softened. She put a hand on my arm. "Oh, hon. That must have been awful, finding her like that."

I nodded. There was a big heart hidden under those double-D implants. I knew she wouldn't allow competition to come between us if I was upset, or if there was a good story to be had. As far as stories go, it didn't get much better than finding a dead body. She carried her coffee to the table, sat, and patted the chair next to her. "So, they think the fiancé did it?"

I brought my cup over and sat too. "They always think the boyfriend or the husband did it, but I don't know. In this case . . . But I shouldn't say anything."

Maddy took a sip from her cup, then ran a pinkie over her glossy red lips. "You don't think he did it?" She sounded nonchalant.

I shrugged. "I'm not a cop."

"He was there, wasn't he? When you found her?"

"Yeah." I stretched out the word like it wasn't entirely true.

She clicked her purple finger nails together with excruciating patience for a long moment. Then, like she couldn't stand my silence any longer, she said, "If he didn't do it, who did? Tell me that."

I glanced at her and gave her a tepid smile. "I wish I knew. I'm having bad dreams. I'm afraid to be alone at night."

Maddy flicked her hennaed hair over her shoulder and leaned closer. "You think the murderer thinks you know something?"

I widened my eyes and whispered, "That's what I'm afraid of."

She patted my arm again and said, "Don't you worry, honey. The police will figure it out."

"They never figured out who murdered Trudy."

That set Maddy back in her chair. "Trudy had a heart attack."

I shook my head. "According to her daughter, there was nothing wrong with her heart. Trudy had just had a doctor's appointment."

"She was sick, though."

"She had seasonal allergies."

"Allergies can kill you." She shrugged. "If they turn into pneumonia."

I shot her a disbelieving look. "If you're old and feeble, maybe. Trudy was neither."

"You don't think it's connected? Trudy and Rita? Who would want both of them dead?"

I stirred my coffee with a stir stick for a long moment, like I was hedging. "I heard something the other day. I won't say who told me, so don't ask. But I heard everyone Doris takes under her wing dies."

Maddy sucked in air. "Oh my goodness, don't say that. She's my client again. I just saw her last week."

"Not someone like you," I said. "I mean old people who are already sick."

A thoughtful look crossed her face, not a common occurrence with Maddy. I knew I was getting through to her. "You should talk to Flora. She's my 9:30. Flora is friends with Birdie. Do you know Birdie?"

I shook my head.

"Birdie's husband, Donald, died last year. I think Doris was helping out over there while he was sick."

"How could I bring it up? I don't even know Flora."

Maddy chewed her lower lip and gazed at the ceiling for so long I wondered if she'd forgotten the question. "Got it." She cut her eyes to me. "Tell her your grandmother is sick, and Doris offered to come by and take care of her. See if she bites."

"Gran would kill me if she found out I told people she was sick."

Maddy waved a hand. "How's she going to find out?"

That was true. Gran and Flora didn't know each other, and Gran never came into the salon. I did her hair at home. "Okay, I'll wander over when she gets here and casually bring it up. See what she says."

We left the break room closer than we'd ever been. We were co-conspirators now. As the morning progressed, I'd catch Maddy looking at me from across the salon. When our eyes met, she'd give me a knowing look and an almost imperceptible nod. I wondered if the other stylists were getting suspicious. She wasn't the most subtle person on the planet.

My nine o'clock was still wet when Flora came in and took a seat at Maddy's station. "This won't take long," Maddy said in a booming voice, glanced my way, and wiggled her penciled-in eyebrows.

"I'd like to try a new process with your hair," I said to the woman seated in my chair. "You have such nice natural curls, I'm only going to give your hair a quick shot with a diffuser and let it dry the rest of the way on its own."

"But my old girl always used a round brush," she said.

"You know, that's kind of passé. Natural curls are being featured in all the style magazines," I lied. The woman's hair was actually more frizzy than curly, but I had to get moving if I was going to talk to Flora.

"I don't know." She looked skeptical.

"Tell you what, if you don't like it, come back tomorrow, and I'll wash and style for no charge." I started the dryer before she could answer.

Three minutes later, I was pulling her toward the door while she repeated the phrase, "My old girl always used a round brush." I had a feeling I'd see her the next day.

I hurried to the break room, plugged a pod into the coffee machine and tapped my fingers on the counter for the thirty seconds it took to brew. I snatched up my cup, sloshed coffee all over my sleeve—another reason black was a good style choice—and raced to the door. I barged into the salon and stopped short. *Calm down, girl.* I slowed, sauntered to Maddy's station, and leaned languidly against the wall.

"Oh, Imogene. How's it going?" She said with too much enthusiasm.

I sighed heavily. "Okay."

"What's wrong, sweetie?"

Flora's eyes slid from Maddy's face to mine.

"Nothing, really. Just have a lot on my mind."

"Is your Gran okay?" Nothing like getting right to the point.

"She's not feeling well. The doctor says it's probably nothing to worry about, but it's really got her down."

"That's terrible," Maddy said, enunciating like a high school drama club ingenue. "I guess it makes for a lot of extra work for you, taking care of her and everything."

"Not really. A friend of hers comes over every day to help out. She's been awesome."

Maddy stopped wrapping foils around Flora's locks and turned toward me. "How nice. Who?"

"Oh, you know her. It's Doris. Doris Miller." I kept my eyes on Flora's face as I said the words. Her eyebrows shot so high they were almost hidden by the foils Maddy had already inserted.

"You know her, too, don't you Flora?" Maddy said.

Flora nodded, tinfoil bobbing. "She took care of my friend Birdie's husband when he was sick."

"She's so thoughtful," Maddy said.

"She's a saint," I said.

"Birdie's husband died," Flora said.

Neither Maddy nor I responded for a moment. Then we both spoke at once. "That's so sad," I said.

"It wasn't like it was Doris's fault," Maddy said.

I thought Maddy was being a little obvious, but I shouldn't have doubted her. She had gossip down to a fine art.

Flora shrugged one shoulder. "Who's to say?" I tried to look shocked. "Birdie never liked Doris. Felt she was too familiar, if you know what I mean."

"No, what do you mean?" Maddy said.

"I hate to gossip."

I almost laughed and ruined my cover. Gossip flowed like shampoo at Harry's. People who didn't like it only came once.

Maddy combed through a hank of Flora's hair. "It's not gossip. Imogene needs to know. For her gran's sake."

"Well, if you put it like that." The dam broke. "Birdie would go out to the store and find Doris in the house when she got back—had no idea how she got in. One time, she went to pick up Donald's prescription from the pharmacy, and Doris had already picked it up. Which sounds nice, but no one had asked her to. She made all their meals, even though Birdie was perfectly capable of cooking. Birdie put up with it for a long time, but she finally drew the line at the bath."

"Bath?" Maddy and I said in unison.

"Doris offered to bathe Donald. Said she did it all the time when she was a nurse." Flora pinched her lips into a sphincter. "I think that's how she gets her kicks."

"Should I be worried about Gran?" I said.

"I wouldn't have her near anyone I cared about," Flora said with finality.

"What should I do?" Alarm bells rang in my brain. I had to remind myself Gran was fine, and Doris wasn't taking care of her. I have a strong imagination.

"You should talk to Birdie. She knows a lot more than I do. She had her nephew—he's one of those computer birds."

"Nerds," I said.

She shot me an annoyed look. "Nerds, birds, whatever, a computer guy. He looked into Doris and found out some very interesting things."

Maddy stopped wrapping a foil. "Like what?"

"I don't remember, but it wasn't good. Doris tells everyone she retired, but I think she got run out of her last job."

"Do you think Birdie would talk to me?" I said.

"I'm sure she would. She's over at the senior living center on the golf course now."

"I thought she lived in Liberty Grove," Maddy said.

"Sold her place after Donald died. Didn't want to live alone. Good thing too. Fell and broke her hip three months ago. She's moving slow these days." Flora caught my gaze in the mirror. "She'd probably enjoy the company."

Flora gave me Birdie's address just as my ten o'clock arrived. I planned to go as soon as I was done. I might be a bit late for Greener Pastures, but it wasn't a big deal. That was another plus about post-life services, nobody was in a hurry.

30
UNNATURAL CAUSES

I stopped at the grocery store on my way to Maison de Bonheur Living Center to pick up an African violet and a get-well card. I didn't want to show up empty-handed.

The senior care home was in a low U-shaped building. Its lobby was located in the center of the U. I pushed through heavy glass doors. The room I entered looked like it belonged in a five-star hotel. It had floor-to-ceiling windows dressed in pricey floral drapes. There were plush carpets on the floor and gold-framed landscapes on the walls. It was lovely in an overblown way. I wondered why Gran made a face whenever anyone mentioned moving in.

I approached the information desk. A brown-haired woman with a bubble cut that went out of style about thirty years ago smiled at me. "Welcome to Maison de Bonheur."

"Hello, I'm looking for Birdie McBride."

The woman checked the computer on the counter. "Room 305," she said. "Should I buzz ahead and let her know you're on your way up?"

"No. I want to surprise her." I held up the African violet. If Bubble-head insisted on letting Birdie know I was coming, Birdie would say, "Imogene who?" and things would get complicated.

I marched to the right, like I knew where I was going. When it comes to directions, if there's a fifty-fifty chance of being correct, I won't be. I've even tried tricking myself. If I think A, it must be B, so I'll choose B. I'm still wrong.

"Miss. Excuse me, miss." Bubble-head called after me. "That's the dementia wing. Three-oh-five is that way." She pointed left. "All the odd numbers are in the well-patient wing. We don't want to stigmatize our patients who struggle."

I pivoted and headed the way she'd pointed. So much for looking like a frequent visitor. At least she didn't insist on calling ahead.

I found a bank of elevators down a short hall and took one to the third floor. The doors opened onto another world, another planet. Gone were the drapes and the carpets.

The floor was linoleum. The walls papered in an old-fashioned geometric print that glinted with metallic shapes except for the places the sheen had worn away. The air smelled of bad cafeteria food and things I'd rather not think about. Now I understood Gran's reaction.

I followed the numbers on the wall to room 305 and knocked. I heard a muffled voice that may or may not have said, "Come in."

I opened the door a crack. "Mrs. McBride?"

"Who's there?" The voice was strong and deep.

I entered. The woman who sat in the mauve easy chair by the window could not have been more misnamed. She was the least bird-like person I could imagine. She had a broad, pleasant face, and I guessed she'd be close to six feet if she were standing.

"Hi, Mrs. McBride. I'm Imogene Lynch, I—"

"Suzanne's girl? What a nice surprise." She knew Gran, then. "To what do I owe the honor?"

I crossed the room and handed her the African violet. She took it with large hands that looked like they might have once kneaded dough or driven a tractor. "How do you know Gran?"

"We took Aqua Aerobics together for years. She's a kick. How's she doing?"

I had planned to tell her the same story I'd told Flora, that Gran was under the weather, and Doris was hanging around. But something about Birdie's wide, steady gaze told me I shouldn't. I'd better tell the truth. Where to start?

I took a deep breath and dove in. "I don't know if you read in the paper about Rita Tarkington's murder?"

She nodded.

"I was the one who found the body." I perched on the edge of an easy chair and told her about Norman's arrest, about my suspicions that Trudy hadn't died of natural causes, and the letter I'd found from Trudy's brother. I did not tell her the twitching corpse bit or about the hair analysis. Being truthful didn't mean I had to spill my guts.

She held a hand up when my narrative slowed. "Forgive me, honey. I love a good story as much as the next person, especially in here, but I don't see what this has to do with me?"

"Maybe nothing," I said. "It's just, I'm having some second thoughts about Norman's guilt."

"Based on what you told me, it sounds like he had a motive."

I nodded. "It does, but he was so broken up over Rita's death. He was devastated."

"Love and hate are different sides of the same coin."

"Doris Miller was involved with both Trudy and Rita."

Birdie stiffened. Her face grew hard. "You should have said that straight out."

"Flora told me you had problems with Doris."

"I did." She looked past me, as if seeing a film I wasn't privy to. "At first I thought she was a godsend. When Donald had his stroke, I was still helping with the grandkids. My daughter relied on me. I didn't know what to do."

"That's understandable," I said.

She gave me a wan smile. "Then I met Doris. She told me about her nursing background and offered to stay with Donald on the days I went to Caroline's to sit." She shifted in her chair. "Pretty soon, she was coming over on other days, too. She'd be there when I got back from an errand."

"Did she have a key?" I asked.

Birdie shot a glance at me. "I never gave her one. I think she may have borrowed Donald's set and had one made. They went missing for a day or two."

"What did you do?"

"I wanted to get rid of her, but I couldn't afford to hire a real nurse and, like I said, Caroline needed me. I was stuck. Finally, I told Caroline about it, told her she was going to have to find someone else to watch the kids until her dad recovered. He was recovering, by the way. The doctors expected he'd have almost full function within a few months."

I thought about Phil's statement that people in Doris's charge seemed to die despite doctor's reassurances they were on the road to recovery.

"Caroline suggested we call my nephew. Hal is a wiz on the computer. He does research for an insurance company—he's in the claims investigation department."

I sat up straighter. This is what I'd come to hear.

"Turned out Doris was let go from three hospitals. There weren't any formal charges, but loads of suspicion. Death seemed to follow her around."

"How scary."

"It was. When we heard that, Caroline and I both agreed she had to go. I told Doris that night. I said Caroline had found someone else to watch the kids, and I'd be taking care of Donald now. A week later, he was dead. The doctors said it was another stroke, but I never believed it."

"Did they do an autopsy?"

"No. I looked it up. There are plenty of poisons that mimic the symptoms of a stroke. I wanted them to check, but Donald was eighty, already had one stroke. They thought I was a blathering old lady."

Her story lent credibility to Phil's suspicions. This was evidence. Real evidence. I was anxious to talk to El. Before I left, I filled Birdie in on Gran's upcoming wedding and assured her I'd visit again soon.

On the way down the elevator, I checked my watch. It was two o'clock. El was probably having breakfast and getting ready for work. I'd wait to talk to him in person. That seemed best after the awkwardness of our last meeting.

I walked through the lobby in a daze, so distracted by my whirling thoughts, I didn't see Doris until it was almost too late. It was the name that got my attention. "Birdie McBride's room, please."

I spun toward the information desk. What was Doris doing here? Why was she visiting Birdie?

I darted behind a potted palm, my heart thudding like it was trying to beat its way out of my chest. I looked around for a better hiding place and saw a restroom behind me.

I glanced toward Doris. Her back was still turned, so I made a run for it. The door exhaled closed behind me. I leaned my forehead against the cool wood.

What should I do? Should I head straight to Greener Pastures so I could fill El in on what I'd learned? Or should I protect Birdie somehow?

Did Birdie even need protecting? Doris took her time with her victims, if they even were victims. It was possible the deaths were coincidences. Doris was a nurse. She worked with old, sick people. I told myself that, but I didn't believe it. I had a very bad feeling about Doris.

The bathroom door began to open, and the drumbeat in my chest started up again. If it was her, how would I explain my presence? I took a step toward a stall. The only place to hide. Before I reached it, a white-haired gentleman stepped into the room. He saw me. His eyes grew round. His cheeks flushed. He murmured something I didn't get and backed out.

I looked at the interior of the bathroom for the first time. A row of urinals were lined up before me like the letters on a marquee. All my anti-rule-breaking instincts sang, but I forced myself to wait a full minute before sneaking a peek out the door.

The lobby was empty. I dashed to the car and drove to the mortuary. On the way, I rang the information desk at Maison de Bonheur. When Bubble-head answered, I lowered my voice, hoping she wouldn't recognize it. "Have someone check on room 305. The woman who's visiting is dangerous."

"What? Who is this?" Bubble-head said. I hung up.

31

A COLD, COLD WORLD

El wasn't in his office when I got to Greener Pastures. I realized it was too early, but I had work to do to keep me busy until he arrived. Rita Tarkington was downstairs waiting for me.

I pushed open the heavy door of the embalming room. Amy Lee glanced up but didn't smile. Rita's corpse lay on a gurney in front of her. The giant blender sat on a table nearby. She'd obviously just finished the embalming process. Rita's body shone from the oils Amy Lee had massaged into it to force the fluids through veins and arteries since Rita's heart would no longer do the job.

"Sorry I'm late," I said.

Amy Lee shrugged. "As long as you finish."

"How many do you have for me?"

"Two. That one." She jutted her chin toward a draped table I hadn't noticed. "And this one, when I'm done." She meant Rita. My heart dropped a floor or two. I had prided myself on the fact I was getting better at this gig. I'd stopped shuddering every time I came into Death Valley, but working on someone I'd known, that was different.

I walked to the cupboards at the back of the room, donned a gown and gloves, retrieved the cosmetics box, and carried it to a table near the draped gurney. I pulled back the sheet and gazed at the face I'd be bringing to life.

It was a man. Early sixties, I'd guess. Thin. A runner maybe? Three photos sat on the table. I looked at them one by one. In the first, the man stood with his arm around an attractive woman of about the same age. His wife? In the next, he looked tired but happy in running shorts and shoes, race numbers pinned to his shirt. I was right. He had been a runner.

The last photo was a family shot. The man, the same woman—definitely his wife—and three adult children: a beautiful blond young woman and two handsome young men. A pang of sympathy shot through me. I knew what it was like to lose a father.

Amy Lee had set his features well. His expression was contented and serene. I chose a slightly darker foundation than I'd normally use, but he was an outdoors kind of guy. He should have color.

I got so lost in my work, I jumped when Amy Lee spoke. "I'm leaving." She had her hand on the door.

"Oh. Okay," I said. "I'll see you—" but she left before I finished my goodbye. Amy Lee was missing the social chip. It wasn't a problem with her usual clientele, but it would take me some getting used to.

I glanced at my cell phone. I'd set it next to the cosmetics box so I could keep track of the time. It was 4:15. El should be in his office by now.

I put the final touches on the runner. He looked healthy, like he had in life. I knew it wouldn't comfort his family. There's nothing about the dead body of a loved one that's comforting. I only hoped to avoid jarring or shocking them and adding to their grief.

I wheeled him into the big freezer, walked to the counter, stripped off my gloves and turned on the tap. Water bounced into the steel sink. I stuck my hands under the flow and began to scrub.

Something squeaked behind me. It sounded like the rubber sole of a shoe. I glanced over my shoulder, expecting to see Amy Lee. No one was there.

I blinked, then realized it must have been an auditory trick—something to do with the noisy stream of water and the tile walls—and returned my gaze to the sink. I wasn't used to the unique sounds of the embalming room yet, not like I was the salon's. I rinsed, turned off the tap, and reached for a paper towel.

Pain.

Blinding, excruciating pain.

It started from a point at the back of my head and blossomed until it filled my skull.

Then blackness.

I don't know how long I was out. An eight-count drumming in my head brought me to. I winced with each beat, wishing for unconsciousness again.

The awareness that someone was watching me was the first thing I noticed after the drum beat. I read somewhere that skill comes from our amygdala—the part of our brain assigned the task of protection from predators. I opened one eye. Then the other. They wouldn't work in unison. I hoped this wasn't permanent.

There was movement in my peripheral vision, but when I attempted to roll over to see what made it, I discovered another even more disturbing problem. I was tied up. My hands were pinned behind my back by something sharp that dug into my wrists. I glanced down the length of myself and saw my ankles were secured with zip ties.

The third and most upsetting thing I noticed was the cold. I lay on the floor of the freezer.

"You're awake," Doris said.

"What's happening?" I asked, but was afraid I already knew the answer.

She smiled. It wasn't a nice smile. "Freezing to death is one of the least painful ways to go. Did you know that?" I shivered. "When I was a child, I had a pet rabbit. Until he bit me."

I didn't want to hear the end of the story, but I had no choice. Captive audience and all that.

"We had a chest freezer in the garage. My father was a hunter. He used it for deer steaks and roasts, and venison sausage. Anyway, I didn't want my rabbit anymore, so I put him in on top of the meat. It only took a few hours. He looked so peaceful when I took him out."

I strained at my ties, but they held tight. "Why are you telling me this?" I don't know why I asked. The answer was obvious.

"I'm sorry, Imogene. This is an unfortunate turn of events. It's not personal."

"You won't get away with it." Stupid. That sounded like a line from one of the old thrillers I liked to watch.

"I think I will. I generally do." Doris wrapped her arms around herself. "It's chilly in here."

"This is pointless, Doris. There are too many people who are on to you. They'll tell the cops. They'll figure it out."

"They'll think it was an accident."

I laughed. Not a happy laugh—I'm not a masochist—a throaty guffaw to show her how absurd she was. "What about the zip ties, Einstein?"

I shouldn't have mentioned Einstein. It was juvenile, and it pissed her off. She aimed a kick at my gut. More pain. I curled up like cheap shrimp on a barbie. "I'll take them off as soon as you're dead," she said.

"Why?" I grunted the word.

"I assume you're not asking about your own demise. My guess is you're asking about Trudy and Rita."

I nodded. I had to keep her talking until the pain subsided enough for me to come up with a plan. The only thing I could think of at the moment was trying to talk her out of killing me. That wasn't going so well.

"I didn't intend to kill Trudy. I just wanted to make her sick." Her eyelids fluttered. "Norman didn't really care about her. He'd always been besotted with Rita—although, for the life of me, I can't understand why. I figured if Trudy was ailing and moping around all the time, Norman would tire of her. Then she'd need me again."

"Rita?" I groaned.

"Oh, Rita. That was sloppy. I'd replaced a bottle of her digoxin with aspirin. I needed her meds for Trudy."

Doris paced the small space, rubbing her arms with her hands. "She began having symptoms within a few weeks. No surprise. But instead of going to the doctor and having a new, stronger prescription written like any sane individual would," she paused and glared at me, "Rita marched into the pharmacy and accused them of giving her the wrong drugs. They took a look at the pills and knew exactly what they were."

"How did she know?" I was able to breathe again, shallow breaths, and had enough air to form short sentences.

"That I took them, you mean?"

"Yes."

"Takes one to know one, I guess." Doris resumed her pacing. "Once she knew her pills had been switched, it wasn't a far leap to know who'd done it. She was delighted, despite the physical discomfort. Norman is such a tightwad, and she wanted more money for the wedding. She saw the whole thing as a financial opportunity."

I took stock of my surroundings as she filled me in on her evil deeds. There wasn't much in the way of weapons in the freezer, only clients. If only I was in the embalming room with our gallon of poisons, scalpels, and tools.

"She tried to blackmail me." Doris checked a fingernail as she spoke. "*Me.* Stupid move on her part." She dropped her hand to her side. "But, enough about me. I'm out of here. My toes are going numb."

So were mine. And my fingers. And the side of my body that touched the frigid floor. I rolled onto my back and lifted my head to get a better look at her. I don't know what I thought would happen. Maybe that the pleading look in my eyes would melt her frozen resolve. "Why me?" I tried to sound pathetic.

"You're the rabbit, Imogene. Soft and cute, but then you bit. If you hadn't gone poking around, hadn't riled up that awful Birdie, you wouldn't be lying here now."

"How did you know?"

She rolled her eyes skyward and shook her head. "You asked Flora about me in the salon this morning. The. Salon." She said the last two words slowly and forcefully, like she was attempting to explain physics to someone with an IQ of 60. "News travels, dear. Annabelle Flornoy was having her hair done by Clarissa two chairs over. She couldn't wait to tell me what she'd overheard."

That was the wrinkle in the carefully thought-out plan Maddy and I had come up with. We'd counted on the gossip mill feeding us, but we'd overlooked the fact that it wasn't selective. It fed anyone who came hungry.

"I'm going to wait outside. Don't want to catch cold." She turned toward the door.

My gaze skittered around the room and came to rest on the gurney of my running man. It stood between me and Doris. I scooted as close as I could get, lifted both legs, and kicked. The table flew.

Several things happened in succession. The table came to a crashing halt against the back of Doris's legs. She buckled to the floor. My running man, still slick with massage oil, slid off the metal table and onto Doris. She shrieked and began flailing her arms and legs, a useless effort. My man must have weighed at least one-hundred and eighty pounds in life, but now—well, you know what they say about dead weight.

I knew my opportunity for escape was brief. It wouldn't be long before Doris disentangled herself. I eyed the open door and rolled. Every three or four revolutions, I glanced up, righted myself, then rolled again.

When I reached the doorway, I turned onto my belly and began inching myself through. I'd taken a few break dancing lessons at Neutron. It wasn't really my thing, but I'll try anything. The worm was the only move I'd been any good at. I'd never expected it to come in so handy.

I heard a grunt and thud. Doris was on her knees. My running man's legs rested on her back. I had to hurry. I flipped my legs, mermaid like, planted them on the outer edge of the freezer door, and pulled with my heels. The door began to close.

Doris swatted running man's legs away, and rose with arthritic motions. I pushed the door with as much strength as I could muster. It closed with a *fwomp*. The last thing I saw before it did was Doris, mouth agape, hair on end, reaching toward me with claw-like hands.

I slid my butt close to the door, planted my feet against it, and got ready to hold it in place. Doris battered and banged and screeched, but I held tight. I was a swing dancer and had the legs to prove it.

Long minutes later, I began to wonder what would give out first, Doris's heart and its ability to pump increasingly cold, viscous blood through her veins, or my legs. I'd been through a lot, and they were quivering. Just as I thought I'd run out of strength, the door to the embalming room opened.

"Imogene?" I'd never been so happy to hear anyone's voice in my life.

"Here. I'm here," I said.

El couldn't see me. I was hidden behind Rita's gurney.

"I was thinking about the Norman thing," he said. "About what you'd said. Maybe you're—"

"El." I panted his name.

He rounded the gurney. "What are you doing on the floor?"

"Help me, please."

Doris threw herself at the door. It exhaled outward a terrifying few inches, reminding me of the doors in the Haunted House at Disneyland. I slammed it into place. My thighs burned with the effort.

El stopped and stared. "There's somebody in there." Sometimes he states the obvious.

"It's Doris. She tried to kill me. Call the cops."

He sprang into action then. He pulled his phone from his pocket, hit 911 and barked information as he wedged a chair under the handle of the freezer door. He glanced at me. "You're tied up." Yet another obvious observation.

"I know."

He ran to the back of the room, rummaged through a drawer, returned with a scalpel, and cut the zip ties. I closed my eyes as the blood flowed into my hands and feet. It hurt so good.

"I need to meet the paramedics and bring them downstairs. They'll be here any minute," he said.

"Yeah."

"You shouldn't be down here alone. With her."

I didn't like that idea any more than he did, but my limbs were only just starting to feel mobile again. "I don't think I can walk yet."

He scooped me up like I was a child.

"Hey," I said.

"I'm not leaving you." It didn't sound like the topic was open for discussion, so I threw my arms around his neck and let him carry me upstairs.

32
ALL'S WELL THAT ENDS WELL

Three hours later, I sat on the edge of an exam table, head and wrists bandaged. Gran held my hand, and Phil stood in the corner with an anguished expression on his face. The doctor, a guy about my age by the look of him, had just finished telling them how to care for a concussion patient. He said they'd need to keep me awake for a while. I didn't like the sound of that. I wanted more than anything to collapse on my bed, close my eyes, and shut out the world.

"How's it going?" El stuck his head into the room.

"She's going to be fine," Gran said.

"Are you up to talking to Detective Sherman?" he asked.

I started to nod, but winced. Head nodding was definitely out for a while. Gran answered for me. "No."

"I didn't think so. I'll tell him to call you tomorrow." El's head disappeared. He'd been doing this Cheshire cat imitation for the past two hours, sticking his head into the room and pulling it out again without ever actually entering. I guessed he was handling the law for me.

"Let's get you home," Gran said. She held my arm as I pushed myself off the table. I grunted when my feet hit the floor. Movement hurt. I wasn't looking forward to the drive home.

It wasn't as bad as I'd feared until we hit Liberty Grove. I'd never realized how many speed bumps there were until this moment. Each sent a jarring pain through my head. The city's obsession with safety was totally unhealthy.

When we got to Gran's, she led me to my favorite chair in the living room, pulled up an ottoman for my feet, and covered me with a throw. It was a warm night, but I couldn't seem to get the chill of the freezer out of my bones. She bustled off to the kitchen to make soup.

Phil sank onto the couch and stared at me. I gave him a quick, toothless smile so he'd know I was okay, but he continued to stare. It was so unlike him, it made me jittery. "Don't you have some pearl of wisdom for me?" I said.

He didn't respond, so I supplied a couple of options. "Fools rush in where less stupid people fear to tread. A fool and her head are soon parted." He didn't crack a smile. I'm not even sure he blinked.

"Come on, Phil. I'm okay. Stop looking at me like you're expecting me to keel over any minute."

He gazed at his hands. "I feel terrible. We could have lost you, and it's all my fault."

"Your fault?" I was incredulous. Doris's fault was the obvious conclusion. My own stupid fault was another possibility. But Phil's? No way.

"If I had reported Doris's behavior to the police at the time . . . "

I started to shake my head, then thought better of it. "They wouldn't have done anything, Phil. What would you have said? She sneaked into my condo through the back door and was messing around with my stuff."

He continued staring at his hands, so I went on. "She would have said she was looking for Trudy's cat, or looking for you. She could even plead confused little old lady. I'm telling you, there was nothing about this that was your fault."

"But I knew the kind of person she was. The kind of people she spent time with."

"How? How did you know?"

"Doris, Norman, and Rita, they were cruel. Each of them in their own way. I think that's why they spent time together. They understood each other."

"Cruel how?" Even my fuzzy brain understood I should pay attention. I was about to learn something important.

"Poor Al Rogers. He was in love with Rita, you know."

"Yes."

"Norman and Doris convinced him she returned his feelings, but they said she was insecure and wouldn't believe a bachelor as eligible as he was would be interested in her. They set him up. Over and over." Phil massaged his hands with his thumbs.

"At times, Rita would return his advances, and other times she'd shun him. It could be what caused his heart attack. The stress, the disappointment, the humiliation."

I sat up straighter in my blanket, suddenly uncomfortable. "Why would they do that?"

"For laughs. They don't call old age your second childhood for nothing, Imogene. It's as bad in here as it is in your local high school."

"How did you find out?"

"Al told me. Trudy told him she'd confronted Norman because of things she'd witnessed. Norman admitted what they'd done but laughed it off. Poor Trudy, she was sickened by the idea that she'd been all set to marry a man like Norman." Phil looked up from his hands and into my eyes. "Me and Al figured that was what killed her."

It wasn't. Doris had killed her, but I didn't want to stop the flow of information.

He cradled his head in his hands. "She was a good woman, Imogene. I shouldn't have talked to her the way I did, but I didn't realize. Not until it was too late."

"You were upset about the cat," I said, trying to comfort him.

"It was more than that. I'd seen what that gang had done to Al and others and thought Trudy was a part of it." He shrugged. "She and Norman were seeing each other. My assumptions were wrong. She didn't know the half of it."

An ember of warmth started behind my sternum and spread outward. "She forgives you, Phil." What was I saying? Trudy was dead. Gone. Yet I knew that glow in my chest didn't belong to me.

"I'm grateful to hear you say that, but I shouldn't have involved you. Shouldn't have put the whole thing into your head. We almost lost you." He choked back a sob.

"Would it have been better if Norman Fielding went to prison for a crime he didn't commit?"

Phil shrugged. "Norman isn't my concern, and Norman isn't a nice man. Besides, blood is thicker than water."

I didn't bother mentioning that he and I had no blood in common. I got his point. "Doris had to be stopped," I said.

"Didn't have to be you that did it."

"Someone had to."

He thought about that for a long time. So long, my eyelids fluttered and closed.

"Hey." They shot open. Gran stood before me with a tray of food. "You were supposed to keep her awake, Phil."

"I didn't see . . ."

"I wasn't sleeping. Just resting my eyes." I had nodded off, but I didn't want Phil to have anything else to feel guilty about.

Gran put the tray in my lap, sat next to Phil, and picked up the TV remote. "I recorded *Jeopardy*."

"That'll keep her awake," Phil said.

We watched two episodes and, although I didn't get as emotional about it as I usually did, it did keep me awake.

Gran switched off the TV and looked at her watch. "I think you can sleep now," she said. "I'll check on you every few hours."

"Want me to stay?" Phil looked hopeful. "On the couch, of course."

Gran patted his thigh. "No, I can take care of my girl. I've been doing it since she was little."

The glow in my chest was all mine now. I was happy here at Gran's. Tonight, I didn't want to think about moving out. I didn't want to be a grown-up. I just wanted to curl up and sleep in the place I'd always felt safest.

Gran disappeared into the kitchen and returned carrying Harley's bed. He'd been dozing in the middle of the living room. When he saw the bed, he looked at Gran with a question in his saggy, brown eyes. "You're sleeping with Genie tonight, boy. She needs company."

He raised himself with stiff movements, stretched, yawned, and waited for me at the bottom of the stairs. Phil pulled himself off the couch with about the same speed and enthusiasm.

"I guess I'd best be getting home," he said.

Gran gave him a kiss on his cheek. "See you in the morning."

"I'll bring bagels."

"It's not Saturday," I said.

"But I feel like celebrating." I raised my eyebrows. "You're okay, and Doris is in the hoosegow."

I reached out and grabbed his hand. "You're a good guy, Phil. I'm glad you and Gran are getting married."

Phil looked at our conjoined hands. "All's well that ends well."

33

TRIBAL ALLIANCES

My headache was down to a dull roar. It was the first day caffeine and ibuprofen made a dent in the pain. I hauled myself off Gran's couch and headed to my room. I had to get dressed and go to the apartment. Moving day was fast approaching, but there was still so much to do. I needed to put two coats of paint on the floor, and I'd just realized I didn't have anything to sleep on. I'd imagined a couch and easy chairs in the living room forgetting there was no bedroom. Hopefully, a futon would fit.

Gran assured me she was in no hurry for me to move out, but the wedding was coming up. I wanted to give her space, and there was only so much of this senior romance stuff I could take. It was cute, to a point. Then it wasn't. And there was the rent. Call me cheap, but I hated the idea of paying for an empty apartment.

As I dressed, my phone rang. It was Detective Sherman. "Just wanted to let you know we got the results of the autopsy."

I'd told the police to send someone to check on Birdie as soon as they arrived at Greener Pastures. She was fine, but only because she hadn't drunk the tea Doris had insisted on making for her. She gave it to the uniforms when they showed up. It was tested and found to contain a large dose of narcotics. The half-bottle in the bathroom that Birdie had left over from her hip surgery had been seriously depleted.

Given her age and her health, it most likely would have done her in. Her death would have been attributed to forgetfulness or suicide. In light of Doris's attempts on my life and Birdie's, the DA agreed to exhume Donald's body and have it tested, as well.

"That was quick," I said.

"It's beginning to look like Doris Miller might be the most prolific serial killer in Orange County since Richard Ramirez, the Night Stalker."

"You're kidding?"

"No. I can't go into the details, but let's just say it's the worst case of Munchhausen by adult proxy we've ever seen."

"Munchhausen by proxy, isn't that when mothers make their kids sick so they can feel important?"

"That's one manifestation of it. Munchhausen by adult proxy often involves either adult children, spouses, or senior citizens—people who can be easily manipulated by the perpetrator."

"So Doris was making people ill and then killing them to get attention?"

"More or less. She's got a pathological need to be needed. She's a very sick woman."

"What did they find in Birdie's husband's body?"

"Lead. Lead poisoning mimics stroke symptoms. Apparently, Miller made stained glass as a hobby. We think she ground the lead used to connect glass pieces into powder and doctored his food with it."

My eyes shot to the hummingbird in the window. *A friend made it for Mom*, Megan had said. "Thanks for letting me know." I hung up.

I finished dressing, grabbed the hummingbird from my windowsill and headed out into the sunshine. I blinked. After five days indoors, I felt like a newly released prisoner—weak and wobbly, but overjoyed by the outside world.

I didn't have to make the usual trek to my car. It was parked in the lot near Gran's place. No one complained, not even Mr. Rogers. I was a hero in Liberty Grove. Once the story about Doris hit the papers, people started coming out of the woodwork to tell the police their suspicions and horror stories.

I tossed the hummingbird into the dumpster at the edge of the lot. I didn't think I needed to save it. There was going to be enough evidence to put her away for a very long time.

I turned up Elm Street and parked at the curb in front of the big house. A car pulled up behind me. Chad popped out of the driver's side door and ran around to the passenger side. He opened it and pulled out a pair of crutches. McKenzie emerged, took the crutches from him, and leaned into them. A white cast covered the lower part of her right leg.

I exited my car. "What happened to you?"

"She fell," Chad said.

"You threw me, you mean." She glowered at him.

He spread his hands. "It was a move. We'd rehearsed it."

"We rehearsed it but decided not to do it."

"We weren't going to win if we didn't do something showy. Kathy and Curtis were crushing us."

McKenzie thumped toward her parent's house. "Didn't help, did it? They crushed us anyway."

"If you'd have landed right, we'd have blown their doors off," he called after her.

"If I'd have known you were going to throw me across the room, maybe I would have." She hobbled faster.

"I thought you'd feel it. Like, you'd know what was coming."

She stopped at the front door and pivoted. "Right. Like I'm a friggen' psychic or something."

"It happens." Chad looked at me.

"Goodbye, Chad." McKenzie placed the tips of her crutches across the threshold, swung into her parent's house and slammed the door.

Chad stared at the pavement for a long moment, then glanced at me. His hair hung in his eyes in a tousled bed-roomy kind of way. His expression was wry. He reminded me of James Dean most when he'd just done something stupid. "You'd have known," he said.

A single black butterfly flew into my stomach. I shrugged. He was right. I would have known. We were that kind of dance team. I didn't miss him, but I missed dancing with him. I missed the confidence and security that came from knowing what was going to happen next. This whole detecting, mystery thing didn't work for me. I liked sure things.

Chad took my hand. "How's your toe?"

I don't know what came over me, but five minutes later I had plans to meet him at Neutron the next week for Samba lessons. There would be no romance. I'd promised Gran, and more importantly, I'd promised myself. El may not be my type, but spending time with him had taught me that guys can be nice. Next guy I dated was going to be nice.

Chad drove away, and I walked upstairs. I kicked open the red door. The smell of fresh paint wafted out. I stood in the doorway and gaped. The floor shone like new gel nails. Light poured through sparkling windows and glinted off its deep gray surface.

What had happened here? I knelt and touched the wood. It looked wet. It wasn't, but its glossy surface was smooth beneath my fingers. I wandered inside in a daze. In the center of the living room was a faux-Oriental rug that picked up the colors of the walls and floor. In the center of the rug was a beautiful, old rocking chair. It had been Trudy's—the one El had admired the day we'd gone to her place.

I spun toward the kitchenette, wondering if he'd been at work there as well. A gift sat on the counter. I picked up a card that leaned against the large box. On its cover was a mouse holding out a wedge of cheese. It read, *Congratulations on your new home!* It was signed, *Best, El.*

I pulled the wrapping paper from the gift box. Inside was a single-serve coffee maker. The one I'd wanted, although I didn't remember telling him I wanted it.

I heard a creak of wood, and a moment later El's broad form filled the doorway. He grinned at me when he saw my expression. "Like it?" he said.

I wasn't sure if he meant the coffeepot, the rug, the rocker, or the floor, but I liked it—all of it. "Oh, my gosh." It was all that came out of my mouth.

"Is that oh, my gosh good, or oh, my gosh bad?" His forehead creased.

"Good. Really good. Too good." I said.

He relaxed. "I was worried. I know you said you wanted me to ask you before I did things to your place, but you were laid up. I knew you were supposed to move in soon, and I just thought . . . "

"How'd you get in?"

"Gran pinched your keys. I told her I wanted to finish things up for you and keep it a secret. She thought it was a great idea."

"I love it. But I can't keep the chair."

"You don't like it?" His eyebrows knit together.

"No, it's beautiful, but it's yours. You were the one who wanted it."

"I don't have room for it."

I looked at him from the corners of my eyes. "You're just saying that."

"I don't, really. Could you hold on to it for me?"

I didn't believe him, but I said, "Okay."

"Did you see the bathroom?" His forehead rumpled again.

I walked across the living room with quick strides. "You did the bathroom?"

"If you don't like it, I can . . . "

I lost the end of his sentence. The jungle was gone. In its place were cherry red walls and fresh white trim, but it was the shower curtain that gave me a lump in my throat. Rosie the Riveter hung from a bright stainless rod.

"It would look better with white fixtures, but the green is kind of striking against the red. Christmas-y anyway." El was babbling.

I turned to him and threw my arms around his neck. "It's absolutely perfect." I hung on for a joyful moment before feeling his muscular arms surround me.

I froze.

Emotions that didn't belong coursed through me: contentment, security, and something else. Something that felt proprietary, like coming home to a beloved and familiar place.

I backed out of the embrace and wiped my hands on my jeans. I didn't want to give El the wrong idea. We were friends. I had developed a deep affection for him, like a sister loves a brother. We weren't right for each other romantically. At least, I wasn't right for him. I plastered a smile on my face. "I think I owe you about five years-worth of haircuts."

The happiness faded from his eyes. "You don't owe me a thing."

I left the bathroom and crossed to where my purse sat on the counter. "You hungry?" It was a safe bet he was, and food generally cheered El up. I pulled out my phone and ordered a pizza.

"There's beer in the fridge," he said when I'd hung up. He sounded hurt.

"Let's celebrate. I have news."

We each grabbed a beer and sat in my new living room, El on a camp chair, me in my new rocker. "What's your news?" El said.

"I spoke to Carlton on the phone yesterday. He asked me to come on permanently."

El's eyebrows raised.

"He wants to hire me as Amy Lee's assistant. Apparently, she likes me. Who knew?"

"You're not afraid of the place after everything that happened?"

I waved my beer. "Nope. I faced the worst and made it through. Besides, he made me an offer I can't refuse. The starting pay is good, but when I get my mortician certification, it goes up exponentially."

El's mouth dropped open. "Mortuary school?"

"I've given it a lot of thought. It isn't the kind of thing you dream about as a little girl."

"It's not like being an elf."

"Right. If I'd had dreams about it, they would've been nightmares, but the job has its perks." I lifted a hand and began ticking them off on my fingers. "The clients are quieter, not a lot of gossip going around. They won't run after coupon deals and leave me high and dry. They aren't opinionated, won't complain about their cut or color. Which means I'll have more artistic license. They don't have bad breath."

I dropped my hand into my lap. "Bad breath is a real problem with some of the Liberty Grove crowd. Older folks are more susceptible to gum disease, did you know that?"

"I did not," El said.

"It's true. Sometimes the halitosis around Harry's knocks my socks off."

El nodded sagely. "So, that's it?"

I lifted a shoulder and let it drop. "Well, in a strange way, I feel like I'm actually doing something good at Greener Pastures. Something important. You know?"

He nodded. Of course, he knew. He'd tried to tell me that from the beginning.

I continued, "After the way Running Man defended me, how could I leave? These are my people."

El looked at the gleaming floor. "I hope you think of me as one of your people."

"Of course," I said, keeping my voice light. "You're in the live tribe."

El held up his beer bottle. "Here's to finding your tribe, alive or dead."

I clinked.

"Pizza," a voice at the door called out. I brought in the box and kicked the red door shut behind me.

Eight months later, El and I stood in the Jubilee Chapel at Greener Pastures, staring into an empty casket.

"She's run off," he said.

"Where . . . Where . . . " I couldn't seem to finish a sentence. El, Amy Lee, and I had put Karin Swanson in her casket that morning. Now she was gone. Who would steal a corpse?

Thanks for joining me on Imogene's first adventure. The saga continues with *Hair Today, Gone Tomorrow*, book two in the series.

If you'd like to know what happens when she goes to *Mortuary School*, you can grab a free community exclusive novella on my website.

You'll also get bi-monthly newsletters where I share what's true, what I completely made up, and weird things I learned while researching. And you'll be the first to hear about deals, new releases and in-person events.

Get your copy of *Mortuary School* at Gretaboris.com/gift

ALSO BY GRETA BORIS

The Mortician Murders

To Dye For

Hair Today, Gone Tomorrow

Bald-Headed Lies

A Permanent Solution

Buzz Cut

Splitting Hairs

An Almost True Crime Series

The Cliff House

Printed in Great Britain
by Amazon